Swept away by the prairie wind...

She crossed the floor to their bedroom; the emptiness here was not the same. Although there was nothing for the eye to see, the air throbbed with remembered rapture, whispers of love, inexpressible emotions so powerful they still lived. Leaning heavily against the doorjamb, she closed her eyes. Never again. Even as she listened, the sounds died, and then there was nothing. She turned away in desolation...

Other books by Barbara Bonham

DANCE OF DESIRE
PASSION'S PRICE
PROUD PASSION
GREEN WILLOW

BITTERSWEET

BARBARA
BONHAM

A JOVE BOOK

BITTERSWEET

A Jove Book/published by arrangement with the author

PRINTING HISTORY
Jove edition/March 1984

ISBN: 0-515-07601-5

Jove books are published by The Berkley Publishing Group,
200 Madison Avenue, New York, N.Y. 10016. The words
"A JOVE BOOK" and the "J" with sunburst are trademarks
belonging to Jove Publications, Inc.

PRINTED IN THE UNITED STATES OF AMERICA

{1}

"THAT CLOUD ISN'T going to get any bigger or move any faster for your watching it," Ward called out to her. "Come in and eat your supper."

Susan heard him but didn't move. Staring off into the southwest, she was willing the distant thunderclouds to bring rain to their parched corn crop. From the point where she stood, she could see Hawthorne, two and a quarter miles away, and beyond it the Republican and the round-topped bluffs that rose so suddenly south of the river. The prairie grasses and scattered cornfields that lay before her were beginning to die. Only the trees that marked the river's course, their roots drinking of its life-giving waters, remained green.

She wasn't aware that Ward had come out of the house until she felt his arms go around her waist, drawing her against his hot, hard body. They stood there, a lean young man with blond hair as thick and tightly curled as sheep's wool and his bride of five months, a girl with hair the color of the bleached prairie grass whose pretty face dipped from wide cheekbones down to a narrow chin. At the moment, her gray eyes were dark with anxiety. "It doesn't look any different than it did half an hour ago," Ward said. "It must be a long way off."

"It's probably dumping all of its rain over there, and there won't be any left for us." That had been happening all summer long. No matter whether the clouds built up in the northwest or southwest, by the time they arrived overhead, there weren't more than a few drops left in them.

"It's too late anyway," he declared. "The crop is ruined."

"No, it isn't! There's still some green in the stalks. A rain could bring it on again."

"What ears it made are so small we wouldn't have much of a crop even if they filled."

"Don't be so gloomy," she cried, breaking free of his arms and confronting him. "There's still hope!"

"Of course there is. But not for our corn. I'll find a job in town. You're the gloomy one, not me. I'm not worried about making our payment to the railroad." He put his arms around her again and kissed her. "Now come on in and eat your supper and forget about that cloud."

Susan regarded this man she had fallen in love with a year and a half ago. His square, sharp-featured face glowed with vitality and optimism. There were no shadows of worry clouding the clear blue of his eyes. He really believed they had no cause for worry, and she realized she had every reason to trust him. Raised in a family of nine boys back in Pennsylvania, he had had to work since he was a child.

He had learned a variety of skills, one of which was how to get the most out of every dollar he spent or made. He had steered them through a steamy courtship for a year after they met, determined not to get married until he had saved enough money to buy a quarter of a section of railroad land out West. Born too late to find good land to homestead, he nevertheless dreamed of owning a farm in one of the new states, land that had never felt the bite of a plow.

"It's like choosing a girl to marry," he told her, with a puckish grin. "I don't want one that some other man has had."

The Burlington and Missouri Railroad had thousands of acres left to sell in the Republican River valley, one of the most fertile areas in Nebraska. It was here that he decided he wanted a farm. Married in March, they had come by train to Hawthorne, bought 160 acres of land on time, built a sod house, plowed up 20 acres of virgin prairie, and planted their first corn crop. Unfortunately, Nature had, in her inscrutable way, decided that 1890 should be a year of drought in southern Nebraska. The money they had counted on from the sale of their first crop would not be forthcoming. Yet Ward did not view this as a disaster. If he could not acquire the cash needed to make his annual payment to the railroad from his corn crop, he entertained no doubts about his ability to get it by going out and working. And if he had no doubts, why should she?

Smiling up at him, she said, "I like being married to you."

"Of course you do. I'm a great fella." His graceful, well-knit body ducked the light blow she aimed at his chest. "I'm also hungry. Let's eat."

Having filled his plate earlier, he returned to the fried

potatoes, squash, snap beans, and tomatoes with gusto. There was no meat. Susan used their salt pork only for their noon meal. Their hog wouldn't be ready to butcher until fall, and she saw no need to spend what little cash they had on meat bought in town when her garden was producing all the vegetables they could eat, and more. She had carried enough water from their well to her garden to float a ship, but her labor had been rewarded. They had been living off the produce for two months, and meanwhile she had been preserving the surplus. Watching the rows of jars and crocks grow in the new storm cellar gave her a deep sense of satisfaction. Housekeeping in the sparsely furnished soddy required only a minimum of her energy and time. Gardening and laying up food for the winter made her feel like a true homemaker.

Ordinarily, the sod house with its two-foot-thick walls remained cool on the hottest days, but heat had accumulated in the two rooms as a result of her preserving today, and her supper fire had not yet died out in the small iron stove that sat on the opposite side of the room from the table. It was no cooler outside. July's heat had carried over into August without a break. The breeze blowing through the open door did little to cool them, although it was strong enough to flap the blue checkered tablecloth against the legs of the table.

While she filled her plate, Ward said, "I'm going into town tomorrow and see if Henry Sims has decided to give me a job. You want to go along?"

"I can't. I've got to put up beans. No matter what happens, we aren't going to starve next winter."

"If Sims decides he can't use me at the lumberyard," Ward said, "I'm going to try the broom factory again. If I make enough of a nuisance of myself, somebody around town is sure to loosen up and hire me."

Susan had thought it strange to find a broom factory out here in this little prairie town until she learned how well broom corn grew in the area and how much Conrad Wirth paid the farmers who raised it. Housed in a simple one-story frame building, it furnished employment for nine men. The brooms they made were shipped by the carload to Denver as well as being sold locally.

She said, "Everybody surely knows by now you're looking for work."

"I'm still a stranger in this community, and there are going to be other farmers looking for winter jobs. They might get first chance."

"You're the only new farmer in these parts. You don't have the cash reserves the others do. You need a job worse than they do."

Ward grinned. "Are you sure you can do better putting up beans than coming along and making a pitch for me?"

"If I thought anyone would listen to me, I'd go with you. When the garden is gone, I'm going to look for a job, too." It was the first time she had announced her intention, although she had been considering it for weeks. She wasn't sure what Ward's reaction would be.

Buttering a slice of bread meditatively, he asked, "Do you really want to work in town?"

"What sense would it make for me to sit around this soddy all winter doing practically nothing when we need money so much?"

"There aren't very many jobs for women in town. What kind of work would you want?"

"I'm willing to accept almost anything. I could clerk in

a store or help out at one of the hotels or at the lunchroom." She asked pleadingly, "You aren't going to say no, are you? This farm is my dream, too."

The idea of coming West had never occurred to her until she met Ward. She had known him only by sight until, bored with life on the farm where she lived with her parents and her older sister, she moved into town after persuading their family doctor to hire her as a replacement for the man who had been running his drugstore. For the first two weeks she found herself at sea. Finally, deciding there was no better way to learn where things were, what stock was kept on hand, and how much of it than by cleaning every shelf and dusting every bottle and book, she undertook the prodigious task. When she was finished, she had a thorough grasp of her job.

"I don't see how you do it," her sister exclaimed one day. Coila and her parents had come to town to do their trading, and her sister was seated on a chair behind the counter, where she could visit with Susan between customers. Admiration and wonder shone on her cheerful, placid face. She already looked matronly at twenty-two. Plump, heavy-breasted, her blond hair pulled back into a bun, she was the picture of a serene wife and mother when, in fact, she did not even have a suitor. It was a situation that would have caused most women her age acute anxiety. Coila Eberly, however, was content to continue living at home with her parents. "How can you remember where everything is?" she asked, surveying the crowded shelves and display cases.

"You know where everything is in the pantry at home, don't you?" Susan asked. "This isn't any different."

"The smell is," Coila said, wrinkling her nose. "How do you stand it?"

"I don't notice it any longer except when I first come in in the morning."

"Don't you get lonesome boarding here in town? I'd miss Mama and Papa something awful."

"I do. And I miss you, too, but I like living in town and having a job."

By that time she had caught Ward's eye. They met when he came in to buy a Christmas present for his mother. She had been struck at once by the male lustiness that emanated from his trim, muscular body and from his brilliant blue eyes when they met hers. He was wearing a moustache at the time, as blond as his tightly curled hair; instead of hiding his mouth, it accentuated its firm curves. His effect on her was so unnerving that she started showing him a tray of brooches until he interrupted her and said with an amused sparkle in his eyes, "I wanted to look at gold pens, not pins."

"Oh, I'm sorry." Knocking the corner of the tray against the display case as she hastily tried to put it back, she spilled several of the brooches and had to bend down to pick them up. When she straightened she knew her face was burning, and the knowledge deepened her blush.

He was back the next day to buy a pencil during the noon break at the sawmill where he worked. For the rest of the week, he came in without any excuse at all, making no attempt to hide the fact that he had come to see her and for no other reason. When he asked if he could call on her Saturday night she said yes, and told her parents and Coila when they came to town to do their trading that she wouldn't be going home to spend Sunday with them. When she told them why, her mother looked pleased, but her father looked grave, and Coila was as ecstatic as if it were she who was being courted. They had scarcely left the boarding house where Susan lived when Ward arrived. Because she was not permitted to have male visitors in her room, and because the parlor was always occupied by one or more boarders, she and Ward went for a walk in the sharp winter night. What snow had fallen previously was nearly gone, the ground frozen and dry beneath their feet.

She was shivering, not from the cold, but from the excitement of being alone with this man whose physical presence sent such strange sensations through her body. When he heard her teeth chattering, he expressed concern and put his arm around her shoulders, drawing her so close to his side that her cheek pressed against the rough wool of his coat. The moon was so bright they could easily see their way along the paths that fronted those houses whose owners had not troubled to build walks. In one yard an enormous old oak cast a wide dark shadow. Ward pulled her into it and kissed her. She had been awaiting it, hoping for it, and when it came it drove the breath from her lungs. After a few moments she slid her mouth free, gasping his name against his cheek. He claimed her mouth again almost immediately, kissing her as if his thirst for her lips would never be satiated.

When at last he drew back, she felt as if the bones in her body had melted. He remained holding her while he looked long and hard into her face. "There's something you need to know," he said, and began to tell her about his dream of moving West. "I've read about it. Everything out there is different, new. I want to go there and see what it's like. I want to get a farm. Some of that land will grow pumpkins too big to fit in a barrel." Susan heard the keen hunger in his voice as he declared, "I've been working for someone else since I was ten years old. I want to be my own boss."

Her spirit of adventure responded immediately. Asking eager questions, she became fascinated by his plan to move to a place she had scarcely heard of. Nebraska. True, it had a harsh, unlovely sound and she had always pictured it as a wilderness, but Ward assured her there were towns, even railroads, out there.

"There isn't any good free land left," he explained, surprised by her interest. "That's why I haven't gone out there yet. I'm saving my money to buy some railroad land."

"It would be like going to a foreign country, wouldn't it?" she exclaimed. "Everywhere you looked, you'd see something new." She saw the gleam in his eyes in the faint light. He pulled her close again, kissing her with an exhilaration that seemed to have its basis in wonder and relief. "Will you go to Nebraska with me?"

Her reply was clear and strong. "Yes."

His breath escaped in a cloud of steam, and he hugged her, explaining that they couldn't be married yet. He would have to work another year before he saved enough money to make a down payment on a farm and have a little left over to buy a team and some machinery. Her savings, she told him, would buy what they needed for their house.

And so she adopted his dream with the zeal of a convert. Never had a year passed so slowly for her. Coila couldn't understand her impatience to leave. "You might as well be moving to China. We'll never see each other again."

"Of course we will. The Burlington and Missouri Railroad runs through this valley where we're going. You can come and visit us."

"I'd rather have you come back here to visit us. It scares

me to think of going out to that wild place, doesn't it you?"

"A little, but that doesn't mean I'm not looking forward to it. Building a new life out there will be exciting."

"We're going to miss you so, Papa and Mama and I. Oh, I do wish Ward didn't have this crazy idea of running off to the edge of nowhere!"

As it turned out, there was only Coila and her father to leave. Her mother died eight months before she and Ward were married. At first Susan felt guilty about leaving her sister alone to keep house for her father. Soon it became evident, however, that Coila did not consider it a sacrifice. "I'm glad Papa needs me. This is my home, and I don't ever want to leave it. Watching you prepare to marry and go away has made me sure of it."

"But surely you'll want to get married someday."

"Why should I? I'm perfectly happy as I am."

Susan couldn't believe any woman would choose to remain unmarried. She found the wait until she and Ward could be married excruciating. Being so much in love and having to be satisfied with only kisses was maddening. There was the promise of fulfillment one day, however. Contemplating a future in which one was forever deprived of a man's love was the dreariest prospect she could imagine.

She marveled at Ward's self-control. There were times when, ignited by their kisses, her senses clamored for the release that only union with his body would bring her. His own quivering muscles told her his passion had reached the same explosive point, yet he always pulled back. "A hurry-up marriage would ruin my plans," he explained to her once after a particularly erotic series of kisses and caresses that he ended abruptly by getting to his feet and bathing his face in the pond along whose banks they had been walking. "I'd never be able to save enough for a farm if I had to begin supporting a wife and baby." Time and again he displayed this rigid discipline, breaking the spell most often with some lighthearted remark that brought laughter to her trembling lips.

Deeply, bemusedly in love as she was, saying good-bye to her father and Coila was still a heart-wrenching experience.

Her father didn't go to the train station with them, preferring to say his good-byes in his own home. Susan buttoned her coat slowly, putting off the moment as long as she could. When she raised her eyes, she found her father waiting, his face pale and drawn. She went to him. "You must come and see me, Papa. . . . I can't bear it if you don't." Her voice shook.

He nodded and embraced her. They clung together wordlessly. Then, holding her away from him, he gazed at her with red-rimmed eyes. "You're so like your mother," he said hoarsely.

She broke into sobs and felt her father pass her over into Ward's arms.

She and Coila held hands as they rode in the rented carriage to the train. "You can get out there in four days' time," she reminded her sister, "and it will be easier for you and Papa to get away than it will be for us. We won't be able to afford to come back here for quite a while."

"Oh, Susan, we're going to miss you so!"

"Write to me," she pleaded.

"You know I will."

"Take care of Papa."

"Yes."

Tearfully, Susan boarded the train, knowing it might be a year, perhaps longer, before she would see her family again. If Ward felt the same sadness at leaving his parents and eight brothers, he gave no sign. His eyes were already turned toward the west, destination: Hawthorne, Nebraska, chosen from a promotional booklet circulated by the Burlington and Missouri Railroad.

They found southern Nebraska in the grip of a February cold spell. Temperatures scarcely rose above zero during the day, they were told by the proprietor of the Commercial Hotel in Hawthorne.

"Welcome to the Lord's house," was his greeting to them as they came through the door, their faces stinging from the drive up from the depot on the open hotel hack. "My name is Rufus Lord," he said, shooting out a bony hand at the end of a long, thin arm. From a skinny neck that supported a small skull, his Adam's apple thrust out like a wedge.

When he discovered they were looking for land to buy, he charged them the special low rate he had for land seekers. "You'll like it here," he told them. "This is a friendly town, and you'll never find nicer people anywhere. Do you play high five? Some of us fellows have a game here in the parlor every night. If you're not too tired from your trip and you feel like a game, you're welcome to join us."

"Thanks, but we'll turn in as soon as we've had supper," Ward replied. "We've had a long trip. Could we have some hot water brought to our room? We need a wash."

"I'll tell my wife. I could bring the tub if you want a real bath. That'll be a quarter extra."

A bath sounded heavenly, but knowing how reluctant Ward was to spend even a cent of their money for anything except the sheerest necessities, Susan didn't expect him to ask for the bath. To her delight, he did.

"I'll bring it right in," Rufus Lord promised. "Your room is number two. The last room on the right," he said, indicating the short corridor that ran from the parlor to the rear of the building.

The room was plainly furnished with a painted iron bed, a washstand, and blue gingham curtains. The blue bedspread was threadbare but clean, the floor so well scrubbed the boards were almost white.

After a quick glance around, Ward groaned. "No stove. And it's like an icehouse in here. We'll freeze trying to take a bath."

"I don't care. I feel like I've got a thick layer of soot all over me."

"You look good enough to eat to me." He pulled her into his arms, nearly crushing her with his urgency. The railroad car had offered them no privacy. They kissed wildly, their hands desperately seeking, knowing that only moments separated them from the fulfillment they had denied themselves so long. Hearing steps in the corridor, they broke apart. Susan went to the window, hiding her flushed face as she pretended to be interested in the street scene outside.

Mrs. Lord, a husky woman with thick muscular arms, arrived with two buckets of hot water, which she poured into the tin hip tub her husband had wrestled through the door. Despite the frigid day, her ruddy face was slightly moist. Heartily friendly, she nevertheless gave the impression that she was too busy to stand around and visit. Not so, her husband. Ward finally had to remind him that the water in the tub was cooling off and, if they didn't take their baths at once, they'd have to call for more hot water.

"I'll wait in the parlor," Ward told Susan as soon as the

hotelkeeper left them alone. Cupping her face with one hand he gave her a burning, lingering kiss. "Don't be long."

She bathed thoroughly but quickly, nearly freezing in the chill air of the room as she dried herself and pulled her nightgown over her head. Snuggling under the bed comforters, she felt deliciously clean and light after four days of never having her clothes off. Her body tingled from the brisk toweling, and from anticipation.

Moments later Ward came in. Saying nothing, he stood at the bedside, looking down at her as he undressed. She saw that he was ready, and her heart began to pound. Both remained silent while he bathed. He was still slightly damp when he slipped into bed beside her. His hand, cold from the frigid room, pulled her gown up over her head with her help. The hard, naked length of his body pressing against her set her on fire. As his finger teased her nipple with short, rapid strokes, her mouth went slack beneath his. Her hand sought and found his hardness. He gasped and rolled over on top of her. Dimly she noted that her body knew instinctively what to do. Desire directed it. She scarcely noticed the instant of pain, so carried away by the passion was she. At its peak she cried out his name, clutching him tightly as wave after wave lifted her into a realm of sensation beyond anything she had imagined.

Incredible as she found it to be, their lovemaking grew into an even more powerful experience as the weeks passed. Their love and intimacy bound them so wholly together that Susan couldn't conceive of herself as an independent individual any longer. Body and soul, she was part of Ward and he a part of her. Worrisome as their financial situation had become, it lay on the surface of her life. Underneath was the bedrock of their love.

"Let me help. Let me get a job," she argued intently, leaving her supper of vegetables untouched. "I've got the time, energy, and strength. Isn't it foolish to let all that lie around unused when we need money so bad?"

Laughing, Ward said, "If you could get a job as a salesman you could make a million dollars. . . . All right. If you can get a job that pays well enough, I'd forget the garden if I were you and start right away."

"I didn't suppose I could get one that paid very much. It wouldn't be permanent. Just for the winter."

"If I can't find a job maybe you'll be the one to go off to work to save the homestead while I stay home to cook and keep house."

"That wouldn't bother you? I mean me working and you staying home?"

"If you mean would I worry about what people might say, no, it wouldn't. You've worked like a slave in the garden and helped me ever since we moved on this place. Why should that be all right and working in town, at a job that would probably be easier on you, be wrong? You and I have too much to do to let ourselves be hobbled by cockeyed ideas."

"Yes, we do, don't we?" She felt the pull of excitement. They were young and healthy, and together they could achieve anything they set out to do.

The Solomons came over that night for a neighborly visit, and the major topic of conversation was the drought.

"The corn on our place looks worse than what we planted on Widow Brown's place," Charlie Solomon said, his calm, quiet-spoken manner giving no hint of the disaster that faced all of them. To look at his tall, spare body one would think he had never known anything except lean years. His wife, too, was thin, almost ascetically so. It was impossible to believe they ever indulged excessively in anything, except their efforts to perfect their characters. Without a doubt they were the most upright, moral people Susan had ever met, and they accomplished this without appearing intolerant or self-righteous.

"I'm glad it's not the other way around," Solomon continued. "Not that she'd say anything. She's a real fine woman, almost a part of our family."

The widow lived a mile south of Ward and Susan along the trail that led into Hawthorne. A shy, sweet woman, she left her farm only to attend church and to do her Saturday trading, driving her buggy, a rare possession for one who lived out in the country, but since her husband's death fifteen years earlier, she had rented out her land to Charlie Solomon, and so had no need of a team and wagon. It was commonly believed that her husband had left her well-off and that she had money hidden somewhere on her place. Slightly eccentric, she nevertheless aroused the protectiveness of the closely knit community of Hawthorne and its environs. Living only a mile and a quarter from town, she was regarded by its citizens as one of their own.

Susan understood the community's protective feeling for her. She found the older woman as guileless as a child. Had it not been for the widow's extreme shyness, Susan would have liked to visit her often. It was plain, however, that Susan's visits were a strain for her. A faint mist of perspiration invariably broke out on her face at the sight of her visitor and persisted through tea and cake. Although her friendliness was genuine enough, there was an awkwardness about it that made conversation difficult. After several neighborly calls, which Widow Brown never returned, Susan confined her visits to quick chats as she and Ward stopped on their way into Hawthorne to ask if she wanted them to bring her anything from town. She seemed to appreciate their concern even though she was well looked after by the Solomons.

"From what I hear, she's got money enough to see her through several hard years," Ward remarked.

"Those are the rumors," said Solomon. "I don't know whether she's got money hidden around her place or not. I've never seen any of it. I hope she has because she's likely to need it. Even if we get some rain soon, her crop is going to be mighty small."

"You don't suppose she'd want to make a loan, do you?" Ward asked, only half joking. "I've got to scare up some money to make the payment on my farm by next March. The bank doesn't seem to want to loan me any."

"I couldn't say," replied Solomon. "I wish I could help you, but my boy wants to get married and I've got to find a quarter for him to start out on."

"Sure, I understand. I'm not really begging for money, but I have been begging for a job. Nobody in town seems to need any help right now."

"Business is slow, I hear, and it will get slower. Everybody's going to be hurting."

Ward left for town right after dinner the next day. While he was hitching the team to the wagon, Susan went into the cellar and brought up a quart of the pickles Widow Brown had exclaimed over at the church dinner several Sundays earlier.

"Put it under the seat," Ward said when she appeared with the jar. The horses stood patiently in the searing sun while he finished fitting the harness over their powerful bodies.

Susan wrapped the pickles in an empty feed sack and tucked it in a corner where it wouldn't roll. "Tell her hello for me and tell her how much we enjoyed her currant jelly."

Ward wound the reins around one hand and climbed into the wagon. "You're sure you don't want me to bring you anything?"

"The promise of a job."

"I'll do my best. Mac puts in awfully long hours at the saloon. Maybe I can get you a job helping him tend bar."

She wrinkled her nose at him. "I can just see you letting me work in a saloon."

"Mac's business would probably double. That's a good selling point. I'll use it when I go in to see him."

"Be sure you don't spend too much time in there."

Grinning, he slapped the reins on the horses' rumps and pulled out of the yard.

Susan watched him for a long time even though she had a big pan of beans waiting to be snapped and put up. Seeing him drive off the place always made her feel lonely. So long as he was somewhere on their 160 acres, out of sight though he might be, she felt that he was nearby. The track leading into town was very nearly a straight line. In those two and a quarter miles the land sloped gradually down toward the river valley. Their place stood higher than Widow Brown's, and hers stood higher than the Solomon place, which was located only a quarter of a mile from town. From where Susan stood, Hawthorne was a smudge on a plateau that rose from the narrow river valley. The only other set of buildings visible from their place belonged to John Kimball, a widower with a son not quite right in the head. Susan had been over there once with Ward and had been impressed with two things: the neatness of the farmyard and the filth of the house. She had quickly turned away from the unwashed plates on the table, one with a chicken feather caught in the yellow stain of an egg.

The Solomons and Kimballs had offered to help Ward build the sod house. Ward, however, had turned them down, with thanks, but John Kimball had taken offense and had never been friendly since. "If I accept their help," Ward explained to Susan, "I'd have to return the favor, and I don't want to be working on someone else's place." He had hired someone with a grasshopper plow to cut the sod bricks and lay them, spending some of their badly shrunken cash reserves to do so. The Solomons had also offered to help him plow. Breaking prairie sod, a tangle of soil, grass, and grass roots so dense it could be used to build houses, was an arduous task for men and horses. Such help by their neighbors would have enabled Ward to prepare and plant more acres, but he said he wanted one day to tell his children that he had broken every acre himself. He couldn't wait to get started at it mornings. Tireless himself, he chafed at the necessity to rest the horses and to work them no more than eight hours a day. After the corn was planted, he continued to plow, breaking ground for crops to be planted next year. Observing his seething energy, Susan realized how safe her future was, and her love for him assumed a new dimension.

When he and the wagon dipped into a draw out of her sight, she started back into the house, stopping to examine the two small cedar trees she had planted in the front yard. The absence of trees on the prairie had dismayed her when they arrived. One rainy day in April when Ward was unable to plow, they had driven to the river and dug up the little trees and brought them home. She had watered them every day since, and they never knew they had been moved. Widow Brown had told her to expect very little growth the first year. "They'll be doing a lot of growing underground. They form a deep root system, you see. By next year you'll never have to water them again. They'll live through the driest of summers."

The older woman had given her some hollyhock and zinnia seeds to brighten up her yard, and the sight of the bright blooms around her door brought a smile to her lips. Much as she loved their place, she found the sod buildings and empty expanse of prairie ugly. Didn't she have plans, though. A white frame house, a big flower garden with plenty of roses, and more trees to shade every foot of the house and yard. A board fence, too, painted white, to enclose it all. For now, the zinnias and hollyhocks broke the drabness that met her eyes no matter in what direction she looked. Humming, she went back to her beans.

Hawthorne's business section was built around the courthouse square. The courthouse, a two-story wooden building facing west, had not been considered solid enough to contain a jail. A stone building large enough to hold three cages had been built to the south of it. On each of the four sides of the square stood an almost unbroken line of stores; only two or three vacant lots left gaps between the buildings. The trail Ward followed entered town at the northwest corner of the square. He continued down that street, then turned left and headed for the lumberyard. Situated on the corner, it could be entered from two sides. He hitched the team out front and went in. Finding no one in the office, he went out back to the yard. There among the long sheds filled with lumber, Ward found Henry Sims, the owner, sitting on a low stack of new boards. Open on all four sides, the shed offered shade and plenty of ventilation. Nevertheless, there was a sheen of sweat on the coarse, pitted skin of Henry Sims's face and on the ample bridge of his hooked nose. A pair of gloves lay on the board beside him.

Grinning, Ward said, "You need an extra man, Henry. If you'd hire me, you could sit in the shade all day and never have to move a board."

"If I were a rich man, that's what I'd do. You still looking for a job?"

"Still looking."

"I wish I could help you, but things just keep tightening up." Sims struck the pile of boards he was sitting on. "This is the last load I'm going to order till business picks up. I need a good soaking rain as much as you do."

"Don't know of anyone else who might give me a job, do you?"

"You might try the broom factory. Con has the edge over the rest of us businessmen. He doesn't have to depend on local trade."

"I tried there once, but I'll try again. I'd like to work for you, though. I don't know anything about making brooms, but I know quite a bit about lumber. I learned it working in a mill back in Pennsylvania."

"So you told me. If times were good, I could use you."

"If times were good, I'd be looking at a big corn crop and wouldn't need a job in town." Ward put his hands on his lean hips. "I'm a good worker. Most times I can do the work of two men."

"So I've heard." Sims regarded him sympathetically, then heaved a resigned sigh. "I can't hire you. I wish I could."

"You wouldn't have to pay me much. My wife and I probably have enough food to get us through the winter. I'd only need to earn enough to make my farm payment next March." He let the words carry his plea; he kept his tone even. All the same, it made Henry Sims uncomfortable.

"Go see Con Wirth. He may be able to use another man."

With a crew of nine men, the broom factory was filling its orders easily. Turned down there, Ward tried the feed store, the creamery, and the livery barn. No one was hiring. Pat Seavey, owner of the barn, was complaining. Ward sat in the dirty office to the left of the door, listening with little patience.

"Everybody seems to be walking these days. The only rigs I can rent anymore are to drummers who need to go to the north part of the county." A frown creased the handsome Irish face beneath the prematurely gray hair. "And farmers let their teams stand out in the hot sun instead of bringing them in here where we could feed and water them and keep them cool."

"We can't afford to bring our horses in here. What money we've got has to see us and our families through the winter."

"I can poor-mouth with the poorest of you. I've got eight kids to feed, four of them boys who eat more than my horses do."

Ward managed not to glance at the half-open drawer in the desk from which a few moments ago Seavey had pulled a flat bottle of whiskey and had drunk deeply from it. Seavey wore two hats—respectable businessman and drinker. Under the first hat he served on the town board; under the other, he frequented the saloon and counted among his friends the type he found there. He kept the hat of respectability by never appearing drunk. Ward had heard that his capacity was astounding. He was never without his bottle. It was an expensive habit whose cost would have fed his hungry sons, if not all eight of his children.

"Now I've got a lawyer to pay," Seavey went on. "I suppose you heard about my oldest boy?" When Ward shook his head he explained. "He broke in here the other night and stole a two-seater. He and one of his friends picked up Joe Stewart's girl, gave her a wild ride, and wouldn't let her out when she got scared. They finally let her out two or three miles from town, and she walked home. Joe's so mad he's trying to get Mike charged with kidnapping. He can't do it, of course, but it's going to cost me a lawyer's fee. Damned kids!" he exclaimed. Then with a laugh and a wink, he said, "I never pulled any crazy stunts like that when I was a kid, did you?"

"Never once." Ward stood up quickly before Seavey could get wound up again. "Business ought to pick up when it turns cold. Farmers won't let their teams stand out in freezing weather all day while they do their trading. Maybe I could help out then."

"I'll keep you in mind."

"I'd appreciate it."

Ward left and made his way slowly to the general store to buy the baking powder Widow Brown said she needed. He wasn't quite as optimistic about their situation as he let on to Susan, and being turned down by four businessmen in one afternoon was a real test of his spirit. Of course, it was only August. Surely something would turn up in the fall. He wasn't particular. He was willing to do any kind of work to save his farm. All he needed was another year and one good crop to give him a cash reserve. After that he could borrow on the equity he had in his place.

An hour later he drove into the Widow Brown's yard. She must have been watching for him; she came to the back porch as he jumped down from the wagon. He waved the tin of baking powder at her. "I got it," he announced.

"Come in," she said, holding the door open for him. There was real pleasure on her face at seeing him for a second time that afternoon, yet there was a nervous tremor in her lips as she spoke. "It hasn't cooled off any, has it?"

"No, it hasn't." Ward followed her small, slender body into the large kitchen, which she also used as a sitting room. A cot stood along one wall, and at its foot was a wooden rocker with cushions tied to the seat and back.

She took the tin from him and set it on the table. "How much do I owe you?" When Ward told her, she said, "Have a seat while I get the money."

Preferring not to appear as if he meant to stay for a visit, Ward remained standing. Although the widow had won his affection as she had everyone else's, her extreme shyness made him uncomfortable. No amount of friendliness seemed able to overcome it.

He glanced around the large room and through the doorway that led to the living room. Both floors were covered with worn linoleum; all the furniture looked much the worse for wear. The wallpaper in both rooms was stained and dark and cracked in the corners. If she had money hidden someplace, she sure wasn't spending any of it.

"I sure do thank you," she said a few minutes later, handing him the coins.

"It was no trouble at all." He dropped the coins quickly

into his pocket, and smiling to cover his eagerness to leave, he said, "I'd better get home and do chores."

The widow took a towel-covered pan from the cupboard and handed it to him. "Take these home for your supper. They're cinnamon rolls. I baked them just this morning."

"They sure smell good," he said, and thanked her.

"Say hello to Susan for me and thank her for the pickles."

"I will."

As he started out of her drive, he pulled his old snap-lock purse from his back pocket and dropped in the money the widow had given him. John Kimball and his son, returning from town, turned off the road near the widow's drive where a trail angled toward their place, located a mile to the northeast. Ward merely waved, knowing Kimball wouldn't bother to stop; the only greeting he got in return was a curt nod. He scarcely noticed. The near emptiness of the small, deep pocketbook recalled his financial plight, and he dug out what money there was to count it, although he knew to the penny the amount that was in it. He wasn't going to have enough left by spring even to buy seed.

He was lost in thought when he drove into his own place. Susan waved from the door and ran to the barn a few minutes later, in time to kiss him when he got down from the wagon. Seeing her joy at having him home, he felt his optimism return. He swung her around and gave her another kiss before starting to unharness the horses.

"Did you find a job?" she asked eagerly.

He told her in detail about his turndowns. "And no job for you, either. I told Mac I didn't mind you tending bar, but taking the boys into the back room was out. He said if I changed my mind, to come back and see him. I might have to. You wouldn't mind that little extra—"

"Ward, be serious," she broke in. "What are we going to do?"

He hated seeing those eyes of hers clouded with worry. "I'll keep tormenting everyone in town until somebody hires me. I never give up, as you should know by now." He winked broadly at her.

"Do you always get what you want?"

"I always have so far."

Later that night, while they were getting ready for bed, Susan found it impossible to defeat the doubt that persisted despite Ward's confidence. "We could always go back to Fieldsboro and live. You might even get your old job back at the mill."

He had stripped off his clothes, and as always, Susan was struck by the fact that his chest was so much wider and more heavily muscled than it looked when covered by a shirt. Glancing across the room at her in surprise, he exclaimed, "What are you talking about? I'm not going back to Pennsylvania. There might not be any jobs around here right now, but something will turn up." He blew out the lamp and lay down beside her, turning on his side so he could caress her. The cross breeze from the windows, still hot, did little to cool them as it blew across the bed. His hand on her breast failed to arouse her.

"Aren't you giving any thought to what we can do if no job turns up for you?"

"Of course I am. I haven't come up with any ideas yet, but I'm working on it. Leave everything to me. I'll take good care of you, I promise."

Feeling disloyal, she said, "I believe you. It's just that I'm still getting used to you. I haven't lived with you long enough yet so that I don't worry. After we've been married ten years I won't be like this."

"Well, just be careful how you change. I like you just the way you are. Especially here. And here."

Soft fire licked through her. She turned, seeking his lips, her anxiety retreating before this assault on her senses.

2

IT WAS TEN O'CLOCK the next morning when Sheriff Enoch Van Alstine came to their place. Having just heard the clock, a wedding gift from her father and sister, strike the hour as she went out to water her garden, Susan knew the time precisely. She recognized the swarthy, melancholy face under the big hat at once. Leaving her garden, she walked to the front of the house, greeting him as he parked the buggy a few yards from their front door. Although he touched the brim of his hat politely, it was obvious from the hard set of his face that this wasn't a casual social call.

"Morning, Mrs. Maddox. Having touble keeping your hog in?"

To his right and slightly behind the house, Ward could be seen fixing the fence around their hogpen.

"She got out this morning about the time Ward was ready

to leave for the field. She broke one of the boards somehow."

Climbing down from the buggy, he said, "They always manage to find a way to get out, don't they? I'd like to talk to your husband."

Susan watched as he made his way toward the hogpen. For a big man he moved with extraordinary lightness. Wondering what business the sheriff could have with Ward, she hesitated for only a moment before following him. They were exhanging greetings when she reached the pen Ward had built around the A-shaped house that was just big enough for the hog to get into and lie down. The sun was already hot at this early hour, drawing the stench from the dirt that the hog was forever rooting up. The sheriff waited until Ward pounded in the final nail and had straightened before coming to the point of his visit.

"Did you stop by Widow Brown's place yesterday?"

"I was there twice," Ward replied. "Once right after dinner on my way into town and once on the way back. She needed some baking powder, and I brought her some." He was bareheaded. Even on the hottest or coldest days, he seldom wore a hat over his thick, woolly hair.

"What time did you see her last?"

"Last? Has something happened to her?"

Ignoring the question, the sheriff said, "John Kimball says he saw you drive away from her place about four. Is that right?"

"It was about that time, I guess." Ward exchanged a puzzled glance with Susan.

"Was she all right?"

"She seemed all right to me. Thanked me and sent home a pan of cinnamon rolls with me."

Susan couldn't stand it any longer. "Has something happened to her, sheriff?"

"She's been murdered."

The word rang as strangely in the shimmering prairie air as if it belonged to a foreign language. Susan felt a sudden chill on the back of her neck. Over in a corner of the pen the hog grunted as it pushed up a mound of soft dirt with its snout.

Never taking his melancholy eyes from Ward, the sheriff elaborated. "Charlie Solomon found her when he went over to her place this morning. Somebody bashed her head in with an iron skillet."

Susan's glance froze in horror on the sheriff's face. In a stunned voice, Ward asked, "Who could have done that?"

"Someone who wanted her money. They tore up the house and must have found it because they left the outbuildings alone." He spoke with controlled anger.

"So she really did have money hidden someplace," Ward said.

"But how could anyone kill her?" Susan asked in a shaken voice. "She was so sweet. I thought everybody loved her."

Van Alstine pulled a folded piece of paper from his shirt pocket and handed it to Ward, who took it as if he didn't know what to do with it. "It's a search warrant," the sheriff said curtly. "I'm going to have to search your house."

Incredulous, Ward glanced from the paper to the sheriff. "You think I killed her?"

Frightened, Susan flew to Ward's side, clutching his arm with both hands. "My husband couldn't kill anyone, sheriff, least of all a sweet old lady!"

Unmoved, Van Alstine retorted, "John said when you drove out of her yard you had a pocketbook in your hands and you were counting money."

"It was my money! And there wasn't much of it. I had my pocketbook out because she'd repaid me for the baking powder I brought her." Tight-faced, flushed, Ward exclaimed, "I didn't kill her, sheriff. She was alive when I left. It could have happened at any time after that. Maybe somebody sneaked in there during the night and did it."

"Nobody around here would have done such a thing. We've all known her too long. And it's no secret that you're hurting for money."

"And you think because I've lived here only a few months, I could do it?" Ward was angry now. "You've got the wrong man, sheriff. Go search the house. Maybe when you don't find the money you'll believe me." He led the way, his heels striking the ground sharply, his whole body expressing his outrage.

Susan followed at Van Alstine's side, explaining urgently, "My husband isn't a violent man. He doesn't get into fights like so many other men do. I've never known him to hit anyone. If you knew him better, sheriff, you'd know he couldn't have murdered Widow Brown. A stranger passing through might have robbed and killed her."

"There was no way anyone could have known about her hidden money unless they lived around here." At the harshness of his tone, Susan fell back, following him through the door.

His search of the house was thorough and, in the sparsely furnished rooms, took no time at all. The only money he found was their small store of cash in Ward's pocketbook, which was kept in a trunk in the bedroom.

"Now are you convinced?" Ward asked, standing with his hands on his hips in the doorway between the two rooms.

"I'd like to take a look at the barn."

Ward muttered an oath and stepped back, but made no move to leave the house. Van Alstine, whose bulk had seemed to fill the soddy, left to search the barn alone.

In frightened bewilderment, Susan swung her eyes from the now-empty doorway to Ward, as he gave the cob bucket a kick. "He won't arrest you, will he, when he doesn't find the money?"

"Who knows? The damn fool thinks I'm the only one in the whole damn county who could have done it. If he does arrest me, I'm going to need a lawyer. You'll have to go into town and hire one. Get Sy Harris."

"Maybe you won't be arrested," she said with desperate hope.

He was, however. Despite the sheriff's failure to find the stolen money, he took Ward to jail.

Angry but cool-headed, Ward kissed Susan good-bye. "Go tell Sy Harris the whole story and don't worry. Between us, he and I will get this straightened out. I may be home for supper."

Susan didn't wait to watch them drive away. She flew to the barn, let out the horses, and hitched them to the wagon with shaking hands. Notwithstanding Ward's expressed confidence, she couldn't believe this situation would be easily resolved. It was incredible to her that anyone could suspect Ward of murder, but none of these people knew Ward very well. How did one get around that? How could he and Sy Harris convince the sheriff or a judge or whomever that he was innocent and should be set free?

The horses were stamping impatiently before she finally got them harnessed. She hurried into the house to change her dress.

Scarcely bothering to tidy up her hair, she ran back outside and scrambled up to the wagon seat. Shaking the reins and issuing a sharp command to the horses, she started the two-and-a-quarter-mile drive into Hawthorne.

A mile from home she passed Widow Brown's place. Set back from the trail some two hundred yards, the house appeared eerily quiet. The small flock of white chickens that usually scratched about the yard were nowhere to be seen. Nor was there a sign of life around the large red barn. Shivering, Susan averted her eyes and urged the team to move faster.

A quarter of a mile farther on, she passed the Solomon farm, with its air of careful neatness and prosperity. The sun glared off the white, two-story house, its fenced yard filled with flowers. Behind it, the outbuildings sat solidly in good repair; a windmill pumped water into an overflowing livestock tank. Hogs sought shade in an open-fronted shed while chickens searched the dirt of the pen for kernels of corn. This was what Susan hoped their farm would look like someday and never passed it without a surge of impatient energy. Today, however, the immediate future was all that was on her mind.

Sy Harris had been one of the first persons Susan and Ward had met upon coming to Nebraska. He lived at the Lord's house, as everyone called the Commercial Hotel, and was to be found nearly every evening in the parlor playing cards with Rufus Lord, other bachelors, and assorted drummers, as traveling salesmen were called. Originally from South Carolina, he spoke with a soft drawl and possessed a courtliness of manner Susan had never seen before.

During the month she and Ward had lived at the hotel, he had become friendly with them, and when Ward finally decided on the piece of land he wanted, Sy Harris had done Ward's legal work. After moving to the farm, they seldom went to town or attended a social event without encountering him and exchanging pleasantries for a few minutes. Invariably he had a young woman at his side at the social events. He was the town's most sought-after bachelor, and Susan could understand why. He was the type of man any woman would find fascinating. In addition to his unusual elegance of manner, there was sensitivity in his handsome face, a sensitivity that was offset by the firm, long jawline, the glint of self-assurance in the dark eyes, the sheathed energy one sensed in his tall, slender body.

Harris's office was in a large brick building a few doors from the Lord's house. Occupying the first floor was a furniture and undertaking business; upstairs were a lodge hall and several offices. The second floor was reached by a steep, enclosed stairway entered from the street. Susan's heart was pounding by the time she reached the top. The open door to her right bore a sign that said S.Y. HARRIS, ATTY-AT-LAW.

The bare-floored room smelled of dusty wood and books. Two glass-fronted bookcases stood on opposite sides of the room. The desk faced the door, and behind it, his back to the window, sat the attorney, his long legs propped up on the messy desk. In contrast to the untidy office, Sy Harris was neatly dressed and barbered. His white shirt was spotless, his boots freshly polished. The coat of his gray summer suit hung over the back of his chair.

He lifted his head and saw her, but before he could say

anything, she blurted, "The sheriff has arrested Ward. He thinks Ward killed Widow Brown. But he didn't. Can you get him out of jail?"

Samuel Yancy Harris sprang to his feet when he saw her, pulling his coat off the back of his chair as he did so. He knew why she had come to him. Through his window, which looked north across the courthouse square, he had seen the sheriff drive up a short time before and lead Ward Maddox, handcuffed, into the small stone jail. Someone coming out of the courthouse had asked the obvious question of the sheriff, then had spread the word around the town square. Ward Maddox, the new young farmer from north of town, had been arrested for the murder of Widow Brown.

Sy Harris's first thought had not been of Ward, but of his wife. He had been dazzled by her loveliness that first night in the hotel when she and her husband had arrived in Hawthorne. Engaged in his nightly game of high five in the hotel parlor, he had forgotten his cards and stared at her, exquisite even in her travel-rumpled clothes. After becoming acquainted with them and discovering that she was a fascinating mixture of sweetness and strength, he knew for certain that if she were not already married, he would be prepared to give up his bachelor freedom without a twinge of regret.

"I've just heard about Ward's arrest," he said, pulling up a chair for her. "I'm sorry."

Ignoring the chair, she looked straight into his eyes and said, "He didn't kill her. It's crazy for anyone to think he could do such a thing."

Even though her features were stiff with tension, she was lovely. Her honey-colored hair framed a face flawed only by a few freckles on her wide forehead. Smooth flushed skin was stretched taut over high cheekbones. Her eyes, which could appear brown from a distance, were actually a flecked gray and, at the moment, were feverish with worry. Beneath the bodice of the pink gingham dress, her full, firm breasts rose and fell rapidly. Even in her fear, there was an unconscious sensuality about her—the way her lips moved, the tone of her voice, the way she held her body—that set Sy's blood racing. He found her the most desirable woman he had ever met.

"Of course it's crazy," he said unequivocally. "I've been sitting here trying to think who the real murderer might be."

"You have?" Some of the tension drained out of her. She closed her eyes for a moment in relief. "I was afraid everyone would think he was guilty. The sheriff seemed to believe that since we hadn't lived here very long, Ward was the only possible suspect."

"Please sit down, Mrs. Maddox. You look done in. And no wonder."

Sinking into the chair he was holding for her, she gave him a tremulous smile.

After he had settled himself behind his desk, he said, "Ward impressed me as the type of man who could solve any problem by his wits. The loss of one corn crop wouldn't have driven him to desperation."

Gratitude flooded her face at this accurate evaluation of her husband. "I'm so glad you understand. He told me to come to you. Can you help him?"

He would have liked to believe she had chosen to come to him on her own. No matter. She was here, and she needed him. "I'll do everything I can. What makes the sheriff believe Ward is guilty?"

Patting the sheen of moisture on her forehead and upper

lip with a linen handkerchief, she said, "John Kimball saw him leaving Widow Brown's place yesterday afternoon." She explained the circumstances of that visit and what it was Kimball had seen. "The sheriff said everyone knew how much Ward needed money. He's been all over town for several weeks trying to find a job."

"Is that all the evidence Van Alstine has?"

Helplessly, she spread her small, slender hands. "That's the only evidence there is. He hunted through our house and barn for the money and couldn't find it for the simple reason it isn't there."

In the three years he had lived in Liberty County, Sy had observed that law enforcement and legal justice on the frontier did not match the standards existing in the older sections of the country. His work frequently took him into the next county, where he found the same deficiencies. Still, he was appalled that Van Alstine would arrest an individual for murder with no more evidence than he had in this case. Questioning the suspect was in order, but no more than that. "Let's go over and see Ward. I'll talk to him and then I'll talk to Van. Unless he has more evidence than this, he can't hold Ward in jail."

It gave him pleasure to see her face light up with hope, and further pleasure to take her arm and lead her down the steps and across the street to the small stone building beside the courthouse that served as the jail.

The jail was divided into two sections, an outer office and behind it the cell area. The narrow office had a desk at one end, a cot at the other. In between them, its pipe entering a chimney in the back wall, was a two-burner stove no larger than the one Susan had on the farm.

Deputy Sheriff Hap Turner was seated behind the scarred

desk, his booted toes scarcely touching the bare floor as he tilted back his swivel chair. Short and squat, he was on the point of running to fat. Susan had seen him frequently on trading days, and never had she seen him that his hair did not look as if he'd just got out of bed. Coarse and short, it clung to his skull in untidy whorls. In the six months since he had been hired as deputy, there had been several complaints about his abuse of authority. He sat and watched them come in, leaving it to Sy Harris to speak first.

"How are you, Hap? Where's the sheriff?"

"Over at the county attorney's office."

"Mrs. Maddox has hired me to defend her husband. I've come to see him."

Buried in his brown beard was a slight sneer as Hap said, "She didn't waste any time, did she?" A flick of his eyes over her was his only acknowledgment of her presence. Sharp dislike for the deputy made her drop her glance quickly. Ward was at his mercy. It would not be wise to let Hap Turner know how she felt about him.

Curtly Sy Harris said, "Are you going to let us see him or not?"

Hap drew a ring of keys out of the desk and sauntered toward the barred door that separated the office from the cell area. With deliberate slowness he unlocked the door. Sy Harris stood aside to allow Susan to enter first. The door was closed with an authoritative clang behind them and locked. Three cages ran along the windowless rear wall, their tops a foot or two beneath the ceiling. At either end of the corridor that ran in front of them was a small barred window set close to the ceiling. Both were open, but the room was stiflingly hot. Another small iron stove sat under one of them. In the poorly lit room, Ward was pacing back and forth in the middle cage, the small space giving him room for scarcely three steps before he had to turn and reverse his direction. His shirt was damp with perspiration; drops of it ran down his face. The spectacle of Ward, with his driving energy, confined in a cramped cell brought a cry to Susan's throat that she couldn't choke off. When he saw his wife and the lawyer, his square, deeply tanned face broke into a smile. Oblivious to Sy's presence, Susan rushed to the cell, Ward's name trembling on her lips. Her hands clutched at him through the bars. Ward grabbed her shoulders and squeezed them tightly.

"I didn't expect you so soon, either of you."

She touched his cheek. "Are you all right? It's so hot in here!" With her handkerchief she blotted the sweat on his face. "And that cell is so tiny!" Remembering Sy, she spun around. "How soon can you get him out of here? This is terrible!"

Sy, who had hung back to allow them a private greeting, came forward and shook Ward's hand. "I'll talk to the sheriff as soon as I leave here and try to get you released. First I want you to tell me all you can remember about yesterday afternoon."

Eager to be able at last to tell his story to someone, Ward described his actions during those hours, his first visit to the widow, buying the baking powder for her, his inquiries for jobs, and finally his return to the Widow Brown's. Susan knew exactly what had happened. Hearing it again only added to her frustration. Tuning out the words, she thought instead how dear his face was to her, how achingly familiar that hard muscular body. How could anyone believe him guilty of murdering a pathetic, lonely woman? The absurdity of it drove her nearly wild. How were they going to prove his innocence? Could they prove it? The necessity to convince those who already thought him guilty sent terror rippling through her again.

Sy, who had listened intently, asked, "Did she appear nervous or frightened or disturbed in any way?"

"No, none of those things," Ward stated firmly. "Did you know her? You know how she was, then, like she was tickled to death to see you but had a hard time thinking of things to say. There was nothing wrong—I'm sure of it." Wiping trickling sweat out of his eyes, he added, "She gave me some rolls to take home. Does that sound like I murdered her?"

"The prosecution could claim you helped yourself to those rolls after you killed her." Sy took out a handkerchief and wiped his streaming face but made no move to remove his coat. "Tell me exactly what John Kimball might have seen when you met."

Frowning with the effort to remember, Ward recounted to him the stiff exchange of greetings and how he had put away in his pocketbook the coins the widow had given him and then contemplated his small reserve of money.

"I wish you'd left the widow's coins in your pocket," Sy drawled.

"So do I."

"Well, I don't want y'all to worry. I'll run over to the courthouse and see if I can't persuade the sheriff to release you. I won't be long."

As he left, Susan turned back to Ward, who pulled her as close as he could, but it was impossible to kiss through the bars. He took her hand and pressed fervent kisses into her palm. With her other hand she caressed his hair and neck and traced the planes of his face. "I feel as if we're separated by miles instead of a few inches," she whispered.

"Isn't this a hell of a note?" He glanced at the bars above his head. "I've never been in jail before. I didn't know the cells were so damn small."

"It's awful. I don't know what they're thinking of. How can they believe you did anything so terrible?"

"If only John Kimball hadn't seen me driving out of the widow's yard. And counting my money! Why the hell did I do that? I knew to the penny what I had."

Susan had to admit that it would look bad to anyone who didn't know Ward well. Wouldn't the real murderer laugh when he found out another man had been arrested for the crime he committed? For a moment Susan forgot Ward's plight and thought with horror of the brutal attack on Widow Brown. Had there been time for her to feel terror, or had she been caught unawares? Trusting as a child, she would have let anyone in. It would have taken someone without an ounce of human feeling to have hurt her in any way.

Ward was thinking the same thing. "Who could have done a thing like that? No wonder the sheriff is sore as a boil."

"Why doesn't he go out and find who really did it?"

"He thinks he's got him."

"Oh, Ward!" She clung to him, more frightened than she had ever been in her life.

The door to the county attorney's office was open, and Sy went in. The sheriff was sitting forward in a wooden chair, one hand placed on his knee, the other resting on the dusty desk. His shirt was dark with perspiration. His hat was on the floor beside him. Across the desk sat Jess Frazier, the county attorney. Frazier didn't know it yet, but the opposition was going to back Sy against him in next year's election.

"Guess who's been hired to defend Ward Maddox," Sy said as he took another chair.

"You're not going to be a very popular fellow around town," Frazier said with the defensive air of a man who knew his ability didn't match his job and was ever on guard against anyone else finding it out. "Everyone I've talked to thinks hanging is too good for him." A dark, drooping moustache broke the expressionless expanse of his face. Never without a cigar, he rolled a half-smoked one now between his fingers.

"They've judged him already?" Sy took out a cigar of his own and bit off the end. "Hasn't it occurred to anyone that someone else may have killed the widow?"

"None of us would have killed her," Van Alstine declared. His dark eyes were hard and sure. "We all looked after her. I think hanging is too good for the bastard, too."

"Guilty or not, you don't have enough evidence to hold him," Sy said easily.

"The hell I don't."

"Tell me what you've got." He lit his cigar and puffed at it vigorously to get it going while the sheriff repeated essentially what Ward had conveyed to him. "Van," he said in a reproachful tone when the sheriff had finished, "that's not enough to hold him on, and you know it."

A faint flush rose in Van Alstine's swarthy face. "He has to be some kind of animal to do what he did. I'm holding him no matter what you say."

Regarding the sheriff through a cloud of blue smoke from his cigar, Sy realized that both sides of the man's nature had been aroused by this crime. He was shocked by the cruel killing of a sweet, harmless old woman and grimly determined to punish the man he believed had done it. It wasn't going to be easy to persuade him to release Ward. "What if someone passing through here killed and robbed her? Some farmers have already given up on their crop and are going west to try to find work to get them through the winter. They wouldn't necessarily have had to have heard what we all suspect—that she had money hidden someplace. An old woman alone is an inviting victim for anyone with robbery in mind. She was sure to have at least some money on hand." They were listening with little patience or interest. "Or let's take another look closer to home. We've got some young rowdies in this town. Phil Osborne is one of them. He'd rather be in town drinking and loafing than out there on his farm working and looking after his wife and baby. He cheated his last landlord out of a hundred-dollars worth of wheat, and he's probably in even worse shape financially than he was then. He could have killed the widow for her money."

"Phil's no good," the sheriff declared tersely, "but he'd never have murdered Widow Brown. He's lived around here too long and knows her too well."

"Maybe someone just like him from somewhere else in the county, someone who'd heard the rumor about her money and needed it because he wasn't going to have a crop or for whatever reason, maybe that someone sneaked over here last night and did it."

Jess Frazier said around his cigar, "You're casting about pretty wild, aren't you? We've got the best suspect over there in jail right now."

"No, you haven't. Ward Maddox is one of the hardest workers I've ever known. That man has been out in his field every day since March, from almost before it was light until it was too dark to see. Anybody who's willing to work that hard isn't going to murder for money just because he hasn't found a job in the first few weeks he's looked for one."

Frazier eyed him sourly. "You've only known Maddox a few months. What makes you such an expert on him?"

"I don't have to have known him for ten years to be confident that he didn't kill Widow Brown." Sy turned to the sheriff. "How long did Doc Long say she'd been dead?"

"All night," Van Alstine replied, finally leaning back in his chair. He was sweating profusely. They all were. Although the two windows were open, the second-story office was like an oven.

"All night," Sy repeated. "That means anyone could have gone to her place after dark. As a matter of fact, if Maddox had killed her in the afternoon and the body had lain there that much longer in the hot weather she would have been in terrible shape by the time Charlie Solomon found her this morning."

Jess Frazier snorted. "You're a regular Pinkerton, aren't you?"

The sheriff wasn't any more impressed than the county attorney. "You can make up all the stories you want, Sy, but I'm not turning Maddox loose."

"You don't have enough evidence to hold him," Sy insisted again.

"He's got enough," Frazier snapped.

Realizing he would get nowhere with these two, Sy decided to save his arguments for the judge. "When is the hearing?"

Jess Frazier replied, "I'm going to see Judge Allen in a

few minutes. He'll probably hold it at one o'clock as usual."

Levering himself up with sweaty hands against the wooden arms of his chair, Sy said, "Well, gentlemen, I'll see you in court."

The Maddoxes were holding hands and standing as close to one another as they could get when he returned to the jail. Expectation lit their anxious faces as he came in. Regretting the necessity to disappoint them, he informed them of his failure to gain Ward's release. "But," he hastened to add as their faces fell, "there's a very good chance that I can convince the judge at your hearing tomorrow that you should be set free."

"What time will the hearing be held," Susan asked, "and can I be there?"

"Probably one o'clock; certainly no earlier. Because of his rheumatism, Judge Allen never does any business in the morning. It takes him half a day to get his joints working. And, yes, you can be present if you like." He shook Ward's hand. "I'll see you tomorrow then. I'll wait outside while you say good-bye."

They strained to embrace each other through the bars. "How can I leave you?" Susan cried softly.

Ward said nothing for a moment, holding her. Then he asked, "Can you handle the chores all right?"

"There aren't that many. I won't have any trouble."

"I hope the sow won't get out again."

"I'll check the pen when I get home."

There was nothing more to say. She took his hard, brown hand, kissed it, and held to it as she started for the door. When her forward momentum pulled their fingers apart, she turned for one last look at him. He was pressed against the bars, gripping them. "I'll see you tomorrow," he called.

She nodded and went through the door to the outer office, her throat aching. Hap Turner was sitting like a malevolent presence behind the desk. She barely glanced at him, making straight for the open front door. Sy stood there, his tall body nearly filling the opening. After one glance at her face, he took her arm and led her without a word across the sunbaked yard to the street and across to her wagon, which she had parked in front of his office building. Only after he had untied the team and helped her into the wagon did he speak. "Will you be all right out at your place alone?"

Her voice steady and clear now, she replied, "I'm not afraid, and I can handle the chores."

"If I can do anything at all, don't hesitate to ask."

She gazed down into his eyes. "Just get Ward cleared of this murder charge."

"No jury is going to convict him. And I'll get him released from jail tomorrow. Come to my office before one, and we'll go to the courthouse together."

The drive back home was a mournful one for Susan. Arrival was even worse. Never had she felt so alone, nor had the farmstead looked more forlorn. The ugliness of the sod house and barn jolted her. The six chickens were in the hog pen scratching in the dirt, ignored by the sleeping hog. Off to the right of the barn, the tethered cow lay, chewing her cud of tough but nutritious prairie grass. Not even the hollyhocks and zinnias brightened the place for Susan today. Without Ward's presence, it looked exactly like what it was—a fragment of wilderness.

She unhitched the horses and pumped some water into the tank for them before going in to make herself some dinner. With little appetite, she sat down to eat a sliced tomato and some bread and butter. When Ward was around her days were always full. Now she saw nothing but empty hours stretching ahead of her until she could visit him tomorrow. Finally, despite the blistering heat, she fled the house and went out to work in her garden.

Sy watched her drive off, the image of her distraught expression lingering with him. He would give the Maddox case everything he had. He wanted the satisfaction of wiping the anguish from that lovely face.

He had another visitor to his office later that day. This one wasn't a client.

Nelson Cooper, whose hardware and farm implement business was on the north side of the square, settled his corpulent body in a chair with a grunt. Puffing and sweating from the climb up the stairs, he delayed his greeting until he caught his breath. Nels never looked healthy, but the heat or the stairs, or both, had him looking ill. Sy leaned back in his chair and waited, knowing only a matter of exceptional importance would have brought him up those stairs.

"I hear you've taken the Maddox case," Nels wheezed finally. "You tried to get him out of jail." His tone was accusatory.

"That's right. There's not enough evidence to hold him legally. I couldn't get Van and Jess to see it that way, though."

"What do you want to take that case for? Sentiment against him is running a hundred to one. Almost everybody I've talked to is up in arms. It's too bad we don't have public hangings in this country. People want to see this guy punished."

"What if he's not guilty?"

"Come on, Sy. Who else around here would have killed Widow Brown?"

Sy brought his swivel chair up sharply. "You know, I'm getting damned tired of everybody thinking all the citizens in and around Hawthorne are such saints that they'd never lift their hand to an old woman suspected of having a cache of money. Y'all withhold this sainthood from Ward Maddox because you can't believe he could be as fond of the widow as the rest of you who've lived here for years. Well, I can't believe y'all are saints. Somewhere out there is a murderer, counting the widow's money, while Maddox is being held on evidence so flimsy Jess would be laughed out of almost any court in the country."

Still wheezing, and making no effort to sponge away the sweat that streamed off his face, Nels Cooper said, "Jess would be laughed out of most courts no matter how strong a case he had. He doesn't know a thing about the law. He's cost this county thousands of dollars by taking the wrong cases to court and losing the right ones. That's why we Democrats are going to run you against him."

"I'd appreciate your support, but you're not running me. I made the decision on my own and then sounded you out and some of the other leaders of the party to see if you'd back me."

"We can change our minds."

Sy studied the man who sat across the desk from him. He was typical of the small-town businessmen he found in the West; solid, respectable, with no ambitions beyond making a living from whatever business he was engaged in, a fervent booster of his town, and one who took his politics very seriously. "You'd withdraw your support from me simply because I'd defend Ward Maddox?"

Nels Cooper met his gaze unblinkingly. "Just defending him is enough to lose you votes. Getting him off would lose you three townships. Chances are you will get him off. Jess isn't any match for you in court, which is why we want him out of there and why we'll throw our support to someone else who can win an election that you'll be sure to lose if you get that murderer off."

Sy leaned back in his chair again, but he was far from relaxed. "If I won an acquittal, would y'all still believe he was guilty?"

"He's guilty."

It was incredible. Ward stood convicted in their minds only hours after the crime was discovered and on evidence so weak that no judge worthy of his title would bind him over to district court. Sy pressed his forefingers together and leaned his chin on them. He wanted the job of county attorney; he wanted to improve the quality of legal justice in Liberty County; and he wanted to stretch his skills by prosecuting cases instead of defending them.

Swiveling his chair slightly so that he looked out on the square, his eyes were drawn to the jail where Ward Maddox was probably pacing his cramped cell. He recalled how Susan had rushed to touch her husband in the jail, with what desperate tenderness she had mopped his perspiring face.

Her love for him, so apparent, sent a pang of regret through Sy's belly. You can't have her, he told himself, but you can make her happy. Without turning, he said, "I won't withdraw from the case, Nels. If you withdraw your support, I'll just have to run without it."

"I thought I could make you see reason," Cooper said morosely.

“I do see it, Nels. It’s just that it happens to be different from yours.”

The older man heaved himself out of his chair with difficulty. At the door he grumbled, “I don’t know why anyone wants an office on the second floor.” He left then to tackle the stairs.

Sy remained for a long time gazing out the window.

3

SOMEONE WAS POUNDING on the sheriff's door. Beside him, his wife raised her head. "Van."

"I hear it." He pulled on his trousers over his nakedness and went padding out into the living room to the door. The summer night was light enough that he could find his way without difficulty and easily identify the short, chunky figure on the porch. Instantly alert, he demanded, "What's up, Hap? He hasn't escaped, has he?"

"We'd be lucky if it was that," the deputy panted. "Three men broke in, tied me up, and hung Maddox."

"Hung him?" Van Alstine echoed stupidly, unable for a moment to accept what Hap had told him.

"They blindfolded me and didn't say a word. I don't know who they were."

"Jesus!" He was fully awake now and wished he were

still dreaming. "Get on back there. I'll be there in a few minutes." Knocking into things now in his haste, he returned to the bedroom and lit the lamp.

Turning over, his wife asked, "Do you have to go out at this time of the night?"

"What time is it?"

"Didn't you hear the clock strike just now? It's two o'clock."

Not bothering with socks, Van Alstine pulled his boots on his bare feet and dragged his shirt from the back of a chair. "Some guys broke into the jail and hung Ward Maddox."

She sat up, a plump woman whose long, dark hair hung loose around the shoulders of her nightgown. "Who would do that?"

"Hap doesn't know. They blindfolded him."

"Didn't he even get a glimpse of them?"

"I don't know. I didn't take the time to find out any more. I've got to get down there." He finished strapping on his gun belt over his shirttail, and left.

They had tied the rope to the top bars of the cage. Ward Maddox's naked body swung slightly, his head lolling crookedly, his wrists and ankles bound. Van Alstine had never seen a man hung before. It was all he could do not to turn his eyes away. Thickly he asked, "Have you got a knife?"

Hap pulled one out of his pocket and opened it for him.

"Hold him while I cut him down."

The rope was new and stiff, and the blade of the pocket-knife was none too sharp. By the time Van Alstine had finished, sweat was running down his face and the middle of his back. Hap staggered under the weight of the body as it collapsed. Together the two men carried it to the cot and put it down. Van Alstine felt sick to his stomach.

"How long ago did this happen?"

"Seems like hours, but it was only one. It took me that long to get my hands free. They snuck in here while I was asleep and stuck a rag in my mouth and turned me over on my stomach and tied my hands behind my back. They tied my feet together, too."

"Couldn't you make out anything about them? Didn't they say anything?"

"Not a word, and they didn't light a light until they had me blindfolded. I could tell they'd lit the lamp. I heard them get the keys out of the desk and open the cage. It woke Maddox up, and he put up a fight."

"They must have talked to him. Told him to keep quiet or something."

"If they did, they whispered. I didn't hear a thing."

Something in Hap's tone when he denied hearing anything started a small suspicion growing in Van Alstine's mind. "Show me how they tied you."

His deputy pocketed his knife and led the way back to the office. Two short lengths of new rope and two red handkerchiefs, one of them wadded, lay on the sheets that were the only bedding on the cot. Van Alstine picked up both pieces of rope and examined them; it was the same stuff used to hang Maddox, narrow, tough, and stiff, so stiff that if a knot had been tied in it there would still be kinks left. These pieces were slightly curved, as if they had been cut from a large spool or roll and not yet known a loop or knot. Absently, he commanded, "Go get Doc Long. As coroner, he'll have to see this."

With Hap gone, he looked around. The desk drawer that

usually held the keys was still open. All the others were shut; the desk top showed no signs of disturbance. The door showed no signs of being forced, but that didn't mean anything. He wouldn't have locked it either if he'd been guarding the prisoner. It was too hot to have it closed. Maddox couldn't have broken out of his cage, and who would have suspected that anyone would want to get at the prisoner. Going back into the cell area, he examined the floor, the bars, everything, avoiding as well as he could looking at the corpse. Finding nothing, he went back to the cot. It didn't look to him as if the handkerchief that supposedly was used as a blindfold had ever been knotted. He picked up the two stiff lengths of new rope again, carried them back to his desk, and sat down, examining them thoughtfully.

Hap hurried through the dark streets, fighting the impulse to look back over his shoulder. He'd have died rather than admit his fear of the dark to anyone; it was a holdover from childhood that, try as he would, he couldn't rid himself of. And tonight the dark held a new terror for him. He could almost feel the cold breath of Ward Maddox's ghost on the back of his neck. Being strung up like that was a hell of a way to die. If dead people could come back, Maddox would for sure haunt the four of them.

Passing one particular house, he wondered if its owner was sleeping or whether he was lying awake seeing again that jerking body, those bulging eyes, that protruding tongue. For an instant he paused, wanting to run inside and be told they had done the right thing, that Maddox had got what he deserved, and that they had made sure he didn't slip through the fingers of the law.

He had awakened with a hand clamped over his mouth and someone bending over the cot, whispering, "We want Maddox. Are you with us or do we have to tie you up?" He had recognized the voice immediately. The gray light of the summer night coming through the window and the open door showed him two more shadows. When he nodded to indicate he would cooperate, the hand was taken from his mouth. He got the keys from the desk and unlocked the door into the cell area. It was very dark in there, the two small windows high in the walls giving little light. Once they were all inside, someone lit a candle. Only then did he recognize the other two men. Their fury over the murder of Widow Brown was evident when they roused Maddox out of his sleep and hung him with such dispatch that Hap was led to wonder if they had done this before. Not to be outdone, he had helped hold the struggling prisoner while they tied him up, then watched without once turning his eyes away while Maddox jerked and twisted as he slowly strangled.

A whisper of movement behind him made Hap whirl, choking back a cry that rose to his throat. It was only a skunk on his nightly foray, his broad white stripe glowing as he ambled across someone's yard, paying no attention to the two-legged creature also abroad in the warm darkness. With two blocks still to go before he reached the doctor's house, Hap began to run.

Susan's step was heavy as she carried the pail of milk to the house. The sun, just inches above the horizon, shone directly into her face. Relishing the early morning coolness after a hot, nearly sleepless night, she wondered if Ward was awake. If he was, he was probably following her around in his imagination as she did the chores. She would wait until noon to go to town. Meantime, she could get some canning done.

She was skinning a panful of scalded tomatoes when she heard a buggy on the road. Moving to the open door, she saw that it was the sheriff. Beside him sat Sy Harris. Rev. England, minister of the church she and Ward had occasionally attended since they had come to Liberty County, followed in another buggy with his wife.

Could they be coming to see her? Susan watched with some puzzlement as the two vehicles pulled into her yard. Shading her eyes against the sun, she went outside and, ignoring the sheriff, greeted the Englands and Sy. Only when Sy got out of his buggy did she see how ashen-faced he was. They couldn't possibly have found more evidence against Ward, could they?

The sheriff removed his big hat slowly, exposing his swarthy scalp with its few strands of dark hair lying across the top. "I've brought bad news," he said quietly and without preamble.

Mrs. England, a stout, buxom woman, came to her side. Her husband, always overshadowed by his wife whenever she was present, hung back, his round pink face wearing an expression Susan couldn't fathom. There was no mistaking Sy Harris's expression, however. Something had shaken him to the core. He, too, moved closer to her. "What's happened?" Susan asked, her heart beginning to race.

"Three men broke into the jail last night and overpowered my deputy." The sheriff paused, turning his hat in his hands. "They hung your husband."

She stared at him uncomprehendingly. "You're not telling me he's dead?"

"Yes, ma'am. I'm sorry."

"I don't believe it." Firmly, she repeated the denial. "I don't believe it."

"I'm afraid it's true, Mrs. Maddox."

"It can't be possible. He wasn't even guilty. It was all a mistake." Her eyes swept their faces and came to rest on Sy's. "A trial would have proved that."

Hoarsely, Sy said, "It's true. Ward is dead. I can't tell you how sorry I am. I should have got him out of jail somehow. It never occurred to me anything like this would happen."

The Englands murmured their condolences, which Susan scarcely heard. How could Ward be dead? Wasn't it bad enough he was in jail, accused of a crime he hadn't committed?

"Who were these men?" Susan demanded.

"The deputy says he didn't recognize any of them," replied the sheriff. "They broke in while he was asleep, tied him up, gagged and blindfolded him. He worked free about an hour after they left and came and got me."

"Why would they want to hurt Ward?"

"Everyone had been upset about the widow's murder. She was sort of a pet around here. They were afraid he'd be set free. Maybe they were drunk besides being mad. I want you to know that I don't hold with vigilante justice. I won't rest until I've found out who did this."

"I want to see Ward. Where is he?"

It was Rev. England who replied with quiet and unexpected authority. "The undertaker has him. We can bring him home when he's ready. Or we can take him to the church."

"I want him brought home." Still unable to believe Ward was dead, she said to Sy, "Did you see him?"

He shook his head, but she wanted confirmation from him. "I want to know how it was done."

Sy turned to the sheriff and demanded harshly, "You tell her."

Hesitating and dropping his eyes to his hat, which he still twisted in his hands, Van Alstine explained in a low voice, "They tied a rope around the bars at the top of his cage."

So it really had happened. Not knowing what to do, she went into the house. The pan of tomatoes still sat on the table. Sitting down, she took them into her lap and began to slip the skins off. She refused to look at any of them. Mrs. England came over to gently lay her hand on her shoulder. "I should get these put up before they bring Ward home," Susan told her.

"Do you want me to see about a cemetery lot?" Rev. England asked.

"No, I'll bury him here. This is where he belongs. Maybe overlooking the draw north of the house. It's been full of wild flowers all summer. . . . I'll think about it. We'll have the funeral tomorrow afternoon. That will give me time to decide and to get the grave dug."

No one said anything. She continued to peel the tomatoes. Finally Sy said, "You have a sister back in Pennsylvania, don't you? Can she come and stay with you?"

"Probably. Yes, I should let her know, and Ward's folks, too."

"If you'll give me her address, I'll send a wire."

"Yes, then she can tell Ward's family. It's Coila Eberly, Fieldsboro, Pennsylvania."

"And if you'll give me Ward's suit," Rev. England said, "I'll take it to town."

"What for? Oh, you mean to be buried in." Setting the heavy dishpan on the table, she got up. "It's in the trunk." Using her apron as a towel, she dried her hands and went to the bedroom. There was nothing in the room except the bed and two trunks. Some of their clothing hung on pegs driven into the sod walls, but her wedding dress and Ward's suit were carefully packed away in mothballs in the hump-backed trunk she had bought before they were married. She shook the mothballs off the black jacket and matching pants. Such fine wool. And Ward had looked so handsome on their wedding day. He had worn the suit on the train trip to Nebraska as she had her light blue wedding dress. After cleaning them thoroughly, she had packed them away where they had remained except for the few times they had been to church.

Rev. England took the suit from her, but when she lifted out the shiny black shoes, he said, "He won't need those."

"All right."

He took the clean linen and socks she gave him and left with the sheriff.

Sy stood near the door, pale and irresolute. "Your sister's name is Coila Eberly? And the address is Fieldsboro, is that right?"

"Yes, Fieldsboro, Pennsylvania." He continued to stand there, looking so wretched that she said gravely, "You'll be helping me a great deal by sending that wire."

He nodded stiffly and left. Susan went directly back to the tomatoes.

Mrs. England, who had been standing beside the table, asked,"Can't I help?" Susan had always regarded her as a formidable woman who, she suspected, was impervious to the sniping criticism most minister's wives had to suffer at one time or another from the female sector of their church membership. There was scarcely a trace of her usual bluntness now.

"Hand me that pan. I'll pour some of these into it. There's a knife in that drawer," Susan said, indicating a low dresser. "Ward and I bought that dresser in Hawthorne. We came out here with only a bed and some bedding and that clock, which was a wedding present from my father and sister. We bought this table and the chairs and stove and not much else. We had to make our money last until we sold our first crop. I haven't minded doing without things. I haven't even minded living in a sod house. These solid walls and deep windowsills make it seem cozy."

"You have it fixed up real nice."

"I didn't even mind the dirt walls, but Ward came home one day with a wagon full of old newspapers he'd bought at the *Echo* and helped me cover the walls. It did make it lighter in here." She surveyed the room fondly. "I told Ward I could put up with a sod roof and dirt floor for a while. I knew it wouldn't be long before he built us a frame house. Ward is very wise with money, and he's the hardest worker I ever saw."

"He was a fine young man."

"He broke eighty acres this summer after the corn was planted. That's about all that can be cultivated. The rest he's leaving in grass. We need some pasture."

"Why don't I get some water and have it heating?" Mrs.

England suggested. "We'll want to wash those jars and sterilize them."

How nice it was to have another woman in the house to visit with while she worked. It reminded Susan of how it used to be when she and Coila and their mother used to work together. She hadn't realized it, but she missed that companionship.

They had carried the newly canned tomatoes down to the cellar and were returning to the house when the hearse arrived. Behind the somber black vehicle with its polished silver side lamps came Rev. England in his buggy. Sy Harris was with him.

She thanked the undertaker and his assistant for their expressions of sympathy and looked blankly at the undertaker when he asked where she would like the coffin placed.

"In the bedroom, don't you think?" Mrs. England suggested gently to Susan. "You have plenty of room in there."

"Yes, that would be best." She went inside, and together she and Mrs. England moved one of the trunks to the other side of the bedroom, leaving the area in front of the north window empty. The undertaker and his assistant brought in the catafalque and set it up, and a few moments later the four men carried in the plain wooden coffin, staggering under its weight. When it was in place and the lid had been raised, everyone stepped back to permit her to see her husband.

Susan went forward quickly. It seemed such a long time since she had seen Ward. He looked so pale. "Ward," she whispered, and bent to kiss him. His lips were as cold and hard as marble. Recoiling, she stared down at the waxy face, the nose that seemed too sharp, the closed eyes that shut her out forever. She shrieked, then crumpled to the floor, moaning, "No . . . no . . . no . . . no."

After they had lifted her from the floor onto the bed, Sy went outside. He had had scarcely a moment alone since Van had come to the hotel that morning and told him in the midst of his shaving that Ward had been hung by parties unknown. He wanted Sy to go with him and the Englands to break the news to Susan. With shaking hands Sy had finished shaving, dressed, and, still dabbing at his nicked and bleeding face, he had come out here with the others.

Oblivious to the searing sun, he walked aimlessly about the farmyard, torn with guilt and aching because Susan was in such pain. It seemed as if there must have been something he could have done to have got Ward out of jail. Was there some argument he had neglected to use that would have convinced Van and Jess to let Ward go? He stopped at the hogpen and pounded his fist against the board fence. Inside her tiny shelter, the sow grunted and raised her head.

Who in God's name had done this? Was it men who were afraid the law wouldn't punish a man they believed guilty of a heinous crime? Or did they want the satisfaction of punishing Maddox with their own hands? If he knew why it was done, maybe he could figure out who had done it.

The sheriff hadn't been any help. He had gone to Van's office after getting the wire off to Susan's sister. By that time he was gripped by a violent fury. "You held him without sufficient cause and then left him guarded by a man you never should have hired as deputy in the first place! His blood is on your hands, Van, as surely as it's on the filthy hands of the man who hung him!"

Van had sat there at his desk and taken it as Sy raved on, castigating him as a law officer and as a man. At last, having run out of words, Sy sent his arm sweeping across Van's desk, scattering papers, pencils, ashtray, and sundry items to the floor. The action served as a final release; he straightened, out of breath, his head pounding.

Looking slightly yellow, the sheriff made no move to pick up so much as a pencil. "Maybe I don't know the law as good as you do, but I had a murder to solve, I had a good suspect, and I did my job as I saw it. I never once thought any of the men around here would take the law into their own hands—did you?" he demanded.

Sy refused to answer. "Who do you think did it?"

"I haven't any idea."

"Are you going to try to find out?"

Van Alstine snapped, "I won't bother to answer that."

"I want to talk to Hap. He must have noticed something that would help identify them."

"I arrested him. He's in there."

"Arrested him!" That had taken Sy by surprise.

"I don't believe his story. I don't think he was ever tied up and blindfolded. There was some rope and some handkerchiefs on the cot, but they didn't look like they'd been used. Especially the rope." Van Alstine opened a drawer and took out two short lengths of hemp cord. "Do those look to you like they've had knots tied in them?"

"No, they don't."

"I think Hap knows who did it; he just ain't talking."

"You think he just stood by and let them hang Ward?"

"That's what I'm thinking."

"There must be some way to make him talk."

"If you come up with one, I sure hope you'll tell me."

"If you're right about Hap, he's an accessory. He could be prosecuted along with the rest."

"I can't see him talking, then, can you?"

The sow struggled up to her knees, grunting. She looked toward the fence at Sy, then at the pen baking in the midday heat. Changing her mind about leaving her shelter, she lay down again, her mounded side heaving as she panted.

Also aware now of the broiling sun, Sy made his way to the barn, stepping gratefully into its shade. The horses and the cow had been turned out, leaving it inhabited by a half dozen chickens who lay about the dirt floor, their wings held away from their bodies, their beaks open. Susan's bonnet hung from a nail driven into one of the support poles in front of the cow's stanchion; she must have hung it there that morning while she milked, and then forgotten it. Taking it down and holding it in his hands, he gazed at it for a long time.

Suddenly it occurred to him that someday soon she would be leaving. With nothing left here for her, she'd sell the farm and return to Pennsylvania, going out of his life forever. For the first time he realized she was free. If she were to stay around Hawthorne, he would wait until the proper time and then try to win her heart. What irony that the same event that made such a plan possible would also take her away from him.

Shame that he could be contemplating his own future happiness while she was suffering the agony of grief made him hang the bonnet back on the nail quickly, as if he were taking a liberty he had no right to take.

• • •

Van Alstine held the long rope that had been used to hang Ward Maddox up to the end that hung from the spool in Cooper's Hardware. It was impossible to tell, as it had been with the two short pieces, whether it had come from that store. "Who'd you sell some of this rope to last?"

Seated nearby in a chair where he was always to be found when he wasn't waiting on a customer, Nels Cooper thought a minute and then said, "Pete Hittering bought some just the other day."

"Quite a bit of it?"

"Yes, as I remember it," Cooper wheezed.

"Anybody else you can remember?"

"Nobody just recently."

Coiling up the pieces of rope again, Van Alstine said, "I'll go out and see Pete."

"Are you going to go off and leave Hap locked up there by himself?"

"I hired Earl Crowder as my deputy. I sent word to him before dinner. Shorty hasn't been needing him regular the last couple of months. The carpenter business has fallen off like everything else. He's over to the jail keeping an eye on things."

"Has Hap admitted anything?"

"He's sticking to his story of being tied up. If you or your boy should remember selling any more rope lately, get word to me. I mean to find out who hung Maddox. I won't stand for people taking the law into their own hands."

Van Alstine's check of the rope at the other hardware store was just as inconclusive. One cut rope end looked like practically every other. A sale the day before, the first in weeks, had been made to Carl Wagner. An investigation led from Wagner's house to one of the churches, where, as

Wagner had stated, the new rope hung from the church bell. A trip out to Pete Hittering's farm was no more productive. Hittering took him to the barn and showed him the brand new lariat he had fashioned from the rope he'd bought from Cooper. As he drove back to town, Van Alstine cursed, knowing that tomorrow morning the coroner's jury would have no choice except to find that Ward Maddox had met his death at the hands of persons unknown.

The rays of the setting sun were striking her pillow before Susan returned to some sort of sanity. From the kitchen came a murmur of voices. Shakily she sat up and went to Ward. She needed to touch him. Avoiding the marble coldness of him, she laid her hand on his arm. Through the crisp wool of his sleeve, she felt the muscular strength that had been so much a part of him, a quality she had grown so intimately familiar with these past five months. She began weeping again, quietly now.

"Can you eat something, my dear? You really should, you know." Hearing her up, Mrs. England had come to the doorway between the two rooms.

Shaking her head, Susan said, "I'm sorry. I should have thought about feeding you."

"We're not going hungry. I gathered the eggs, and you have plenty of stuff in the garden. Do you feel well enough to come out here for a few minutes? Sy Harris is still here. He'd like to talk to you."

Straightening her twisted dress, she went into the kitchen. Sy and Rev. England sat at the table, the remains of their supper still before them. Sy rose immediately to pull out a chair from the table for her. He was still white-faced, and his drawl sounded more pronounced as he said, "I wonder,

Mrs. Maddox, if you wouldn't like to reconsider your decision to bury your husband here on the farm. It will pass into other hands when you return to Pennsylvania. You might rather have him buried in the Hawthorne cemetery."

She and Ward passed the cemetery every time they went into Hawthorne. Lying just outside the north edge of town, it had been planted with cedars brought up from the river twenty years ago when the town was taking shape. It was a nice place, as cemeteries went. They had attended Decoration Day services there in May, watching while flowers were placed on the graves of the four Civil War veterans. But nothing tied them to it emotionally; none of their loved ones was buried there. The farm, on the other hand, had absorbed their sweat and been transformed by their love. Its virgin sod had been broken by Ward; he had created a farm out of wilderness. No matter how many future owners it might have, none would have that special relationship with this piece of land.

"No, I want to bury him here." She hadn't the strength to explain why. "Above the draw to the north of the barn. No one will ever plow there. It's too rough."

"Do you feel like showing us now?" Sy asked. His eyes were dark with an intensity of emotion Susan found difficult to understand; he was taking Ward's death very hard. Maybe he saw it as a failure on his part to protect his client. Whatever his reason, his distress formed a bond between them; no one else in Hawthorne would be affected so deeply by Ward's murder. "There are several hours of daylight left," he went on. "We could start digging the grave and finish tomorrow morning."

Forcing her legs to move, to hold her upright, she took the three of them out to the spot she had chosen. Even at this late hour of the day the draw they gazed down upon was vivid with color. Sunflowers that had followed the course of the sun during the day now faced west, their brilliant, heavy heads drooping slightly with their own weight. Purple flowers, several different varieties, grew closer to the ground; somehow they had managed to pierce the thick prairie sod and grow among the grasses. "Right here," she said, picking a level area back from the edge of the bank.

"Isn't it pretty," Mrs. England observed approvingly.

Sy Harris agreed. "I can understand why you chose this place."

She showed them where she kept her gardening tools, and the two men went back to dig the grave. Darkness had fallen before they quit and drove back to town, leaving Mrs. England to spend the night with her.

She slept very little, yet she lay so still beside Mrs. England that the older woman asked once, "Are you all right?" and had to be assured that Susan was.

Rev. England came out for dinner the next noon after conducting funeral services for the Widow Brown. He brought with him a wire from Coila saying she was leaving immediately and would arrive Saturday afternoon. Sy Harris came out at two-thirty. With him was the sheriff. Behind them came several other vehicles bearing mourners, among them Mr. and Mrs. Lord and some members of Rev. England's church. Even the Solomons were there, all three of them, expressing not only their sorrow but also their condemnation of the vigilante justice that had deprived Ward of his right to a court trial. It was a small group, yet Susan was surprised that anyone came. She assumed everyone in the community believed Ward guilty of the murder of Widow

Brown. Through her numbness and fatigue, she received their condolences and thanked them for coming when the service was over. She declined Mrs. England's offer to stay with her again that night. "I'll be able to hold together until my sister gets here."

"Are you sure?" Sy Harris asked. "I think you ought to have someone with you." Mrs. England expressed equal concern.

"I'm fine, really. Don't worry. I'm numb and I'm very tired. I'm sure I'll sleep well tonight."

Mrs. England left reluctantly with her husband. They were the last to leave, and when they were gone, Susan sat for a long time trying to come to terms with this traumatic change in her life. She would have liked the routine of the evening chores, but some of the men had done them before they left. Eventually she wandered out to the barn and spoke softly to the cow and the horses. Her small flock of chickens were coming in and settling on the roost for the night. She stood among the animals for a few minutes, listening to their sounds, before going back out into the fading light. The new grave drew her, and she went to say good night to Ward. As she stood as close to him as she would ever be again, she was glad she had insisted he be buried here instead of in town. It was going to ease her loneliness to be able to come to this spot and be with him while she remained on the place. Finally she returned to the house and, without lighting a lamp, got ready for bed.

She slept soundly until four in the morning. Awakening suddenly, she remembered at once that Ward was dead. The knowledge was a pain that spread to every part of her being. Rendered powerless by its assault, she lay there until the clock struck six. By that time the sounds of the animals were growing insistent. They were hungry and thirsty, and the cow needed to be milked. With every movement a major effort, she dressed, lit a fire, and set the coffee on to boil.

Soothed somewhat by the physical activity required by the chores, she sat over her coffee an hour later and considered how she would get through the next two days until Coila arrived.

At one-thirty that afternoon, Sy heard someone taking the steep stairs outside his office two at a time. Moments later, the sheriff burst in, red-faced and fuming. "The judge ordered me to release Hap."

Sy closed his lawbook with a bang. "Why the devil did he do that?"

"Hap hired Ezra Black to represent him, and Ezra told the judge Jess would be laughed out of district court if the judge bound Hap over for trial. That's all Jess had to hear. He's no lawyer, and he knows it. He turned pea-green when Ezra said that about being laughed out of court." Van Alstine swore and looked like he'd like to kick something or someone. "The three of them went into a huddle, and a few minutes later Judge Allen ordered Hap released. Not enough evidence to bind him over, he said."

Next to finding out who really killed Widow Brown and clearing Ward's name for Susan's sake, Sy wanted to see the men who killed Ward convicted and hung as they had hung him. It was the only thing he could think of that would help ease Susan's grief. If Hap had felt the noose tightening around his own neck, he might have talked. "We've got to get Jess out of that county attorney's office," he said tersely. "He's a disgrace to the profession and to the county."

"I agree, but the election is more than a year away. What

do I do about Hap in the meantime?"

"Give him a hard time. Keep after him. Maybe he'll give himself or the others away somehow."

"The damned little runt! I can just hear him laughing at me."

"Our day will come. If he hasn't put the noose around his neck by next November, I'll slap a murder charge on him and let's see him get out of that one."

The livery barn was cool, its big doors at either end open, its haymow trapping the heat above the ground floor. The small office was cramped and hot; nevertheless, this was where Hap indicated he wanted to talk to Pat Seavey, making sure the door was closed once they were inside. Hap sat on the edge of the scarred wooden chair across the narrow space from the rolltop desk where Pat Seavey lounged, his wavy white hair falling over his smooth brow. Glaring resentfully at the fair-skinned, handsome face, the tall, well-built body, Hap announced, "I need a job."

"I've got all the help I can afford. Business is rotten."

"You can afford me."

Seavey regarded Hap for a few moments, then took a bottle from one of the desk drawers, pulled at it, and handed it to Hap. "I'd have to let Aldie go. It would look funny if I hired you to take his place."

"Say he wasn't doing his job. Or get him mad so he pops off at you." Hap took a pull at the bottle. "I helped you out the other night. Now I need your help. That's what friends are for, isn't it?"

Seavey held his hand out for the whiskey and took another swallow. "All right. Wait a week, then come in. Meantime, I'll let Aldie go. I'll try to do it so it won't look funny."

He swore. "Van ought to thank us for what we did. We saved the county a lot of money and trouble."

"He sure didn't see it that way."

Hap got up and left, not bothering to thank Seavey. Why the hell should he? Pat owed him.

{4}

GIDEON KIMBALL WAS standing at the ticket window talking to Frank Cook, the depot agent, when Van Alstine went in. The small wooden building smelled like baking lumber. Even at seven-thirty the sun was still cooking the west side of it. Dust coated the floor and the benches; behind the agent the telegraph chattered unintelligibly.

"Howdy, Gideon." The boy had been leaning on the small counter on the outside of the window grille when he saw the sheriff, he straightened his tall man's body slowly, a look of surprise on his usually vacant face. Almost instantly, fear replaced the surprise. Van Alstine spoke past his shoulder to the short, dark-haired man behind the grille. "Curly said you wanted to see me."

The green-billed cap bobbed as Frank Cook nodded. "Gideon's buying a ticket to Denver. I think you ought to ask him where he got the money he's carrying."

The boy cowered against the varnished wooden wall when

Van Alstine swung his eyes back to him. "Does your pa know you're going to Denver?" A tremor went through Gideon's body; he didn't answer. "Have you really got enough money to get you there?"

The reply was a nod; his expression was half fearful, half proud.

"Let's see it."

Gideon pulled an old black leather pouch from his pocket and opened it, showing the silver and paper money inside to the sheriff.

The sight of the money, a considerable amount of it, sent a wave of foreboding through Van Alstine. "How much have you got there?"

"I don't know."

"You can count, Gideon. I know you can."

"Not that far."

Van Alstine raised his eyes to the boy's face. The shadow of a man's beard showed through his skin. Despite his size and strength, no one had ever considered Gideon dangerous; he was a child. Everyone pitied him because his father had never forgiven him for being slow in the head. He vented his fury by beating the boy for the slightest cause, working him like a horse at home, or hiring him out and taking all his wages except for the few cents he left him to spend for candy or ice cream each Saturday.

"Is this your pa's money?" Let him say yes, Van Alstine prayed desperately.

Terror contorted the boy's face. "No! No, it ain't Pa's!"

The sheriff felt a heavy weight begin to press down on his shoulders. He wished he could walk out of there, let the boy go to Denver with the money, and let the matter drop.

"Whose is it then?

"It ain't Pa's!" Gideon cried again. He had begun to shake.

Van Alstine said soothingly, "I believe you. But if it ain't your pa's, where did you get it?"

"If I tell you'll beat me!"

"No, I won't, Gideon. I won't hurt you, I promise. And I won't let your pa hurt you either."

"If you don't let me go to Denver, he'll beat me! You can't stop him." His eyes had taken on a wild look.

"Yes, I can. I'm the sheriff. I can take you away from him so he can't get at you."

"He'd find me."

"No, he wouldn't. I'd make sure he never laid a hand on you again. Not ever again. Tell me where you got the money, Gideon, and I'll take you to that place right now."

"You won't beat me neither?"

"I won't beat you. I swear before God."

Gideon dropped his eyes to the open pouchlike purse. "It's Widow Brown's."

He had known it, figured it out while he walked to the depot. Maddox had been innocent. He had arrested the wrong man and then let him be killed. He released his breath in a long, despairing sigh. He glanced at Frank Cook, whose answering glance was sympathetic.

"How'd you get the money, Gideon?"

"I did something bad," the boy said in a low tone, still not looking up.

"It's all right. You can tell me. Remember, I'm not going to hurt you."

Fingering the money inside the purse, the boy haltingly explained. "I took the money George Buxton paid me for helping him put up hay and went to Sadie's . . . I never been there before, but I been wantin' to go . . . I know what men do there . . . I'm a man and I need to . . . I knew Pa wouldn't never let me; so I told him George said he'd pay me in a few days . . . Pa kept asking me for the money and finally said he was a-going to George himself . . . He'd a killed me if he found out what I done . . . I knew the widow had some money hid, so I went there." His voice had dropped steadily until it was barely audible. He paused and was silent so long it didn't appear he was going to finish.

"She wouldn't give it to you, I guess," Van Alstine said heavily. Gideon shook his head. "So you hit her and hunted for it. Where'd you find it?"

"Under the mattress, where Pa hides his."

Wishing he'd never taken this damn job, wishing he'd gone on working at the feedstore even if it had meant living on cornbread and beans, Van Alstine reached out and tried to take the purse. Gideon hung on. "I want to go to Denver," he said. "Sadie said there was lots of women there. Pa can't never find me there."

"Yes, he can, Gideon. He'll telegraph the Denver police, and they'll find you and bring you home. He'll beat you then."

The boy seemed to shrink; the look of wild terror came back. "You said you wouldn't let him."

"I won't if you'll come with me and let me take care of you." Gently, he coaxed, "Give me the money, Gideon, and I'll take you where you'll be safe for the rest of your life."

The boy hesitated, his glance never wavering as he looked at Van Alstine. His working face, his opaque blue eyes, told the full story of the conflict raging inside that inadequate brain. Then, slowly, he released the purse. Van Alstine patted his shoulder, saying a bit thickly, "Come along now." Not trusting himself to look at Frank Cook, he led Gideon away.

Susan had just set some bread out to rise when she heard someone on the road. Grief threatened to paralyze her, but she had discovered that activity kept her from collapsing. Emotionally she was hanging by her fingertips until Coila arrived. Glancing out the open door, she saw that it was the sheriff. Fear shot through her. He brought nothing but bad news. Then she realized there was no bad news left for her and went with dragging steps to the door.

"Morning, Mrs. Maddox." When he removed his big hat, she could see that he hadn't slept much the night before. His bloodshot eyes were sunken in dark hollows, and his swarthy skin was gray.

Without returning his greeting, Susan asked, "What more can you do to me, sheriff?"

He flinched. Dropping his eyes to his hat he began running the brim around through his fingers as he had the morning he had come to tell her Ward was dead. Susan realized with a sick feeling that he had after all brought some more bad news to her. He cleared his throat. "Coming out here to tell you this is about the hardest thing I ever had to do, but I felt it was my place to do it. Gideon Kimball tried to buy a ticket to Denver last night. When the depot agent saw the bag of money he had, he sent word to me. I went down and got Gideon and made him tell me where he'd got all that money. He finally admitted it was Widow Brown's."

"You mean . . ."

He forged on, repeating the story Gideon had told, only

hinting at how Gideon had spent the wages he was supposed to turn over to his father.

A loud ringing began in Susan's ears. She must have looked as if she were going to faint because the sheriff exclaimed, "You'd best get inside where you can sit down. Can you walk?"

She turned blindly, making for the house with the careful tread of a drunk, shaking off Van Alstine's attempts to aid her. The fire she had built to boil coffee earlier had died out, leaving the coolness of the earth walls to take over once again. Sinking into a chair, she tried to draw the cool air into her lungs. Gasping, she said, "You're all murderers. Just because Ward hadn't lived here very long, you thought he was guilty...you killed him...without giving him a chance to prove he was innocent."

"I was only doing my duty when I arrested him." His hat was taking a terrible beating in his hands. "I fired Hap Turner and arrested him. The judge turned him loose because he said I didn't have enough evidence, but I'm going to try again. I mean to find out who killed your husband." One arm shot out, its hand clenched into a hard fist. "They're going to have to pay for what they did."

The fierceness of his declaration failed to ease her fury. "That won't bring my husband back, will it? Please leave. I never want to see you on my place again."

"I'm sorry, ma'am. About everything." He left then, quickly.

Ward need not have died. Just three days time would have proved him innocent. Driven wild by the monstrousness of the blunder, she sprang to her feet and ran outside, heading for Ward's grave. Chickens flew out of her path as she rounded the sod barn and made for the mound of fresh earth that she could see easily through the prairie grass cropped short by the cow and the horses. Flinging herself down upon it, she cried, "They know you were innocent. Oh, God, if only I could bring you back! How can I stand it?" Pummeling the dry, chunky earth, she poured out her fury at the cruel mistake that had cost Ward his life and her, her beloved. He could be alive and at her side this very minute if those murderers had waited for the law to take its course. "It's so unfair . . . you shouldn't be dead . . . please, God, give him back to me . . . it's a terrible mistake . . . he shouldn't be dead . . . oh, God, what can I do?"

In the draw below the grave, the sunflowers nodded toward the east, their brilliance a poignant reminder of the richness of life that Ward could no longer experience. If only she could see those who murdered Ward brought to justice, she thought, twisting with anguish. She had no faith in the sheriff's achieving that; he had bungled the whole matter from the beginning.

Another onslaught of fury and grief threatened to overwhelm her. She closed her eyes against the beauty that Ward's eyes could not see. She couldn't bear the thought that his killers should be forever free while Ward lay in his grave. She had more reason than the sheriff to try to learn the identities of these men. The dry, lifeless clods on which she rested bit into her face as she contemplated the possibility that she might succeed where the sheriff might fail. It would mean staying here. She could live on the farm until she failed to make the payment in March, but she needed to live in town in order to search out Ward's murderers. That meant a job, and although Ward hadn't been able to find one for her, maybe she could find something next spring when she would be forced to surrender their place to the railroad.

Was this what she really wanted to do? She pulled herself up slowly, brushing the earth from her cheek. It wouldn't bring Ward back. Yet she would die if she didn't do something.

She sat beside the grave until the broiling noon sun drove her to seek shelter inside the house.

Sy Harris came out that evening. He had been in the next county for twenty-four hours, representing a client in court, and had been told about Gideon Kimball's arrest on his return to Hawthorne. Driving out to Susan's farm almost immediately in a rented buggy, he was surprised to find her alone.

"Mrs. England came out soon after dinner," Susan explained. "I sent her home. I don't need to have anyone here with me."

He looked travel-worn and weary. She was touched that he had hurried out to see how she was after this latest turn of events. He waited until she was seated in the rocker, then pulled out a chair from the table and sat down himself. Making some concession to the heat, he was wearing a soft-collared white shirt with a loose narrow tie beneath his jacket. Did men never remove their jackets in the South, no matter how hot the weather, Susan wondered.

"I'm glad that Ward's innocence was proven. I'm sure that doesn't balance your loss, but it must be of some comfort to you."

"It is." Her voice shook, and she dropped her eyes.

"I wish I could have been more help to you!" His tone was bitterly self-accusatory.

"You did all you could, and I appreciate that."

After a pause he asked, "Would you like me to meet

your sister tomorrow and drive her out here?"

"That's kind of you, but I'll go in after her. I have so little else to do."

"If you find that you need help with anything—anything at all—it would please me greatly if you'd call on me."

"I may have to do that. I've decided to stay here and not go back with my sister."

He didn't respond to her announcement immediately. It seemed to her that he was keeping his face carefully blank. "Do you plan to keep the farm?" he asked at last.

"That's not possible, but it will be mine until March. When I don't make the payment, the railroad will put me off. I plan to move into Hawthorne then and get a job."

"If I were you, I'd try to sell the farm before I'd let the railroad take it back," he advised.

"Who could afford to buy it, or would even want it, in these hard times?"

"You never know. You've got until March to find a buyer. Meanwhile, if I hear of a job suitable for you, I'll let you know at once."

"I'd appreciate that, but when I spoke of needing your help I had something else in mind." She hesitated, anticipating his negative reaction to her plan. "I intend to find out who killed Ward. The sheriff says he's going to do it, but he's a bungler. And this whole community is bent on protecting its own. Now that the real murderer has been caught, no one is going to care whether the vigilantes are caught or not. I'm sure they'd like to sweep that mistake under the rug and never think about it again."

He had listened without expression, giving no hint of what he thought about her reason for staying. When she finished explaining, she caught the flare of excitement in his eyes. "If you stay, there will be at least three of us who are determined to bring those men to justice. Don't count the sheriff out. He won't countenance people taking the law into their own hands, and he is fuming because the judge ordered Hap released. He'll do everything he can to nail Hap again and catch the others. And I have some plans of my own." He told her about the possibility that he would be elected to the county attorney's office and his intention to charge Hap with murder and bring him to trial if he won the election. "Meanwhile, we hope some evidence will turn up or that Hap will get drunk and give something away that will give us a lead."

It was so much more than Susan had expected that her eyes blurred with tears. "I had no idea. I thought if I left nothing would be done."

The jingle of harness brought her to her feet. From the open door she saw Charlie Solomon and his wife driving in.

Standing at the door a few minutes later, Solomon said, "Art came home from town just before supper and told us about Gideon. We want you to know how glad we are that Ward's name has been cleared."

"Thank you."

Charlie Solomon was wearing a clean set of work clothes, his wife a fresh cotton dress. Notwithstanding their leanness, there was nothing austere about them. Their faces were filled with simple goodness and, at the moment, compassion.

"Won't you come in?" Susan invited.

After they had exchanged greetings with Sy and seated themselves on the chairs Susan pulled out from the table, Charlie Solomon asked, "What will they do with Gideon?"

Sy said, "They'll hold a hearing tomorrow. He'll be

judged mentally incompetent, and Van will take him to the asylum in Lincoln."

"They won't ever let him out, will they?"

"No, he'll be there the rest of his life."

Mrs. Solomon declared, "None of us ever thought he was dangerous."

"From what I've been told," said Sy, "he's known nothing but violence all his life. He probably thought nothing of hitting Widow Brown when she wouldn't do what he wanted. And he was desperate, too, remember. Terrified of what his father would do to him if he didn't get some money."

Solomon winced with pity. "John has always whipped him like a dog."

"He's the one who should be put in jail," Mrs. Solomon declared with uncharacteristic harshness. "I lay all this tragedy at his door."

Susan's throat grew painfully tight; the air was suddenly heavy with grief and regrets for which there were no words. Charlie Solomon broke the silence by turning to Susan and saying, "Art is getting married in a few months. I'm looking for a farm for him. I'd like to buy yours." He went on to make an offer for a third more than Ward had paid for the farm.

Sy spoke up immediately. "That's a very generous offer, Susan. I'd take Charlie up on that before he changes his mind."

Solomon said, "Ward broke a lot of it. Almost eighty acres. It's worth more now than when he bought it."

What he said was true. With that much money, Susan realized, it wouldn't matter whether she found a job or not. "I'll accept your offer, and thank you." To Sy she said,

"Will you take care of all the legal work?"

"Of course. If you'll stop in my office tomorrow when you go into town to pick up your sister, I'll have the papers ready to sign. Can you come in tomorrow afternoon, Charlie? If two o'clock suits both of you, I'll have everything drawn up."

"I'll be there," Charlie Solomon promised.

Coila was aghast when Susan informed her she didn't intend to return to Pennsylvania.

"You can't mean it!" Her eyes were wide in her plump, placid face. "Why would you want to stay here?" Unconsciously her glance swept the kitchen-sitting room of the soddy, where they sat waiting for their supper of potatoes and onions to fry. Her travel dress was soot-stained and wrinkled. Susan could imagine how much she must have been looking forward to a bath and the freedom of movement a house gave after the cramped and dirty train. She had noted Coila's expression of distaste when she first saw the dirt-floored sod house. When she heard Susan's explanation for her surprising decision, her voice softened. "I can understand why you want to make those murderers pay for what they've done to you—"

"And to Ward," interjected Susan.

"—and to Ward, but what chance do you think you'll have?"

"I don't know. But if I left here I'd have no chance at all. I've got to try, Coila. It's the only thing that's keeping me going."

"I know it's awfully hard for you right now, but I think you'd feel much better if you'd go back with me. Your friends are there, everything is familiar, it's your home."

Susan realized that Coila could never understand that this crude shelter, formed of earth, papered with newsprint, and sparsely furnished, could ever have seemed like home. There was no way to explain that love and dreams had transformed it into a place dearer to her than any place she had ever lived in or expected to live in again.

"And there's Papa and me," Coila continued. "We've missed you so. First Mama, then you . . . both in the same year." Her full lips trembled. "You wouldn't believe how Papa has aged. He grieved so hard the day we got the wire about Ward that I wasn't sure I dared to leave him. He's so awfully lonely . . . he needs you, Susan. Just before I got on the train, he said, 'Bring her back just as soon as you can. Tell her I'll take care of her.'"

Susan's eyes filled with tears. How wonderful it would be to be a child again and run to her father to have her hurt kissed away. Suddenly she yearned to see him. Even though he didn't have the power anymore to kiss away her hurts, his very presence would be a comfort. And he needed her. The abrupt emptiness of her life could be filled.

Now that Coila was here, she realized how much she had missed her sister, too. Ward had filled her life so completely she hadn't once thought that she needed anyone else. It was not true. She and Coila had shared too much of their lives, too much love, to be separated from each other without feeling the loss. Regarding her sister's familiar face, listening to her light, sweet voice, all of the old childhood affection came rushing back. Perhaps she needed her sister and her father now more than she needed to pursue Ward's killers.

Coila was recounting her attempts to break the news of Ward's death to his family. His parents hadn't been at home when she hurried over with the wire and, pressed for time to make arrangements to leave her father and to pack, she had gone to the sawmill and told Ward's brother Jed. Just before supper, Ward's folks had come to the Eberly home, having just heard the news. They were stunned, disbelieving; they had to read the telegram with their own eyes. Absorbing the truth finally, they had wept. Susan could picture them: Ward's mother, whose sense of humor had remained intact through years of work and childbearing, brightening a poor and overcrowded house with her wit; his father, a man with little to say but whose pride in his nine sons was unmistakable and whose appreciation of his wife's sallies was revealed in an almost silent chuckle.

Haltingly, Susan said, "It would hurt to go back there, to see Ward's parents... his brothers. There would be so many memories. There are memories here, too, and they're hurting, but it would be different back there. Oh, I don't know what I want to do!"

In the end she stayed. Taking Sy Harris's advice, she decided not to rent a house, moving instead into the Commercial Hotel, where, he assured her, the price for permanent board was reasonable. He oversaw the sale of her machinery and livestock and helped move what few personal things she kept into her corner room at the Lord's house. When he refused payment for the legal work he did for her as well, she didn't know how to adequately thank him.

"I've done very little, really," he told her, "and besides, friendship doesn't require any payment."

After seeing her settled in her new surroundings, Coila left, reluctant to return to Pennsylvania without her.

"I'll come home just as soon as I've finished what I want

to do here," Susan promised. "I don't know how long that will be. Not too long, I hope. Tell Papa not to worry, and give him my love."

Watching Coila's train pull out of the station that morning, Susan was swept up by a feeling of desolation. Once back in her hotel room, she wondered if she'd made the wrong decision. Small though the sod house had been, it was twice the size of the room that would now be her home. Her patchwork quilt covered the iron bed; the striking clock stood on the new bureau. Beside the window that gave on the square sat her rocker; in front of the other window was the small table she had bought to hold the fern and the geranium she had brought from the farm. These personal touches failed to provide any sense that this was her home, however. If Ward were there to share it with her, even that small room would have seemed like home. She had asked for the one she and Ward lived in for a month before moving to their farm, but it was now occupied by the new jeweler, who was a bachelor.

She laid her hat on the bureau before sitting down in the rocker. The breeze coming through the open window was still fairly cool. Through the lace curtains, she watched the midmorning activity of the town. On the corner to her left a woman entered Salvador Cross's Mercantile. Down a few doors, a man started out of the saloon, turned as if speaking to someone inside, then went back in. Across the square she could see two men sitting on a bench outside Cooper's Hardware. On another corner a wagon pulled up in front of the feed store, a farmer jumped down, tied his team to the rail, and went inside. Everyone had their doors open, letting in as much breeze as possible. It looked so staid and peaceful, she thought bitterly. No one would suspect that beneath that surface lurked the savagery that could murder a man in cold blood.

Her heart began to beat in crazy little jerks. Laying her head back and closing her eyes, she tried to calm herself. Without being bidden, a sweet memory came to her. After Ward had worked from sunup to sundown to get their first field plowed, and after they had both worked at the back-breaking job of burying the seed corn in the turned earth that was still a mass of grass roots, Ward announced that they were going to celebrate: She was to put on her best dress and he would take her to a dance. And so, dressed once more in their wedding clothes, they drove to Empire, the town that lay five miles west of Hawthorne. Tired as they were, they stayed until the last dance.

On the way home, she sat within the circle of his arm while he held the reins with his other hand. There was no need to drive the team; the horses knew the way home. The night was warm and clear, the track clearly visible. A couple of miles or so to their right, down by the river, some coyotes began their hysterical yipping. Two or three of them could sound like a large pack. They broke off suddenly, and the night was quiet again, sweet with the scent of prairie grass. Ward began playing with her breast. She had been telling him about her uncle, a fiddler who used to play for dances when she was a child. Her voice began to trail off as Ward's hand at her breast sent desire spreading through her body.

"Do you realize what you're doing?" she asked finally.

"I was hoping *you* did." He grinned at her and pulled the team off the track.

They parked in a ravine, in the shadow of a bank. Ward tied the horses to a plum thicket and lifted her down off the seat. They lay together in the back of the wagon, loosening their clothing and beginning to make love to one another with leisurely voluptuousness.

Afterward they fell asleep, not awakening until the sun had been up for an hour. Laughing and hungry, they had completed the trip home.

Coming out of her reverie with a smile on her face, Susan opened her eyes only to have reality assault her as she found herself in the unfamiliar hotel room. Gasping with the pain of it, she closed her eyes again and began to rock, seeking some relief from her agony. Never again to share such rapture! Never again to feel his body against hers! The longing to hold him, to be in his arms, wrung a moan from her. Clasping her arms tightly around her breasts in an effort to ease her pain, she paced the bare wooden floor. Finding no easement in movement, she fled her room, seeking human company. Rufus Lord, who always had time to visit, wasn't at the desk. The parlor was deserted. Stepping into the dining room she heard voices in the kitchen. Mrs. Lord and her helper, Lettie Turner, were busy preparing the noon meal. Not bothering to return to her room for her hat, she left the hotel and went down the street a few doors to Sy Harris's office. A man she didn't recognize raised his hat to her and greeted her by name as he passed her. She supposed everyone in town knew she was now living at the hotel.

Sy Harris, coatless, his pale brow moist with perspiration, was almost out of sight at his desk behind stacks of books, which he had removed from his glass-doored bookcases and was intently searching through. He didn't see her come through the door and struggled up quickly when she said, "You look very busy."

"Not so busy that I can't visit for a few minutes. Come

in." He took an opened book from a chair and invited her to sit down. "You've seen your sister off, I guess. I should imagine it wasn't easy to see her go." He had slipped his coat off the back of his chair and was hastily donning it.

"Please," she protested, "don't put your coat on. It's too hot. I'll feel guilty sitting here knowing how uncomfortable you are."

Smiling, he replaced his coat on the back of the chair. "I can't have you feeling guilty, can I?" He ran slender fingers through his dark hair, pushing a damp wave off his brow at least temporarily.

Susan felt herself beginning to relax. Sy had become a good friend. She had leaned on his strength and been comforted by his sympathy. Now that she looked back on it, she wondered how she'd have gotten through these past weeks without his sound advice. Coila had been much taken with him, the first time Susan had heard her express an interest in any man.

"He's so sweet," Coila had exclaimed the day he had helped move Susan into town. "If I were one of the girls in Hawthorne, I'd do everything I could—and still remain decent, of course—to catch him."

Susan took a piece of paper from his wastebasket and began fanning herself with it. The faint breeze ruffled her hair and the lace at the neck of her dress. "A few minutes ago, I was wishing I had gotten on the train with Coila. Even now I'm not sure I've done the right thing by staying here."

"I think you have." He settled himself behind the desk, moving a stack of books to the floor so they could see each other. "You can't help but be very, very angry about what happened to Ward. You need to work it off somehow. I don't know how you'd have done it if you'd gone back to Pennsylvania."

"You don't think I'm just being spiteful to want to stay here and see Ward's killers punished?"

His protest was instantaneous and emphatic. "Anyone in your situation would feel that way. It's perfectly natural. Don't think badly of yourself for wanting to see justice done."

The fierce grief that had driven her to his office was fading to more manageable proportions. She was grateful for his understanding. It made her feel less alone.

Leaning back in his chair, he made a tent of his fingers. "The sheriff has come up with an idea. He's going to ask the county board to offer a thousand-dollar reward for any person who can give him information that will lead to the arrest and conviction of one or all of the men who broke into the jail that night."

A gleam of hope pierced Susan's depression. "For that amount of money maybe Hap Turner will talk."

"I doubt it. He's probably as guilty as the other three, and he wouldn't want to incriminate himself. There's a possibility that someone saw or heard something that night, though. Or they might have heard some talk before or after it happened that would lead us to who did it." Tapping his fingertips together, he added, "I'm still counting on one of them giving himself away in some manner. Something that I consider suspicious has already happened. Do you know Aldie Miller? He worked for Pat Seavey at the livery barn until a couple of weeks ago. He'd worked there for years. All of a sudden Pat fired him. Said he was getting lazy and wasn't doing the work he should. Guess who Pat hired to take his place?"

When Susan shook her head, he said, "Hap Turner. I went to Aldie and talked to him about it. He claims he was doing just as much work as he ever did, and I believe him. He's a good, steady worker, the kind you'd want to hang on to. Hap can't keep a job. He's had several just in the three years I've been here. He's a loafer, he drinks quite a bit, and he can't get along with anybody. I asked myself why anyone would fire a good man like Aldie and replace him with Hap. It looked to me like maybe Pat was forced to, like maybe he owed Hap something."

Susan's hand paused in its fanning. "You think Pat Seavey might have been one of those men?"

"I think it's possible. Pat has a fierce temper. He might have felt that anyone who murdered Widow Brown didn't deserve a trial."

"Why doesn't the sheriff question him?"

"Pat would only deny that he was involved. And I don't think it's a good idea to put him or anyone else on their guard. We need to have someone get careless and give himself away. It's going to take a lot of patience," he warned.

"I can be patient if I think just sitting around waiting will get us anywhere." She began fanning herself again, briskly. "I wish there was something I could do, though."

It was after she left his office and was returning to the hotel that a thought occurred to her. Maybe it wouldn't be necessary to wait for someone to give himself away. Maybe someone else possessed some information, either knowingly or unknowingly. A mounting excitement made her feel more alive than she had felt since Ward's death. She entered the hotel with a tingling sense of purpose.

5

"It will be a lot cooler over here," Lettie Turner said approvingly. "The bed should have been in this corner to start with." Tiny as she was, helping Susan move the bed nearer the room's west window appeared to be no strain for her.

In the few days that Susan had lived at the hotel she had discovered that Lettie's diminutive size and fragile appearance were deceptive. So was the washed-out look created by her pale red hair, white skin, and invisible eyelashes. In reality, she was vivacious and possessed tireless energy. She had volunteered at once when Susan asked for help to move her bed.

"How long have you worked for the Lords?" Susan asked as they slid the bureau across the floor.

"I've been here nine years. I started when I was thirteen.

I worked for room and board at first. I couldn't do anything with Papa after Mama died. He was so messy around the house. Mama managed to keep it fairly clean, but after she was gone he said he didn't want me fussing around. Said a little dirt never hurt anybody. He's a born grouch. I finally had to get out of there."

Frank Bowers, the harness-maker, was a bit peculiar. There were those who swore that when he bought a new pair of overalls, he wore them without ever washing them until they rotted off him. Susan had seen the tiny shack he lived in. No bigger than her kitchen out on the farm, its unpainted siding had weathered to gray, and the yard surrounding it was choked with old bits of iron and wood and similar trash, all of it poking up out of waist-high weeds.

"After I left," Lettie said, lifting the bureau over an uneven board in the floor, "he sold the house and built that little chicken coop he lives in now." She shook her head at the incomprehensibility of her father's behavior. "I quit my job when Hap and I got married and was looking forward to scrubbing my own floors for a change, but six months later Hap lost his job and I asked Ella if I could come back to work here. She'd had two different girls working for her in those six months, and neither one of them was worth shooting. She was glad to get me back, and I stayed on, even when Hap got another job. A good thing, too. Seems like his jobs never last long." Color rose beneath her milk-white skin as she remembered the connection between Hap's last firing and the woman she was now helping. The memory froze her tongue.

"There, that's better," Susan said, dusting her hands and surveying the newly placed bureau and bed to give Lettie a moment or two to recover from her embarrassment. "It even looks homier. If I had some rags, I'd crochet a couple of rugs. One for between here and the bed, and a little one to go in front of the door."

"Ella might let you have some rags. She's always got a sheet or two that's beyond patching. I'll ask her," Lettie offered eagerly. "Did you crochet that back for your chair?"

"I had an old dress that went to pieces right after I moved out here from Pennsylvania. I dyed half of it red and left the rest as it was."

"It's real pretty. I haven't crocheted anything since I left home. Haven't had the time. Our house needs a few touches like that, but I've always got too much to do when I get home at night to sit down and do any handwork except mending. Actually, we're not home enough to hardly need a house anyway. I've got to be here to help get breakfast in the morning, and it's eight or nine o'clock before I get home at night, depending upon how many we serve. And Hap always hangs around downtown until I get off work. If we weren't paying such cheap rent, we might as well live here the way you do. Your geranium is so pretty." Lettie walked over to the window to get a closer look at the orange blooms. "I don't have time for flowers, but I like them."

"Geraniums don't take any time. Just water them now and then, and they go on blooming. I could slip this one and start one for you if you'd want me to."

"Slip it?"

"Break off a leaf and stick it in a pot of dirt. It will root and grow."

"Into a plant like that?" Lettie's sharp-featured face lifted in disbelief.

"Just like that. Would you like one?"

"I sure would if it's no more trouble than that."

"Save me a can from the kitchen about this big, and I'll start you one."

When Lettie had gone, Susan examined her geranium absently. Hap must have said something to his wife about that night. It was possible she knew all about it. Whatever information she might have, Susan meant to coax it out of her. Snapping off a dying leaf from the potted plant, she felt that she had made a good beginning.

That afternoon, lonely beyond bearing, she walked to the farm to visit Ward's grave. Scarcely aware of the intense heat, she made her way along the trail that had become so familiar to her during the five months she and Ward lived on their farm. Less than a road, the rutted track ran across the prairie, over grass worn to stubble. In places the taller prairie grasses had been killed out altogether, leaving only buffalo grass, short, thickly matted and, because of the lack of rain, as tan and dead-looking as it had been when she and Ward had arrived in February.

A mile from town, she passed the Solomon place. It drowsed in the heat, but dampness in the garden rows gave evidence that someone had carried dozens of buckets of water to it earlier. A few chickens scratched in the shade on the north side of the house. Carefully tended, the farmstead appeared prosperous even in the midst of the present drought. The ambitious dream that the sight of it once aroused in her had been buried with Ward. She averted her eyes, unable to look at it today.

In the quarter of a mile between the Solomon place and Widow Brown's farm, the corn looked as it normally would in October at the end of the growing season, dry, crisp, and dead. Instead of seeing an ear on every stalk, she had to look sharply to discern even an ear here and there, stunted cobs that she suspected bore only a few kernels, if any at all.

The widow's farm had been left to a niece in Illinois who retained the Solomons as renters. Everything had been sold. The curtainless windows gaped blackly. Unbidden, the scene leaped to her mind: the elderly woman taken by surprise by a demand for money from a seventeen-year-old boy she had had until then no reason to fear, a boy whom she must have pitied because he was the victim of nature and a brutal father . . . her refusal to give him money . . . the boy's desperation . . . the blow with the skillet that shattered her skull . . . Gideon's terrified search for the money . . . his flight from the blood and death.

Forcing the horrible picture from her mind, she trudged on, her eyes fixed on the crisp grass at her feet.

As she drew near her sod house, her throat began to ache. Her heart was still there, there and out on the hillside in the grave that she was not yet able to see. Not a sound broke the stillness. There was no movement save for the heat waves that shimmered between the house and the barn, making the barn appear as if it were wavering and on the verge of collapsing and returning to the earth from which it had been built.

The wind had blown open the door to the house; subsequent banging had torn loose one hinge. It dragged on the floor as she pushed it open far enough to enter. The emptiness of what had been their kitchen hit her like a spasm. Over in one corner a few fluffs of rabbit fur were all that remained of a wolf's meal; a large mouse's nest made from bits of newspaper chewed from the walls sat in another corner, its owner away from home either for the moment or permanently if it had rounded off the wolf's meal. All human smells were gone, swept away by the prairie wind.

She crossed the floor to their bedroom. The emptiness here was not the same. Although there was nothing for the eye to see, the air throbbed with remembered rapture, whispers of love, inexpressible emotions so powerful they still lived. Leaning heavily against the doorjamb, she closed her eyes. Never again. Even as she listened, the sounds died, and then there was nothing. She turned away in desolation and walked out of the house.

The hogpen had already been torn down, the boards taken elsewhere to be used. The barn looked smaller than she remembered it, the smell of the horses still strong inside. When she reached the grave, she found it untouched, secure behind the iron fence she had had put up before she moved, along with the stone she had bought. The mound of yellowish-gray clay was undiminished; there had been no rain to wear it down. She stood outside the tiny enclosure, waiting for the feeling of closeness she craved. It didn't come. Reaching across the fence, she bent and touched the raw mound.

"I'm here, Ward," she whispered. Overhead a hawk circled silently, riding the air currents. In the draw below the grave the sunflowers were drying up, their brilliance fading. "I'm here," she pleaded, but nothing came to her. She stayed at the graveside for a long time. When it became evident at last that there was nothing left for her here, she returned to town, bereft and utterly alone.

Invited to a farewell party for Bessie Laurence, one of Hawthorne's most popular young women who was going to Chicago to take nurse's training, Susan began to believe that the town was trying to make amends for the tragedy they had brought upon her. For that reason she felt betrayed when Sy informed her the next day that the county board had turned down Sheriff Van Alstine's request for reward money.

"The hypocrites!" she said bitterly. "They don't really want to find out who killed Ward!"

She and Sy were sharing a table at dinner in the hotel dining room that noon. The sheriff had come to Sy's office earlier to tell him there would be no reward. There were only two other diners, two drummers whose glances kept straying in her direction.

Laying down his fork, Sy sought to soothe her. "Don't forget that only one of the supervisors is from this township. The others think this is a local matter and rejected the idea that the taxpayers of the entire county should pay to solve a crime that happened in this town. The sheriff is deeply disappointed. He doesn't know where to go from here."

No longer hungry, Susan felt the depression that she had been holding at bay all morning take possession of her. "We aren't going to find out who those men are, are we? Ward's death will never be avenged."

Hearing the despair in her voice, Sy put his hand over one of hers. "Don't give up, Susan. We've only just started. One of us is sure to come up with an idea or some information sooner or later. And even if nothing turns up, I'm going after Hap if I win the election. I can't believe he will keep quiet if he thinks he's the only one who's going to pay for what he and the rest of them did."

Dully, Susan said, "The election is more than a year away."

He said gently, "You told me the other day you could be patient. Trust me. I'm going to get these men for you. One way or another, I'm going to run them down. I promise."

Gazing into that strong, intelligent face, she was convinced that Sy could do it if there was any way it could be done. But what if it was impossible?

As if he sensed her reservations, he said abruptly, "I'm escorting Queena Cross to the ice-cream social tonight. Come with us. Laura will be with us, too, of course. You've met them, haven't you?"

She hadn't, but she knew each of them by sight. Queena was a strikingly pretty girl of fifteen or sixteen whose father, Salvador Cross, ran a general store and whose mother had been in a state mental institution for years. Laura Knapp, Mrs. Cross's sister, kept house for them and was a surrogate mother to Queena.

"Several weeks ago Queena bet me she could beat me nine games out of ten at high five." Sy gave a self-deprecatory grin. "I fancy myself quite a cardplayer, so I took her bet. She declared if I lost I had to escort her to the next ice-cream social; if I won she said she'd cook me a real Southern meal with turnip greens and biscuits and ham. I lost. Laura will chaperone us, and I'm sure neither of them would mind if you came along."

There could be no harm in it, no fuel for the gossips. And although at the moment she didn't feel like going anyplace where she would have to see and talk to people, she knew she needed something to pull her out of herself. "Queena will probably think you're cheating to take me along as well as Laura, but all right. What time should I be ready?"

• • •

Feeling as if she didn't have strength enough to even sit in the rocker, Susan lay on her bed that afternoon, the two windows open to let a breeze through. Even though she had taken off her dress, she felt as if she were burning up. Strangely, the heat bothered her more in this small room than it had on those days when she had worked in her garden. Her petticoat was sticking to her body and her scalp was perspiring. It was September. Would this heat never end?

September. Ward had died six weeks ago tody. It seemed like a year. Pressing her hand against her heart, she moaned softly with each breath. The need to touch him, to hold him, was so great she felt as if she would die of it. Underneath the pain was rage at the senselessness of his death. The thought that his killers were enjoying life at this very moment—laughing, loving—nearly drove her wild. If it was the last thing she did, she was going to see these men held up before the world for the murderers they were. If Ward could no longer know the joys of life, neither should they. Somehow . . .

It came to her then, in her grief and fury. She would offer the reward herself. She'd use the money she got from Charlie Solomon for the farm. It would mean she would have to find a job, but that had been her plan anyway before Solomon made his offer. She didn't mind working; in fact, the idea appealed to her. Already she had had enough of sitting around this hotel room. She got up and stood in front of the window, looking past Cross's Mercantile down the street leading west to the Congregational church, where the ice-cream social was being held that night. She could scarcely wait to tell Sy her plan.

• • •

They met in the hotel parlor and walked to the Cross house in the east part of town to pick up Laura Knapp and Queena. A northwest wind had sprung up about five o'clock, dropping the temperature by at least twenty degrees. She had changed to her blue-sprigged muslin with the pearl buttons down the bodice. It was not as nice as her wedding dress, but she would never wear that again. She had sent it home with Coila to make over for herself. Sy was waiting downstairs for her, and when he saw her, he exclaimed, "How pretty you look! But you'd better take a shawl. This is the way summer ends in Nebraska. Suddenly. It will probably be chilly when we come home tonight."

He did not greet her plan with the enthusiasm she had expected. "I don't think you should beggar yourself to offer this reward." The wind was blowing hard, and he settled his hat more securely on his head.

His clothing was different from that worn by the other men in town, typical, Susan assumed, of that worn in the South. His summer suits were light in color and material, his hats also light in color and broad-brimmed. Despite his forecast of a chilly evening, he still wore the pale gray summer suit and white hat he had worn earlier in the day. "What if you can't find a job?" he continued. "You know how few there are around."

"I'll have enough money left to last for three or four months," she explained, hoping to win his approval. "Maybe we'll have caught the persons responsible by then and I can go home. If not, maybe I'll have found work by then. Or," she added dismally, "maybe there will never be any reason to pay the reward."

"Why don't you wait awhile? Look around for a job and see what the chances are that you can find one."

"And let the days drag by without anything being done? You've got your work to fill your days. I've got nothing!" His crestfallen expression brought instant regret. "Oh, Sy, I'm sorry. I didn't mean to speak so sharply. I'm afraid I'm becoming terribly self-pitying."

"Who would have a better right?" he said at once, leaping to defend her. "But you're not. You're a strong, courageous woman, Susan. You've handled yourself remarkably well. Your husband would have been proud of you."

Tears sprang to her eyes. Her voice quivering, she said, "Thank you, Sy. You have no idea how much your words mean to me. Since Ward's death I've felt such a nothing. It's as if when Ward died, all that was worthwhile in me died with him."

He put a hand on her elbow and halted their steps. Turning so that they faced each other squarely, he said with forceful gentleness, "Everything about you that Ward loved is still there, Susan. Don't ever forget that. You're a fine, wonderful person. That's the way the world sees you. That's the way you should see yourself, even in your deepest moments of grief."

In a choked voice, she said, "You're such a good friend, Sy. That has meant so much to me. More than you'll ever know."

There was such gravity in his scrutiny of her that, believing it was caused by concern over her state of mind, she sought to reassure him, even managing a smile. "I'm all right now. Shall we go on? Queena is probably waiting impatiently."

Queena Cross did not seem to mind an extra woman in the party. Susan suspected that being over twenty and a widow put her in a category that Queena viewed as no competition for Sy's attentions. Her young girl's crush on the handsome lawyer was obvious, bringing a flush to her face when he told her how enchanting she looked with her blond hair swept up on her head. Deftly she maneuvered so that Susan and her aunt went ahead of them, managing then to walk slowly enough that she and Sy couldn't be overheard.

"I hope you won't get the wrong impression of her," Laura Knapp said to Susan as they fought to hold their hats on in the wind. "She's really a very good girl." Tall, rigid of body, and stern-faced, Laura Knapp gave a somewhat spinsterish image that was moderated by her voice.

"She trapped Sy into this situation. She coaxed her father and me to play high five with her all summer. We had no idea it was to practice and become good enough to challenge him. . . I'm not surprised she beat him. Her hands had to be very bad before Sal or I could win a game from her. She's always been good at card games. If I'd known about her scheme, I'd have forbidden it."

"I'm sure she's perfectly safe with Sy."

"I don't worry about that. It's just that I don't like to have her behaving so brazenly." Apologetically, she declared, "It isn't easy being a mother when you are merely substituting for one."

"It's not a responsibility every woman would take on. Will Mrs. Cross ever be able to come home?"

"She has been home twice—about a year after she was committed and again three years ago. The first time for five months, and this last time for only three. Each time she asked to go back to Lincoln. She doesn't seem interested in Queena or Sal. Her rejection nearly broke Queena's heart. Sal discussed it with the doctors, and they decided it would be best if she weren't sent home again. They assured him she was happy in the asylum and had no desire to leave it, which is a blessing since apparently she'll be there for the rest of her life." She spoke so matter-of-factly that Susan almost didn't catch the sadness underlying her tone.

She had shopped frequently at Cross's Mercantile because she had liked Salvador Cross's sincere friendliness. He had always seemed genuinely interested in the answers to those routine questions everyone asks of people they meet. When she confided to him, shortly after Ward was arrested, her fear that they wouldn't be able to make their payment to the railroad, she had the feeling that he really shared her anxiety. Now that she knew more about his personal life, she suspected that his pain left him open to the pain of others. He would be joining them at the church, Laura Knapp said, after he closed his store.

Plank tables covered with white oilcloth had been set up in the church basement. Sy found them seats, and Queena quickly pulled him down next to her while Laura and Susan took chairs across from them. Sy introduced Susan to the other three people at the table and paid for the ice cream and chocolate cake one of the church women set in front of them almost immediately. Pitchers of water sat on each table, a cluster of glasses beside them. Susan was handing out the glasses and pouring when Salvador Cross entered. She saw his face light up when he saw his daughter across the room. He made his way slowly through the tables toward them, stopping now and then to exchange a few words with someone. Laura Knapp and Susan each moved down one chair so that he could sit opposite Sy at the end. He sank down with a sigh.

Queena said, "You sound tired, Daddy."

"It's not because I've been busy," he replied ruefully. "It's the heat. I'm glad it's finally broken." Beneath prematurely graying hair, his face was furrowed with sadness.

"Business is as bad as ever, I take it," Sy commented.

"The farmers aren't spending any money, even those who have some."

"I think we should write the governor and let him know how bad off we are back here and ask for help," Sy said.

"Can't we handle it at the county level?" wondered Cross. "Or even the township level? Asking the governor for help would give us a lot of bad publicity, and we need to encourage immigration out here. There's still a lot of land to be settled." He had a warm greeting for the woman who brought him his ice cream and cake.

"I agree we ought to handle this ourselves if we can," Sy said, "but I doubt we can do it. These farmers will need seed for next year's planting, as well as food to get them through until the next crop. I don't think many people could respond to a call for donations. Everyone is hurting. Susan would like to find a job, but I've warned her she isn't likely to find one. Not in hard times like these."

"Do we have to talk about the drought and hard times?" protested Queena, her pink-and-white face wrinkling in distaste. "We're supposed to be having fun tonight."

"All right," Sy conceded, "let's talk about how you managed to beat me at high five. You've tarnished my reputation, young lady. I'd like to know how and when you learned to play that game so well."

Susan was watching, amused, while Queena avoided the eyes of her aunt, when Salvador Cross leaned forward across Laura and said, "I've been thinking about hiring a woman to manage my millinery department. Would you be interested in a job like that?"

She almost blurted "I certainly would!" but caught herself in time. With business as bad as it was, she suspected he was making the offer purely out of kindness.

"I worked in a drugstore back home, but I've never had any experience in millinery."

"I'm sure you could pick it up in no time. I've got a bunch of millinery stock, and Mrs. Ferguson has taken away a lot of that sort of business from me since she opened her shop. I'm sure if I had a woman in there, I could get some of it back."

He made a salary offer, and doubting that he could afford to be that generous, Susan asked, "May I think about it for a few days?"

"Take your time."

"Now that that's settled," Queena said in exasperation, "would you please, Daddy, not talk any more business tonight?"

"I'll promise to try, and if I forget, you have my permission to remind me."

Susan said good night when they all reached the hotel, but when she heard Sy come in a short time later, after seeing Queena home, she stepped into the hall and caught him before he went into his room. "I don't think I should accept Mr. Cross's job offer, do you?"

He paused, hand on the porcelain doorknob. "Why not?"

"He's just being kind, isn't he? I'm sure he can't afford it."

He came back down the hall to where she was standing, tapping his hat thoughtfully against his thigh. "His reason for hiring you seemed pretty sound to me. And if you can bring back some of his business, you'll be a good investment for him."

"If the offer had come from someone else, I probably would have accepted it whether or not they could afford it. But he's such a nice man and has so many problems."

"And you don't have any?" She thought Sy's smile was almost tender. "I think you two make a good pair. Good night."

She went back into her room feeling for the first time since Ward died that she was regaining some control over her life.

6

SUSAN FOUND MANAGING a millinery department much simpler than managing a drugstore. When it was clear that she could handle the job and that Salvador Cross was satisfied with her work, she put an ad in the *Echo* and had some posters printed offering one thousand dollars reward for information that would aid in the arrest and conviction of the vigilantes who hanged Ward. Sy placed the posters in half a dozen businesses in town. The day after the offer came out in the *Echo* Susan arrived at the hotel after work to find Hap Turner at the desk talking to Rufus Lord. Only later did it occur to her that theirs was not a chance meeting. He had been waiting for her.

He was only a few feet from the door and facing it when she came in. It had been a golden October day, but the advancing dusk was a reminder that winter would soon be upon them. Hap was in his shirt-sleeves, defying the chill that was in the air now that the sun had set. "Well, if it isn't the lady who wants to catch herself a vigilante."

His tone was so insolent Susan would have brushed past his squat body if Rufus Lord hadn't announced with his usual cordiality, "There's some mail for you, Susan. I brought it over with ours." Handing it to her, he said, "A letter from your sister."

As she took it, Hap Turner declared, "A thousand bucks is a lot of money. Wish I'd seen one of them buggers' faces. I sure could use a thousand dollars." Beneath his brown beard, his expression mocked her.

Shooting him an icy stare, she started for the stairs. Catching a glimpse of Lettie coming through the dining room toward the lobby, she waved but didn't pause. As she started up the staircase, she heard Lettie call out to her husband from the doorway. He had picked up his conversation with Rufus Lord and didn't reply.

"Hap!" she called again. He ignored her.

As Susan reached the landing and turned to go to her room, she saw Lettie walk up to her husband and place herself in front of him. "Hap, would you pick up our milk from Ernie? I haven't had time, and we'll need some for breakfast."

Deigning at last to acknowledge her presence, he turned away from Rufus Lord. Giving her neither a negative nor a positive answer, he said in a surly tone, "Go get me a cup of coffee." When she reached the doorway, he added, "Ask Ella if she's got a piece of pie she could spare. I'm hungry."

Once inside her room, Susan took off her hat and sat down in the rocker. The letter from Coila lay on the bureau forgotten while she thought about Lettie and Hap and the incident she had just witnessed.

It was impossible to believe love could survive treatment like that; if it had it must have accumulated a heavy layer of hostility and anger. Lettie had not proven to be the fruitful source of information Susan had hoped she might be, but perhaps she had found the key that would open her up. She hadn't a single doubt that Hap knew the identities of the men who supposedly overpowered him. He had been waiting in the parlor to jeer at her, confident the reward couldn't buy her the information she wanted. How much loyalty could a wife continue to feel for a husband who treated her as disdainfully as Hap treated Lettie?

It was some time later that she remembered Coila's letter and got up to read it.

Shortly before noon a week later, Van Alstine entered the saloon. He had had his first nibble at the reward. Two drinkers at the bar glanced up from their beers, their expressions suddenly wary. The sheriff never entered the saloon except on business. The broad-set, reflective eyes of Mac McDaniel, the saloonkeeper, showed nothing, however, and his tone was friendly as he greeted Van Alstine. "What brings you in here today, Van? As you can see, everything is nice and quiet."

The sheriff nodded to the two customers, stopping at the end of the bar and waiting for McDaniel to join him. "That drummer, Harry Saunders, the one who sells groceries, came to see me a little while ago. You know him, don't you?"

Resting one elbow and his paunch against the bar, McDaniel replied, "Sure. He comes in here for a beer or two every time he's in town. I haven't seen him yet this trip."

"He just got in last night. Someone at the hotel told him about Ward Maddox's hanging and about the reward his wife is offering. He says he was in here the night it happened and Pat Seavey was spouting off about how Maddox ought to be strung up for killing Widow Brown. He said Pat had everyone riled up and agreeing with him, everyone except you. You spoke up and said maybe Maddox wasn't guilty. Do you remember that?"

Pretending to think, the saloonkeeper rubbed his big, smooth jaws. "Can't say as I do."

Undeceived, Van Alstine retorted, "You should. Saunders said everyone jumped on you for saying it. You don't usually speak up and get yourself in trouble with your customers like that. I think you remember all right. Why didn't you come and tell me about Pat when you found out somebody broke into the jail and hung Maddox?"

With an apprehensive glance at the two men down the bar, who were eavesdropping unashamedly, McDaniel muttered, "If I told you everything I hear in here, I wouldn't have any business left. Besides, Pat spouts off about a lot of things. I didn't want to cause him any trouble if he didn't have anything to do with it."

"And what if he did?"

McDaniel fidgeted and looked uncomfortable. Defensively, he demanded, "Why are you talking to me? Why didn't you go see Pat?"

"I intend to. First I want to know who else was in here that night?"

"That was two months ago!"

"But a night none of us will ever forget."

"Maybe you won't, but I've got fifty nights or more between me and that night. My memory isn't that good."

Van Alstine knew he wasn't going to get any more out of the saloonkeeper. He glared down the bar at the two eavesdroppers, each of whom gave a start, then looked quickly away, anticipating his question. They vigorously denied being in the saloon that night, and McDaniel backed them up.

Van Alstine let his gaze sear the three of them before suggesting to McDaniel, "If you happen to remember who was in here that night, you know where my office is." He left, heading for the livery barn.

"Sure, I was het up about the widow's murder, but so was the whole town." Pat Seavey was seated on a scarred bench on the south side of his barn watching two men pitch horseshoes. The men were retired farmers, members of a loose group that hung around the livery barn and spent their days smoking and visiting and playing horseshoes. Seavey's head was bare, his hair glinting like silver in the sun; his pink face and blue eyes were as innocent as a child's.

Van Alstine stood a few feet away, listening to the ring of the horseshoes but not taking his eyes from Seavey. "Not everyone was saying Maddox should be hung."

Seavey's head shot up. "Neither did I! Did somebody say that? If they did, they're a damn liar!"

"A drummer said he heard you saying Maddox ought to be strung up."

"I never said any such thing! Who claims he heard me say that?"

"Harry Saunders."

Seavey snorted. "Anybody who has sat and listened to

him tell his stories knows better than to believe anything he said. He tells some of the damnedest tales you ever heard. He's good for a few hours of entertainment if you don't get tired of hearing somebody exaggerate."

"I know Harry, and I don't think he was exaggerating."

"Well, I'm telling you he was. If I said Maddox should be hung, I meant by the law, not by vigilantes."

Van Alstine swung his eyes to the horseshoe players. One of them hit the stake; the sharp clink of iron against iron broke a short silence. "Who else was in the saloon that night?"

"I don't remember. I wasn't there very long. We'd had a town board meeting that night, and I stopped in for a drink on my way home. Mac was about to close up."

"And I suppose you went straight home."

Seavey reddened. "I sure as hell did, and if you don't believe me, you can ask my wife. Now get the hell out of here. That star you're wearing don't cut any ice with me. You were voted into office, and by God, you can be voted out!"

His voice had risen, and the two elderly men paused in their game to glance at Seavey and Van Alstine. Knowing it would be futile to expect Seavey's wife to admit her husband wasn't in bed at her side during those early morning hours that Ward Maddox was murdered, Van Alstine accepted defeat, but only temporarily. Seavey appeared to be the best suspect that had turned up since he caught Hap in the lie about being tied up with rope that had never known a knot. Unruffled by Pat's display of his notorious temper, he remarked dryly, "I may be able to get reelected without your vote, Pat." With a wave to the horseshoe players, he left.

The sheriff gave Susan an account of his visit to Pat Seavey and the report of Harry Saunders that had prompted it. "Saunders does have a reputation for telling wild tales, but this wasn't one of them, I'm sure of it. Mac didn't deny Pat had said something about your husband being hung. And I know how mad Pat can get. I think he could very well have picked up a couple of supporters at the saloon. Then there's the fact that he fired Aldie for no reason and hired Hap in his place."

"That still isn't reason enough to arrest him, is it?"

"No, but it's more than we had before you offered the reward."

Fall chilled to winter without any further information being offered. The churches began a drive to collect clothing to help the drought-stricken farmers through the winter. Susan undertook the task of sorting through Ward's things, a task she hadn't had the courage to do earlier. Settling herself in the rocker, she opened the humpbacked trunk. Her summer quilt was on top, and below it, her summer dresses. She removed them slowly, steeling herself for the sight of Ward's clothes, which had been packed on the bottom. There they were, his shirts neatly folded on top of his trousers. She lifted the blue shirt and shook it out, recalling with what proud possessiveness she had made it for him last Christmas. Burying her face in it, she was aware of every slow, ponderous beat of her heart. She had always believed that when people spoke of heartbreak they were exaggerating. She had learned these past months it was not so. There had been times, as now, when she wondered if her heart would find the will to beat one more time.

She laid that shirt and the other two in the box she'd

brought from the store. There were two pairs of long underwear. They would help keep some farmer warm while he did chores this winter. His trousers. How she had always loved the way they fit over his trim hips. How could she give away these things? They were all she had left of Ward. Once they were gone she would have nothing. She contemplated that abyss of nothingness with sick panic.

Stuffed into his good pair of shoes she found his shaving things—mug, brush, and razor. She had forgotten about them. The gold-rimmed mug with a shock of wheat painted on it was the one he had used ever since he began shaving. Some of the gold had worn off, and the painting of the wheat was slightly scratched. She held it in her hands, gazing at it, then put it to her cheek. This she would keep, she decided, and set it on the bureau where her eye would fall on it many times during the day. Why hadn't she thought of it before? It made him seem very near. She filled the box with his other things and set it aside to be taken to the church.

She was invited to the Crosses for Thanksgiving. With some amusement she saw Sy off to share a family dinner with one of the young ladies who, with the determined aid of her mother, was pursuing him. That evening Sy would be escorting the blissful young woman to a dance at the Opera House.

It was the Christmas season she dreaded. Although certain she would not lack for invitations on Christmas Day, she opted to give a dinner of her own. Days of planning staved off depression. On Christmas she took over the hotel kitchen and prepared a dinner for the Lords and the Crosses. She would have liked to invite Lettie, with whom she had become good friends since she had given Lettie the geranium she promised her. No one understood better than Lettie, however, the impossibility of Susan's extending an invitation to Hap.

To Susan's surprise, she learned that Sy had no plans for the day. "You must have dinner with the rest of us," she told him. "I'd have invited you earlier, but I thought you'd be spending the day with one of your lady friends."

He grinned. "Don't give me away. I did have some invitations, but I gave the excuse that you had invited me to your dinner."

"Do you expect my dinner to be that good?"

"After listening to you plan it for two weeks, I anticipated a feast."

The Lords closed the dining room for that day. The dining room in the hotel across the square remained open for those who preferred to eat their Christmas dinner out. Like a fish out of water, Ella Lord wandered about while Susan commandeered the kitchen. Taking pity upon her at last, Susan let her peel the potatoes and set the table. Sy, who was keeping Rufus company in the parlor, wouldn't stay out of the kitchen either.

"Doesn't anyone up here in the North ever make cornbread stuffing?" he asked, watching Susan break yesterday's bread into a bowl as she prepared the dressing.

"Complaining already?" Susan teased. "And we haven't even sat down to eat yet."

Denying hastily that he was complaining, he said, "My grandmother used to make cornbread stuffing."

His tone was so wistful that it set Susan wondering what memories Christmas evoked in him. He had told her very little about himself, she realized. Most of their conversation had been about her and her problems. "How long has it been since you went back to visit your family?"

"I don't have any family left. The war killed my father shortly before I was born. I believe it killed my grandparents, too. My mother died shortly after I was born."

Susan paused in her work to look at him. "I'm so sorry." How selfish she had been to be so engrossed in her own grief that she hadn't been interested enough in Sy to learn more about him. To be so alone! She had Coila and her father waiting for her back in Pennsylvania. Putting a hand on his arm, she exclaimed, "I'm so glad you're going to be with us today. Can you carve a turkey? No? Well, never mind. You shall sit at the head of the table and play host just the same."

The pleasure this brought to his face far exceeded the simple invitation she had offered. "Why, thank you, Susan. I'd be honored to serve as host to your dinner."

"Run along, then, before I put you to work peeling an onion for this dressing."

She had the satisfaction of knowing she had given not only Sy, but all of her guests, a day of special pleasure. None perhaps more than Queena Cross, for whom Sy's unexpected presence transformed a sedate dinner into a party. Late that night, alone in her room, loneliness engulfed her. Memories of last Christmas, which she had been trying to avoid all day, came scuttling back. She and Ward had eaten a noon Christmas dinner at her house. All the time she and Coila had been preparing it, Coila had been tearful. It was their first Christmas without their mother, a situation that brought tears more than once to Susan's eyes, too.

"And who knows when you'll be back here to spend Christmas with Papa and me again," Coila had observed sadly.

It was the prospect of her marriage that kept Susan alternating between sorrow and happiness that day, until she and Ward left her home to go to his for the meal his mother had spent all day preparing. She could still hear the laughter of Ward and his brothers as one after another they found fault with the way the turkey was baked—not done enough, Ward said; not salted enough, said another—bringing forth sharp, witty sallies from their mother that had Susan laughing so hard she could scarcely catch her breath. Ward's laugh was not the loudest, but it was the most distinctive—a gleeful shout. Susan could hear it still.

But she was tired of hurting so inside, tired of grieving. She couldn't go through the rest of her life like this. She should become less aware of her own pain and more aware of other people's needs. Sy's revelation that he had lost all of his family had made her realize how closed in upon herself she'd become. He had been such a good and generous friend to her. What had she given in return? Nothing, so far as she could see. From now on, she'd try to be kinder to him.

One morning near the end of January a red-eyed Lettie served Susan breakfast. "Is something wrong?" Susan asked, studying that pale face.

"Just the usual thing," Lettie replied bitterly. In a voice choked with tears, she said, "I don't know why Hap married me. He can't love me. Not and treat me the way he does."

"Oh, Lettie!" Susan caught her work-roughened hand and squeezed it sympathetically. "What's he done?"

"I can't talk now. Ella needs me in the kitchen. I'll come back in a few minutes."

Sy and Rufus Lord and Carl Dillard, the jeweler, were breakfasting at a table near the kitchen. Several other tables were occupied by men Susan had never seen before.

Lettie returned as Susan was finishing her pancakes, bringing the coffee pot and refilling everyone's cup before sitting down with a cup of her own at Susan's table. "Would it be asking too much of you to start me another geranium?"

"No, it's as simple as can be. I thought yours was doing so well."

"It was. It's been so pretty." Lettie hadn't tasted her coffee. Her lips began to tremble, and she played with her cup. "Hap and I had an argument last night. When I got up this morning, my plant was ruined. He had broken off every stem."

"Surely it was an accident," Susan suggested.

Lettie shook her head. "He does mean things like that when he gets mad. Once he broke a plate that had been Mama's. It was a keepsake. I kept it on a shelf beside the clock. He threw it on the floor, and I found it when I came home from work. There have been other things, but"—her voice wavered and she paused until she had steadied it—"Mama's plate meant the most to me."

"Oh, Lettie, that's terrible."

Weeping quietly now, Lettie covered her face with her hands. Knowing that to open her mouth would be to release a spurt of words that would express her loathing of Hap Turner, Susan sat silent and helpless, and watched her friend cry.

"Sometimes," Lettie murmured at last, "I want to walk out of that house and never go back. I could live here, work for my room and board like I did before I was married."

"Why don't you?" Because of the friendship that had developed between herself and Lettie, Susan had given up using her relationship with Lettie to turn up evidence that

Hap had helped kill Ward, but she saw nothing wrong with urging Lettie to leave a husband who humiliated her the way Hap did.

"Hap is all I've got. Papa hardly knows I live in the same town with him."

Galled by the injustice of fate that would take the life of a man like Ward and let a man like Hap live, Susan burst out. "Life is so unfair, isn't it?"

Lettie understood immediately what she meant. "Yes, you were happily married and lost your husband. And here I am—" She broke off sharply, a distraught look on her face. "I don't mean I'm wishing Hap dead!" She shuddered. "I don't mean that at all." She fell silent, staring at her cup, then began to twist it nervously.

Susan waited, almost holding her breath, sensing that Lettie was engaged in some sort of conflict within herself.

When Lettie spoke, her tears had dried and there was a hard note in her voice. "All Hap ever said to me about that night was that those men did a job that needed doing and he made things easy for them."

So Hap had been in on it! Smothering heat enveloped Susan, and she began to shake inside. If Hap had been in the room, she'd have sprung at him, raking nails into his face to bring blood. When the dining room came back into focus, she said in a suffocated voice, "You realize I'll tell the sheriff this."

"I know that."

Susan whispered, "Thank you, Lettie." She stood up on legs that felt rubbery. Across the room, Sy was engrossed in conversation with his breakfast companions. He glanced toward her at once when she got up, but there was no need to disturb him. This she could do alone. After exchanging a pregnant glance with Lettie, she walked out of the hotel and across the street to the jail.

The sheriff was just unlocking the door. Her face still felt hot, and he gave her a sharp glance as he greeted her and pushed the door open for her. The small building was icy cold. Van Alstine went at once to the small stove and began to build a fire.

"I've just been talking to Lettie," Susan said, refusing the chair he had offered her. "She's very upset with Hap, and she told me something." She quoted to him the remark Lettie had repeated to her.

He paused and straightened to look at her. "She actually told you that?"

"Do you have any idea how mean he is to her?"

"No, I guess I don't."

She repeated to him what Lettie had told her about her mother's dish, the geranium, and that he often committed similar malicious acts when he got angry with her. She also described to him the scene she had witnessed in the hotel parlor one day. "Lettie was crying this morning. She said she didn't see how Hap could love her and do those things to her."

The natural melancholy in Van Alstine's dark eyes deepened. "I sure made a poor choice when I picked him for my deputy, didn't I? Did she tell you anything else he said?"

"That's all she knew. I'm sure of it."

"I knew Hap was lying when he swore he'd been tied up and blindfolded." He bent his big body over the small iron stove and shook down the ashes with such force the stove wobbled on its tin mat.

"You can arrest him again now, can't you?"

"Don't think I wouldn't like to, but what good would it

do? He'd only swear up and down he didn't have anything to do with it." He began stuffing cobs into the firebox. "Lettie couldn't testify that he said this to her, even if we managed to get him into court." Hap has a legal right to prevent the prosecution from putting Lettie on the stand.

"You mean we aren't any farther along than we were?" Discouragement and the icy air in the stone jail began to cool the feverish flush she had brought with her from the hotel.

"Well, we know for sure now that Hap helped them, that he knows who did it, and that he is just as guilty of murder as the others. That's a lot to know even if we can't use it against him yet." He had poured some kerosene on the cobs, and now he dropped in a match. Covering the flash of yellow flame with the stove lid, he said, "I don't think a thing like this can stay hidden forever. Hap's always hanging around the saloon. He likes to drink and he likes to act important. He could very well let something slip someday." He adjusted the damper and dusted his hands before placing them in his pockets to warm them. "And although Pat Seavey and Hap are drinking friends, I don't think they're going to get along as boss and hired man. Hap's lazy, and he doesn't like being told what to do. Put that together with Pat's temper, and sooner or later, there's going to be fireworks. Something could come out of that, too."

"So we can't do anything except wait?" Susan asked in despair.

"Seems to me you're doing more than just waiting."

Susan pulled her shawl tigher around her shoulders and arms. "Lettie is very dear. I don't like using her."

"She didn't have to tell you what she did."

"I know." Shivering now, Susan took her leave and hurried back to the hotel, where she picked up her coat and rushed off to work.

February brought a blizzard that piled drifts four and five feet deep, locking in the town, curtailing trade and social activity. Before the drifts had a chance to shrink, more snow fell. Freezing temperatures continued, preventing any thawing, and the snow grew deeper and deeper.

"I'm glad you're here in town and not out on the farm," Sy told Susan. And so was she. She didn't know how she'd have managed the chores or kept warm with the ground covered with drifts too deep to walk through.

No one really complained about the snow. It would furnish moisture for the parched soil. Earlier forecasts of privation among the county's farmers had not been exaggerated. Requisitions were made on the state relief fund for 134 families; they were given food and seed for their next crop.

On March first the weather changed. The wind veered to the south, warmed, and in a few days, the snow had thawed until there remained only grimy remnants of the deepest drifts. With the frost going out of the ground, there was mud everywhere. Lettie mopped the linoleum in the hotel parlor and dining room several times a day.

"This is Nebraska at her best," Salvador Cross exclaimed one April morning when Susan arrived for work. A rain the night before had left the greening trees sparkling with dew diamonds; the air was intoxicatingly sweet. The various prairie grasses were coming to life, and bulbs were sending up new shoots through the moist earth.

Not two hours later, someone else expressed himself in exactly the same words. Jerry Gibson, the new millinery salesman, was a Nebraska native who lived in Omaha and boosted his home state at every opportunity. "You can't beat Nebraska's weather in the spring," he maintained.

"Providing the wind isn't blowing a gale and kicking up dust," Susan amended. She liked Jerry much better than the drummer he replaced, John Hayden, an older man who was forever urging her to buy more than she needed. Jerry's easygoing manner was a relief. Although he was an outrageous flirt and flatterer, his manner was so lighthearted and innocent, it was impossible to take offense. Even Salvador Cross made no objection when Jerry flirted with Queena. No one took him seriously; no one could imagine Jerry taking advantage of any woman. There were no dark motives lurking behind that fresh face.

As Salvador Cross helped her clear off the counter to make room for Jerry's sample cases, he asked, "Do you ever hear anything about John?"

"He finished the bichloride of gold cure and is traveling for a paint company."

"It's a lonesome life, being a drummer. He'd be better off getting a job where he could be home every night. It won't be easy for him to stay out of saloons if he's got nothing else to do. It's something to watch out for."

"I know. There's nothing more lonesome than a hotel room, and a man can always find somebody to talk to in a saloon."

"You always stay at the Tremont House, don't you? Why don't you try the Commercial? There's a game of high five going on there every night of the week."

Jerry glanced at Susan. "That's where you live, isn't it? Won't people talk if I start staying at the hotel where you live? People love to gossip about pretty women and handsome young bachelors."

Susan laughed. "I'll sacrifice my reputation to keep you out of the saloon.

"Is that an invitation?"

She cast a helpless glance at her employer. "See what you started."

Salvador Cross was smiling as he tucked the last bolt of velvet under the counter, leaving the darkly varnished top bare and ready to receive Jerry's cases. "I'm not trying to talk down the Tremont. It's a good hotel, but I think you'd be better off at the Commercial. Ella Lord sets the best table in town, too."

Lifting one of his cases up to the counter, Jerry said, "Next time I'm in Hawthorne, I'll give it a try."

He didn't wait until his next trip. Susan heard his laugh soon after she'd left the dining room that night and had gone to her room. Taking the rug she was crocheting and her basket of rag balls with her, she went down to the parlor. Rufus, Sy, and Jerry were playing a game of three-handed high five, and when they urged her to join them, she consented.

"Do you call on Mrs. Ferguson?" Rufus Lord asked.

"I do, but it doesn't do me much good. She goes to St. Joe twice a year and buys her stock."

"I know. She used to live here at the hotel. She partitioned off part of her shop the first of the year and moved in there. We never had a milliner who could make it for very long in this town. There just isn't enough business for a woman to make a decent living at it. And this year is worse than usual, what with the drought and hard times."

"It takes a place as big as Omaha to make a go of a millinery shop. Or even South Omaha. Our population there is about twelve thousand. Someday I'd like to go into business there myself."

"The millinery business?" Susan asked in surprise.

"The mercantile business. I'd like to own a store like Sal's. A neighborhood store. My ambition doesn't run any bigger than that. I've got no yen to expand like some of those places have in Omaha."

Jerry proved to be a good player, bold when he had a biddable hand, intuitive when it came to helping Rufus, who took him as his partner. None of them, however, could match Sy's skill. And luck. Jerry asked finally, "Do you always get cards like this?"

It was Rufus Lord who answered. "He gets the best cards of anyone I ever saw. I think he cheats."

"That's libel, Rufus!" Sy protested.

"Sue me."

"Things are so dull I might just do that."

The good-natured joshing was interrupted by the appearance of Lettie, who had walked from the kitchen through the darkened dining room. Her small, slight body was clothed in a faded calico dress. Her red hair hung untidily about her pale, sharp-featured face. Yet Jerry Gibson's own face was instantly alight with interest, and he put up a hand to smooth his hair. Was it her sashaying walk, Susan wondered, or was it the soft, generous mouth curved now into a warm smile that emcompassed all of them?

"Through for the day?" Rufus Lord asked, turning to look at her.

Laying a hand affectionately on his shoulder, she replied, "*I* am, I guess. Ella told me to go on home. She's putting some tablecloths to soak."

Susan introduced her to Jerry, explaining, "He's been staying at the Tremont House on his trips to Hawthorne, but I think Mr. Cross convinced him he should stay here after this."

"If I'd known there were so many pretty women around here, I'd have been here before this."

Rufus Lord asked pointedly, "I haven't seen Hap around all day. He isn't sick, is he?"

Busily securing loose strands of her hair with pins, Lettie replied, "He wasn't when I left this morning. Maybe Pat worked him hard today."

Rufus turned to Jerry, the wedge of his Adams's apple rising and falling as he passed along what he believed was vital information. "Lettie's husband works at the livery barn."

Watching Lettie fuss with her hair, catching the new light in her eyes, Susan realized this chance meeting contained the seeds of complications. Had Rufus sensed that before she had? She glanced covertly at Sy and found him contemplating the tableau with amused interest. Something perverse came to life in Susan, and she said brightly, "Come take my hand, Lettie, while I run upstairs and get a handkerchief."

"I can't stay," Lettie warned. "I have to get home and fix Hap's supper."

"I'll only be a minute."

Making her way to her room, Susan was astonished at her deviousness. Probably nothing would come of it anyway. And who could it hurt except Hap Turner, who was guilty of more than he would ever be called upon to answer for?

She stood for some minutes inside her room, then without

lighting the lamp went to her rocker and sat down. She stared out at the dark street for half an hour before she went back downstairs.

7

WALKING HOME ON that soft spring night, Lettie was aware of a strange excitement that she was sure could be read in her face had it been daylight. Although it was late, she did not hurry. It wouldn't do to let Hap see that she was in a ferment, and she needed time to compose herself. She wasn't sure that her effect on Jerry Gibson had been quite as dazzling as his effect on her, but she knew there had been more behind his words than idle flirting. There had been a spark whenever their eyes met, a silkiness in his voice whenever he spoke to her, and something else she couldn't put a name to but which enclosed the two of them in a bright bubble, shutting out the others even when he flirted with Susan.

No man had had this effect on her before, not even Hap. She had liked Hap's kisses, and his rough hands had aroused a hunger in her so that when he told her that they were going to get married, she hadn't opposed him. By the end of the first year of their marriage, the desire for his love-making had died, killed by the indignities that marked his treatment of her both in public and in private.

Jerry Gibson was an altogether different kind of man. Two hours in his company had shown her that. If his hands touched her, they would not be rough. The mere thought sent a shiver through her and gave rise to fantasies that so bemused her that she went a block past her house before she realized where she was and turned back.

"Where the hell have you been?" Hap demanded when she walked in. "I've been waiting an hour for my supper."

"Ella and I had some extra cleaning up to do. I'll have some food on the table in just a few minutes." Using her secret excitement as a shield, she ignored his sullen silence and began to prepare his meal.

She didn't expect to see Jerry again until his next trip to Hawthorne, when he would be staying at the Lord's house. When she found him in the dining room the next noon, she lost control of her face. He couldn't have failed to notice the effect that seeing him had on her. It wasn't until later that she realized he had chosen a table by himself rather than sharing one with Susan or Sy.

"I supposed you had left town," she exclaimed, trying to draw in her smile to a more modest proportion as she arrived at his table. The light in his eyes when he looked at her was so intimate that her voice trailed off to a whisper.

"I decided to stay an extra day. I'll be eating here tonight, too."

"You're going to like Ella's cooking."

"So I've been told, but that isn't the reason I came over here to eat."

Pulling her glance away with difficulty, she murmured, "I'll go get your food."

Back in the kitchen, Ella Lord was thinning the gravy, pouring milk into the roaster in small quantities and stirring vigorously after each addition. Turning her ruddy, faintly moist face toward the door as Lettie came in, she asked, "Are those two drummers ready for their pie?"

"Not yet. There's another one out there who just came in."

"Where'd he come from?"

"From the Tremont. He's the one who came over last night to play cards." Lettie busied herself cutting slices of the pork tenderloin and placing them on an empty plate.

"That millinery salesman? Rufus says he's quite the ladies' man."

"He likes to flirt." That's all it is, she reminded herself. Don't take him seriously.

"Well, don't let him get out of line."

"I won't. I don't think he's that kind, anyway. He's all talk." And very good at making a woman feel like he's smitten with her. Lettie gave herself a mental shake, and smiled. Even if it was an act, it made her feel more alive than she'd felt in a long time.

Placing the plate heaped with meat and potatoes and sauerkraut in front of him a few minutes later, she said, "Do you think you can get around that?"

"Do I have to clean my plate?"

"Every bite."

"I may be here for a long time, then."

He was the last one to leave the dining room. Lettie and Ella were washing the pile of dishes when he came to the kitchen carrying his empty plate. "All gone," he said, grinning at Lettie. To Ella, he said, "Mrs. Lord, that was one of the best meals I've had since I used to eat at my mama's table."

Without pausing in her washing, Ella said, "I'm sure that's quite a compliment. You want some pie?"

"I couldn't hold another mouthful, but I'll be back for supper. I hope you'll save a piece for me."

"Will you remember that, Lettie?"

"I'll see that you get your pie, Mr. Gibson."

Behind Ella's back, he let his eyes linger on her face a moment and then he left.

Lettie found him seated at a table with Sy and Rufus Lord at supper. Thus restricted, he fell back on the light-hearted boldness with which he treated all women, earning amused smiles from Sy and silent disapproval from Rufus. Lettie countered her disappointment at their lack of privacy, by telling herself it was just as well. She liked him far too much; it was a good thing he was leaving town the next day.

On her way home that night she had just left the square when she heard quick steps behind her. Looking back over her shoulder she saw a man running toward her. It was too dark to see who it was until he caught up to her. She halted then but found that she couldn't speak. Nor did he say anything. She forced her feet to begin moving again; he fell in beside her.

"I'm leaving in the morning," he said, finally breaking the silence.

"I know."

"I won't be back until July."

Three months. She said nothing.

"I want to write to you. Will you write to me?"

"We can't do that. Everyone will know."

"I'll write to Susan and ask her to pass along my letter to you," he said. "You can do the same. Let her send your letters with her name on them."

"Have you talked to her about this?"

"No, I'll just do it. She'll see that you get my letters, won't she?"

"I don't know."

Somewhere close by an owl hooted. Otherwise there was no sound. Windows glowed softly with lamplight.

"She's your friend, isn't she?"

"Yes, but—" She broke off, then cried in a despairing voice, "Jerry, I'm married!"

He halted abruptly and pulled her into his arms. The response of her body to his kiss was familiar enough; it was the strange emotions that accompanied it that were totally new. What was it about this blithe, good-looking man with the honeyed tongue that could fill her with such joy?

"Promise you'll write to me," he demanded urgently.

"I promise," she replied weakly.

He kissed her again, and she knew she would say yes to anything else he asked of her. Finally his arms slipped from around her, but his hands remained on her slight waist. "Someday you're going to belong to me," he declared.

She watched as he walked away. Then, as if in a dream, she turned and started home.

Once Susan's relief at having the winter over had faded, the spring weather brought despondency to her. Memories of the previous spring crowded her days. The fragrance of the morning air recalled those hours when, working in her garden, she would look up from her planting or hoeing to watch Ward plowing in the field, waiting until he reached the end of the row and looked up. She would wave to him then and receive an exuberant wave in return. The clear notes of a meadowlark plunged her into melancholy. Often, as she and Ward worked together, they would pause, smiling at each other, and listen to the sweet, joyous song until the lark rose from the grass and flew away.

Sensing her mood one Sunday, Sy suggested a picnic down at the river with the Crosses. After church, Susan returned to the hotel for the sandwiches she had made from the beef roast Ella had fixed for her. The five of them crowded into Salvador Cross's carriage and drove down to a spot where Sy assured them they could catch a mess of fish. There were no memories there. The Maddox farm had lain more than three miles from the Republican, and only a few times had she and Ward gone to the river. The ground was still cool, and Sy chose a place where the sun, making its way through the new, small leaves of the cottonwoods, warmed them. Seating themselves upon the carriage robes Salvador Cross spread out, they ate their dinner. The unfamiliar setting and the bright chatter of Sy and Queena raised Susan's spirits and gave her appetite an edge it hadn't had for some time. Yielding to Laura's urging, she had a second piece of burnt sugar cake.

Sy cut willows and made fishing poles for each of them with the string and hooks he brought.

"Where did you get those?" Queena wrinkled her nose as she peered into the can Sy placed upon the ground between them. He had shaken out some dirt, exposing a convoluted mass of squirming pink worms that had collected in the bottom of the can.

"Henry Sims had his garden plowed the other day. I went

over and picked these up. Nice fat ones, aren't they?"

"Ugh! I can't stand those slick, squirmy things. You'll bait my hook for me, won't you, Sy?"

"I'll bait your hook and even take any fish you catch off your line, but it'll cost you."

Brushing her blond hair back from her face with a quick, graceful gesture, Queena protested, "I'm not going to clean the slimy things!"

"I didn't mean that. You've got to fry them for supper tonight."

Eagerly leaping at the chance to extend the day and cook a meal for Sy, she said, "Hurry up and bait my hook, then. Let's get busy and catch some."

Susan watched with amused interest as Sy skillfully kept his relationship with Queena on a brotherly basis, deflecting her efforts to turn it into a flirtation. She wondered how anyone so nice as he had remained single for so long, and it occurred to her that in two more years Queena would be ready for marriage. Had that occurred to him? Curious, she paid closer attention to their banter; nowhere in Sy's manner was there the slightest hint that he was aware of Queena in any way other than that of a romantic child. She had his affection, nothing else. Incomprehensibly, she was glad.

Sy sat staring out his office window, absently observing the morning activity in the square below. Time was moving so damned slowly! He knew there was no chance that Susan could begin to see him as a man, rather than a friend, for months yet. He would be surprised if she could, and disappointed, too. When she loved, she loved deeply, and he wouldn't want it any other way, because someday he wanted that passionate womanliness concentrated on him.

Last night, after returning from the fish fry at Sal Cross's house, he had left her at the door of her room and gone back outside to cool the fever in his blood. He had scarcely been able to keep his eyes off her all evening. The day spent out in the warm spring sunshine and the excitement of catching a fish for the first time in her life had brought a glow to her cheeks and a light to her eyes that he hadn't seen since Ward died. He had wanted her so much that to hide it he knew he'd acted like a fool, cracking bad jokes and teasing Laura until she had begun to regard him with silent puzzlement. She and Sal had probably discussed it and divined the reason for his behavior. He didn't mind their knowing. Queena had simply thought he was being amusing. Whatever Susan had thought, he was confident she hadn't hit upon the truth. When she stood at her door telling him what a lovely time she had had, her eyes were as guileless as Queena's. It had taken every bit of self-control he had to keep from pulling her slim body into his arms and kissing her.

He sprang out of his chair and began pacing the large square room that held his law library and everything else he owned, with the exception of his clothes and the few other personal things he possessed. It was as much a home to him as his hotel room; both had been sufficient unto his needs until he fell in love with Susan. Now he yearned for a house with her in it. Not since he was fifteen had he had a home blessed with a woman's presence.

He had no memory of his mother, who had died two weeks after giving birth to him, nor of his father, who had been killed in the battle of Williamsburg in 1862, two months before he was born. Confiscatory taxes cost his grandparents their plantation shortly after the war ended, and they moved to Charleston, where his grandfather opened a private school to teach former slaves to read and write. Ostracized by other white families because of this, the three of them lived an isolated life, but Sy had only happy memories of that time. The loss of the war, of their daughter and their land took its toll on his grandmother. Thinking back after he reached adulthood, he realized she had faded away gradually into death, leaving him, at eleven, and his grandfather in the care of Chloe, who had refused to be freed and had come with them to Charleston to care for him as she had on the plantation.

When his grandfather died four years later, Sy found himself destitute. The modest tuition the blacks had been able to pay had barely covered the rent and other basic needs. Sy's education had been received at home in his grandfather's library. Having decided earlier that he wanted to be a lawyer, he inquired until he found an attorney who agreed to let him read law in his office. He was also permitted to sleep on a couch there. For the next three years he worked at odd jobs to pay for his food and clothing. Knowing enough law by then to be able to serve as a law clerk, he was hired by the attorney in whose office he'd been sleeping and studying. He was admitted to the bar on his twenty-first birthday and practiced one year with his benefactor before departing for Omaha. He had begun to feel the lure of the West soon after his grandfather died, growing more and more certain that this fresh, new land was where he wanted to live. Omaha proved to be a lively city, crude, robust, pulsing with energy, but it was no place for a lawyer with no connections and too young to be able to inspire confidence in prospective clients.

Wanting an office of his own, he searched for a location

where his youth might be less of a handicap. From the first moment he heard about the beauty of the Republican River valley in southern Nebraska his interest was captured. He chose the town of Hawthorne, fifty miles south of old Fort Kearny, chiefly because of its newspaper, the *Echo*. Not only did the paper reveal the life of the town in a friendly, humorous fashion, but it was also literate, a feature he hadn't expected to find on the frontier.

He had never regretted his move. After spending a year in Hawthorne, he knew that this was where he wanted to spend the rest of his life. He was aware now, however, that life would never be complete for him without Susan as his wife. There was nothing he could do but wait.

It was a dream she had frequently just before waking in the morning. The setting might change, but always Ward was making love to her. Her desire mounted to the point that she was wild for Ward to enter her, and then he drifted away, leaving her crying out to him. Sobbing aloud, she awakened and lay there throbbing, aching and weeping. The open window she faced was gray with the summer dawn, and the air coming in smelled clean and damp after the violent rainstorm they'd had late the previous afternoon. By the time her sobs subsided, the square that was the window was much lighter. The clock struck once for the half hour. She didn't have to turn to see that it was four-thirty. She remembered that, by this time each morning last July, Ward had milked the cow, fed the hog and the horses, and was sitting down to breakfast with her. In fifteen minutes he would consume a tall stack of pancakes or a plateful of fried mush, together with two eggs and three cups of coffee. Following him as he hurried to the barn, she visited with him while he hitched the team to whatever implement he was using that day—cultivator or plow—and waved goodbye as he went off, not to be seen again until noon.

Curling her body against the physical pain of remembering, she was aware that it was not as sharp as it had been. Her grief was lessening, but not the loneliness. The emptiness of her life at times made it difficult to get out of bed mornings and make a pretense of living. Contemplating the vista of all the years without Ward stretching ahead of her sometimes left her filled with anger at him for dying and leaving her. Arguing with herself that he hadn't chosen to die did no good. The irrational anger persisted, and she would silently rail at him for abandoning her.

The dream refused to fade. She went down to breakfast, a quivering hollowness inside her body, blaming Ward for this feverish need that he was no longer here to fill. Entering the dining room, she found Lettie lit with the same pink glow she'd been wearing ever since Jerry Gibson checked into the hotel yesterday. Susan had been surprised when in May she received a letter from Jerry, and even more surprised when she found another letter inside, folded and sealed, which Jerry asked her to pass along to Lettie. A few days later a furtive Lettie had asked in a whisper if Susan would mail a letter to Jerry under her own name. Without hesitation she agreed. During the following two months there had been several letters. When the postmaster began to wear an ill-concealed smirk each time he handed a letter from Jerry to her or when she bought postage to send one to him, she told him she was inquiring about some new millinery goods.

When Jerry walked into the dining room while Lettie was serving Susan her eggs, Lettie left with eager haste to take his order. The expression on Jerry's face as he greeted her told Susan that this was no mere flirtation on his part. Jerry had excused himself from the card game last night shortly after Lettie left the hotel; Susan felt sure they met secretly. A close, covert examination of Lettie revealed an electric tautness in her small, slender body that Susan identified all too easily that morning. However unfaithful Lettie had been to Hap in her thoughts, Jerry had not yet made love to her.

Unable to eat more than a few bites of her breakfast, Susan left the dining room unobserved by a couple, who were absorbed in each other. With still a half hour before she had to go to the store, she started a letter to Coila and her father but found that her thoughts went skittering off in directions that for her were now forbidden. The same lack of concentration, the same ungovernable fantasies, persisted during a day that seemed unending. When that evening at supper Sy suggested they walk the mile and a half to the creek whose bridge had been washed out by yesterday's cloudburst, she agreed at once, hoping the three-mile walk would help her sleep that night.

Dark green cornfields bordered the road to the creek, the ears beginning to fatten on the stalks. Water stood in the rows from the rain. The road itself was still muddy in spots. Often rutted by wagon wheels, it was today nearly smooth after the pounding rain. Despair filled Susan at the sight of the luxuriant cornfields. Why couldn't these rains have come last year? If they had she'd be cooking Ward's supper at this hour, waiting for him to come in from the field with horses that were more tired than he was. His inexhaustible energy had amazed her. He could walk all day behind a cultivator or plow and still be as light and quick of step as he'd been that morning. And as ardent and eager to make love to her. That thought took her breath. She had suffered moments like this before, but never had this physical need persisted through an entire day. She turned her face away from Sy, lest he see.

"I walked down to the depot with Jerry this afternoon," he was saying. "I think we can be glad he won't be back for a couple of months."

She had never mentioned the letters to Sy, and apparently he hadn't heard anything about them. "Lettie does seem taken with him, doesn't she? Would it be so wrong," she asked, "if she left Hap for Jerry? You know how Hap treats her."

"I'm not sure Jerry is doing anything except some serious flirting. I'd hate to see Lettie get hurt."

"I watched his face this morning when they met in the dining room. I'm sure he's in love with her."

"If he is, they are playing a dangerous game. Can you imagine what Hap would do if he found out?"

The creek was still bank-full, its rushing water gray with mud. For several yards back from its banks, weeds and grass were flattened, showing how high the water had been. The wooden bridge had collapsed. Its piling on the side where Susan and Sy stood had been washed out, leaving it to fall into the creek.

"I've never seen anything like this storm in the three years I've been here," Sy remarked, surveying the broken bridge and the wide swath on either side of the creek that gave muddy evidence of how high and how swift the water had been. "Jake Haney and the other farmers across the creek are going to be cut off from town until this bridge is rebuilt."

"They surely can't complain, can they? With all the rain we've had this summer, they should raise bumper crops."

Laughing, Sy said, "They'll complain. Farmers always do. Al Brock was complaining this afternoon about all the debris that was in his alfalfa field. His draw was running water like a creek after the rain and carried down a lot of trash with it. He said it would take him a week to clear it off."

Susan clicked her tongue in vexation. "They should be so grateful for these rains!" The fecundity of the earth on that summer evening pierced her heart like a knife and brought hot tears to her eyes. "It's so unfair," she whispered. Hiding her face in her hands, she burst into sobs.

Putting his arms around her, Sy pressed her head against his chest. She felt his lips against her hair, the solid masculine strength of him. He murmured her name, and then he was kissing her. It was what she had been ready for all day. Spontaneously her lips and body opened to him. There was no turning back the tide of passion that swept her mind clean of every thought except attaining the exquisite release she had been denied by her awakening that morning. Sy drew in his breath sharply at the wild urgency of her response, and his kiss deepened. Together they sank to the soft sand at the base of the cottonwood tree, and together they unfastened her clothing. She gasped at the touch of his hands on her body and was only vaguely aware of him murmuring, between kisses, that he loved her. A few moments later the dream that had stopped just short of fulfillment that morning was rushing to completion. "Ward, Ward," she cried, and when the sweet, crimson explosion shook her, she gave another cry, this one wordless and defiantly ecstatic.

To Sy, the sound of Susan's voice crying out her husband's name came as no surprise. What did surprise him was that the sound was not one of ecstasy, but of accusation and protest, and that her final cry was unmistakably defiant. Coming down from his own climax, he felt her silent, convulsive sobs. Kissing her closed lids, he urged, "Marry me, Susan. I've loved you almost from the first moment I saw you."

"No," she whispered.

"Why not?"

Ashamed, she threw an arm across her face to hide from his gaze. "This thing that happened just now . . ." She faltered, then continued. "I can't explain it. I still love Ward . . . but he's dead and I'm alive . . . sometimes I'm so angry at him because he died and left me alone . . . and I need him so . . . today was worse than usual. When you put your arms around me . . . I knew you weren't Ward, but it didn't matter . . . not then, but it does now."

He pressed kisses on her arm and tried to take it away from her face, but she resisted. "Don't hide from me, Susan," he begged. "Don't be ashamed. God, I love you so much! Don't turn this into a shameful thing."

Beneath her arm, she turned her head wordlessly from side to side in despair.

"Marry me, Susan," he urged again. "You're fond of me. We can build on that."

"I can't imagine being married to anyone but Ward. Let me up, please."

He did as she asked, keeping his back to her while she adjusted her clothing. "You can't spend the rest of your life alone. There are many years ahead of you."

Bitterly, she said, "I've counted them."

"They don't have to be lonely. You can have a husband. And children. I know you feel your life has stopped, but you mustn't allow it to. Take what you can, even if it isn't the full measure you once expected."

"You don't understand," she said.

He heard her begin to walk away. Too desperately in love to accept defeat, he caught up to her and spun her around. "You can't live in the past," he said harshly. "You made that pretty obvious a few minutes ago."

Fire spat from her eyes. She kept the full power of that glare fixed on him for several tense moments before she jerked loose and stalked off.

Closing the door of her room behind her, Susan leaned against it, relieved at last to escape the tension of Sy's presence. His apology had not dissolved her anger; his jibe was unforgivable.

She went to her rocker and sat down, leaning her head against the back. Recognizing the reason for the fluid heaviness in her body, her face flamed. But whose fault was it? If Ward had done something sooner about raising money for payment on his land, he might still be alive. He wouldn't take the problem seriously; he kept telling her not to worry. They could have gone back to Pennsylvania. He could have got his old job back at the sawmill. They could have lived safely, and she wouldn't be here widowed, her life in ruins, forced to give in to the demands of her body and fall like a wanton into the arms of any man who happened to be nearby. A woman put her life in the hands of her husband, and if he made the wrong choices, she suffered for it.

She sat there in the fading light blaming Ward and nursing

her fury at Sy until the gold rim of Ward's shaving mug glinted in the dusk, drawing her eye to the bureau. Suddenly she saw the washstand it used to sit on, the one Ward had made and which she had covered with oilcloth. There was the tin basin and the towel, and there was Ward, mug in one hand, brush in the other, lathering his face before the small, wood-framed mirror that hung from a peg driven into the sod wall. Seized with an intolerable loneliness, she recognized the absurdity of her anger, both with Ward and Sy, knew it for what it was: an attempt to escape her guilt and embarrassment. Wishing she could run away under the cover of darkness and never return, she began to prepare for bed. When she removed the combs from her hair, she felt sand between her fingers, and dropped her eyes, unable to face herself in the mirror. She washed quickly and lay down upon the bed, falling almost immediately into a sound sleep.

Too embarrassed to face Sy the next morning, she skipped breakfast and fled to the store. She told Salvador Cross she wanted to rearrange her shelves and remained at the store during the noon hour, lunching on cheese and crackers. Seeking out Lettie in the kitchen that night, she pleaded a headache and asked if she would bring something to her room.

Knowing she could not avoid him forever, she went down late for breakfast the following morning and chose the first unoccupied table she came to without surveying the room. She took a chair and busied herself with her handkerchief, her belt, the brooch at her throat, anything to avoid raising her eyes. She heard his footsteps—she hadn't realized until now that she could recognize them—and then heard his voice above her asking quietly, "Are you all right?"

Without looking up, she murmured, "Yes."

"I was worried about you. If you hadn't come down this morning, I meant to come to see you."

"I'm all right." She straightened the silverware at her place.

He broke a short silence by saying quietly, "Don't forget that I love you." When she didn't respond, he moved away.

She was going home. Ward had been dead almost a year. The reward she had offered had not accomplished what she hoped it would, and in spite of the fact that they were now certain that Hap was one of Ward's killers, there appeared to be no way at present that they could arrest and hold him and ultimately force him to identify the others. There was only Sy's certainty that he would defeat Jess Frazier in November that furnished hope that Hap would ever be made to talk. She could not live on that certainty any longer, not after what had happened. She had so complicated her relationship with Sy that they could never resume it on its old footing. Leaving without seeing Ward's killers was a bitter defeat. She still burned with fury when she saw Hap and thought about those other men, whoever they were, who were going about the business of living while Ward lay in his grave. Would she ever lose this rage if she left without seeing them punished? She knew she would not, but the situation had changed. She had to leave.

Respecting her desire to avoid him, Sy left her alone, greeting her warmly whenever they met, waiting for her to make the next move toward reconciliation. She thought it only fair to tell him she had decided to leave.

One afternoon she asked Salvador Cross for an hour off

and went to Sy's office. The door and window were open, letting in a hot wind that ruffled the weighted papers on his desk, yet did nothing to cool the air. He was in his shirt-sleeves, but made no move toward his jacket, which hung from a hook on the wall. She had managed to convince him some time ago that such gallantry was not necessary around her.

Greeting her with surprised gladness, he came around his desk and held a chair for her. After a few awkward comments about the continuing hot weather, Susan said, "I came to tell you I'm going back to Fieldsboro."

"Not for good?" he asked at once, his smile fading.

"Yes. I want to go home."

His tall, slender body slumped perceptibly as he moved to his chair and sat down. "I thought you wanted to stay and see the men who killed Ward sent to prison."

"I've given up hope that that will happen."

"In six months I'll have Hap in jail, and you can be sure he's not going to go to prison alone. He'll name his friends."

"What if you don't win the election?"

A gust of wind came through the window at his back, disturbing the dark hair behind his ears. "I can't lose. Everyone has had enough of Jess's incompetence." He put his arms on the desk and urged, "Don't leave yet, Susan. If you're doing it because of me, there's no need. We can have any kind of relationship you feel comfortable with, or none if that's your choice. To have remained here this long and leave when a few more months would bring you what you've waited for would be a mistake."

So far she had managed not to look directly at him. With him leaning across the desk toward her it was more difficult. She pressed her handkerchief against her perspiring brow and upper lip, and ignored his remarks about their relationship. "There aren't any guarantees. If I stay here and for some reason you fail to convict Hap and the others, the disappointment will be worse than if I go now." She stood up. "I gave Mr. Cross my notice this morning. I'll be leaving in two weeks."

He stood up, too, and came around the desk. His eyes very dark, he said, "Please don't go, Susan. Give me more time."

More time to catch Ward's killers? Or more time to try to persuade her to marry him? "No, this is best," she replied firmly, and left.

8

THE TWO-STORY FRAME house rose stark and graceless from the flat fields that surrounded it. Van Alstine hadn't been out this way for a long time. Surveying the peeling paint on the house, the graying boards of the small barn, and the decaying chicken house and hog shed, he concluded that Phil Osborne's landlord wasn't one to spend money on improvements. Maybe it was because he lived in Iowa and didn't realize what poor shape the buildings were in. More likely was the possibility that with a renter like Osborne, the owner didn't earn enough off the farm to keep everything repaired. Van Alstine wondered if the landlord knew that Phil spent more time loafing around town—particularly in the saloon—than he spent working the farm.

A hen with a brood of six or eight baby chicks flew out of the path of the buggy as Van Alstine pulled up near the back door of the house. A lilac bush, thick with leaves as a result of the wet summer, grew on the south side of the house. Clusters of brown seeds remained from what had been a large crop of blossoms. There wasn't a sign of another flower anywhere, but near the windmill a huge vegetable garden was flourishing. A shaggy tan dog rose from the shade on the north side of the house and came forward, his tail wagging a friendly greeting as Van Alstine climbed out of the buggy.

Phil Osborne appeared at the back door and peered out. He seemed in no hurry to come outside. Suspecting that Osborne was startled to see him, Van Alstine took his time securing the reins. It wouldn't hurt at all to scare him a bit. At last he called out, "I'd like to have a word with you, Phil," and started toward the house. Apparently preferring to hear what the sheriff had to say outside the house rather than where his wife could overhear, Osborne came out and strode toward the buggy on his long, powerful legs. A big, strapping man, his strength would have insured his success as a farmer had he not had an aversion to work. His blond hair hung lankly about his ears; his bloodshot eyes and pallor betrayed the fact that he was hung over this morning. Van halted a few feet inside the yard. He, too, preferred to hold their conversation out of earshot of Osborne's wife. "Were you at Mac's saloon last night?" he began.

Warily, Osborne replied, "Yeah, why?"

"Was Hap there, too?"

Osborne's pained squint against the bright sunshine hid anything his face might otherwise have revealed. "Sure. We had a few drinks together."

"I hear you had a fight."

"Who told you that?"

"Cal Rivers said he heard you and Hap talking in the privy and when you came out you were so mad you climbed on your wagon and left."

"It wasn't Hap and me. Cal was so drunk last night, he probably couldn't see straight. Or hear right, either. If he heard a fight, it was somebody else."

"What he heard couldn't have been said by anybody except Hap." The dog had retreated from the heat and gone back to the shade on the north side of the house. Pointing to the animal, Van Alstine said, "He's got the right idea. Why don't we go over there and get out of the sun?"

Osborne didn't say a word as they moved into the shade. Now that he wasn't squinting and Van Alstine could read his expression, he dropped it on him. "Cal heard Hap say that he wished he hadn't helped you guys hang Maddox. If he'd let you tie him up, he could have claimed the reward Mrs. Maddox has offered." The bloodshot eyes were squinting again. Was it just his splitting head or was it tension? "Cal claims he heard you cuss Hap and ask him how he could turn on his friends, and when Hap said he could do anything for a thousand dollars, he said you flew mad and pushed Hap out of the privy. He thought you two were going to have it out right there, but Hap got away and ran into the saloon. He said you stood out there cursing for a while and then left."

Osborne had some swear words left over. He used them before declaring, "That's a pack of lies! About me, anyway. And I don't think Hap ever said any such thing, either. If Cal Rivers wasn't hearing things, then he's making it up so *he* can claim the reward."

"When he came to me this morning with this story, he admitted he had had a lot to drink last night, but he swore that what he was telling me was true. He said he recognized both you and Hap by your voices first, and when the two of you came out of the privy, he saw you plain."

"In the dark?" Osborne spat into a bare place in the turf where the chickens had scratched away the grass, then kicked some dirt over the spot.

"Our nights aren't that dark. You'd have been easy to recognize."

"Yeah, if it had been me!"

Van Alstine shifted his weight and put his hands on his hips. "Pat Seavey was in the saloon the night the jail was broken into. He was in a temper and saying Maddox ought to be strung up for killing Widow Brown. According to my witness, he had everybody riled up. You must have been there. You're in there every night."

That made Osborne mad. "The hell I am! I wasn't there that night."

"Where were you?"

"Home, I suppose."

"I'd like to talk to your wife about that."

"You leave Gracie alone! I'm not going to let you upset her."

"I'll try not to do that. Are you going to call her out here or do I have to go in the house?"

Osborne glared at him without moving. The dog, which was lying nearby, threw up his head suddenly and began biting a flea on his rear flank. The clacking of his teeth and his heavy breathing were the only sounds that broke the morning stillness. He was still at it when Osborne stumped around the corner of the house. Van Alstine followed. "Just call to her to come out," he ordered. "Don't go in."

Osborne jerked open the screen door and yelled, "Gracie,

come here!" He let the door bang closed.

Gracie Osborne picked up the baby from the kitchen floor and came out on the porch. A thin, washed-out woman, she peered timidly at the sheriff, who raised his hat and said, "Morning, Mrs. Osborne. I'd like to ask you a question or two."

She glanced uncertainly at her husband, who said quickly, "He wants to know—"

"I'll tell her what I want to know," Van Alstine interrupted. Gently he asked, "Was Phil at home the night the jail was broke into and Ward Maddox was hung?"

"Yes, he was," she said in a small voice.

"Are you sure? That was a year ago."

"I know, but I can remember." Her tone grew firmer. "I can remember because I thought at the time how glad I was he had been at home."

Van Alstine noted the faint flush that had risen to her cheeks. He couldn't tell whether she was lying or whether she was simply nervous about talking to him. "Thank you, ma'am. I don't need to ask you anything else, I guess."

She glanced at Osborne as if asking permission to go back inside. He wasn't paying any more attention to her. He stepped away from the door and confronted Van Alstine. "Does that satisfy you?"

"No, but that'll be all for now. I'll be talking to you again." That last remark was more to worry Osborne than anything else. Questioning either one of them further would probably be a waste of time.

Susan was just leaving her room after washing up for dinner when Sy, who must have been listening for her, came out of his room and stopped her. "I've got good news," he said. His face shone with suppressed excitement.

They had spoken little to each other since she announced to him her intention to leave Hawthorne. She still felt uncomfortable around him. She had forgiven him, but not herself.

"Somebody came to Van this morning with a story that may identify another one of the men who broke into the jail."

She forgot her shame as Sy told her what Cal Rivers had heard and about the sheriff's trip out to see Phil Osborne. "Phil denied it, of course, and his wife backed him up, but that was to be expected."

Susan knew Phil Osborne by sight and sound. His loud voice and laugh could be heard anywhere on the square when he was out on the street. She knew he was a loafer and a drinker and a frequent companion of Hap Turner's. She could easily believe he might have been one of the men involved that night. Her rage freshened. "Who is this Cal Rivers? Can we believe him?"

"That's the one fly in the ointment. Cal is a drunk. Van has had to pick him up out of alleys several times and take him home. He used to put him in jail and let him sober up, but he's harmless. Doesn't give his family or anyone else any trouble, so Van just takes him home and lets his wife take care of him."

Down below they heard Rufus greeting someone who had come in for dinner. Dropping his voice a bit, Sy continued. "Cal has been known to imagine a lot of things when his drinking gets bad. Twice he's been taken to the insane asylum and from there he's gone for the bichloride of gold cure, but he always starts drinking again."

Susan's interest had begun to wane. "Then he may have imagined this, too."

"I happen to believe him." Annoyance darkened his firm-jawed face. "Our trouble is that Jess Frazier doesn't. He's not going to take a case into court that depends on the testimony of a man like Cal."

Susan made an exasperated sound. "What's he waiting for, a confession?"

"You've hit it. Jess is afraid of our district judge. He doesn't want to take a case before him unless he's sure it's winnable. As a result, the court docket here is always pretty brief. If I were county attorney, I'd file charges against both Hap and Phil, farm one of them out to the Harlan County jail to keep them apart, and then let them sweat until the next court term. I'd lay odds one or the other of them would panic and try to save his own neck by talking."

With his gaze holding hers, he said, "Don't leave yet, Susan. I'm going to win the election, and the day I take office I'm going to file charges against Hap and Phil and maybe even Pat Seavey. I won't let up on them until they've identified the fourth man and they're all locked up in prison or hung. The election is only three months away. Is that so long to wait?"

She made herself look squarely at him. Very slender in his tan summer suit, he appeared taller than usual in the low-ceilinged, narrow corridor. His softly curling dark hair was still damp from its recent combing. There was a loose-limbed grace about him in contrast to Ward's taut energy. "No," three months doesn't seem like a long time to wait."

"Meantime we might learn something else." He was watching her.

Information did seem to crop up unexpectedly, and she now knew the probable identity of another of Ward's killers. The case obviously was not dead, and if Sy won the election, she wanted to be here when he pressed the case against Hap and Osborne. "I'll stay."

His face broke into a grin so charming it drew a smile from her. "You won't be sorry."

There was something so boyish in his elation that the constraint she had felt in his presence the past weeks dropped away, exposing once again the easy friendship that had grown up between them since Ward's death. It's going to be all right, she told herself.

Sy was at his desk, roughing out the case against Hap and Osborne, when one of the Seavey kids came in. Red-haired, freckled, looking every inch the scamp that he was, he told Sy he'd been sent by Nels Cooper to ask Sy to drop by his store when he had time. "Thanks, Sean." He tossed the boy a penny, and the snub-nosed face turned angelic—but only for a moment. Then he was racing noisily down the stairs.

Reluctantly, Sy put away his papers. Since Cal Rivers's disclosure and Susan's decision to stay, he had burned with impatience to get Hap and Phil Osborne into jail and into court. In his spare time he had begun to build the case against them. He had been looking forward to another hour of work on it before he closed for the day.

He found Cooper sitting on the bench outside his hardware store. At this time of day, the sun came in under the tin awning to the right of the door, so the bench had been pulled to the other side. Cooper sat in the only position his obesity permitted, back straight, hands on knees, his great stomach heaving with each breath. It was a mystery to Sy how the man could continue to run his store, even with the help of his son. Sitting down beside him, he said, "Sean Seavey said you wanted to see me."

"I hear you're going to arrest a bunch of men for that Maddox hanging if you win the election."

Cautiously, Sy admitted, "I think Jess and Judge Allen made a mistake when they turned Hap loose."

"He's not the only one you're after, though, is he?"

Sy turned his head to one side to study the massive man. His many-chinned face was, as usual, expressionless. Sy had long ago come to the conclusion that emotions required more energy than Nels Cooper was willing to expend. "Who told you what I intend to do if I win the election?"

"It doesn't matter. What concerns me is that these men have families. What happens if you convict them? Who's going to take care of their families?"

"Are you suggesting that I not prosecute them because of what it would do to their families?"

"I'm suggesting that you ask yourself if sending those men to prison or the gallows is worth the misery you'll cause."

"Is that the criterion by which the justice system should judge criminals? By its effect on the families of those who are tried for crimes?"

"This isn't a city, Sy. We can be a little looser about enforcing the law. We know our neighbors as well as we know our own kin. There isn't anybody in this town who's a threat to anybody else."

"That's what you'd have believed before Ward Maddox was hung, but four men killed him. Are we supposed to just forget it ever happened? You've been complaining about

Jess Frazier's incompetence. I'd be guilty of worse than that if I closed my eyes to evidence that might lead to the conviction of four murderers."

"It happened more than a year ago. Let it lay, Sy. It caused a countywide scandal. Do you want to raise the stink again? Every few years, Liberty fights us for the county seat. You might give them the ammunition that will defeat us next time. All our opponents will claim Hawthorne isn't a fit town to have the county seat located in."

"Can you imagine what they'd say if they found out we had covered the whole thing up? I've got some good suspects, Nels, and I'm going after them if I'm elected county attorney."

Eyes flat and dark as an Indian's regarded him from beneath puffy lids. "I can't support you if you plan to hurt all these people and maybe ruin the town, too."

Winning the county attorney's seat had become the most important thing in the world to Sy, next to winning Susan, and he knew he couldn't have her unless he had the other, because he was convinced that until she was free of the past she would never be able to love another man. Nels Cooper was one of the most influential Democrats in the county. A word from him to other Democratic leaders could cost Sy the party's nomination, which up until now he had considered a certainty. Still, what was the good of winning the county attorney's office if he couldn't prosecute the men who killed Ward Maddox?

"I won't pretend that losing your support wouldn't be a blow, Nels, but this Maddox case is something I've got to prosecute. If you decide not to back me, I'll have to try it without your help."

"You're doing it for the Maddox woman, aren't you? You're sweet on her."

"Yes, I am," Sy admitted. "She doesn't feel the same about me. I'm hoping she will once her husband's murderers are caught and she can forget it and start a new life." He added, "I'd appreciate it if you kept that to yourself."

"I won't tell anyone. Are you sure you want to give up the chance to be county attorney for something you only hope will happen?"

Sy grinned. "Who says I'm giving up the chance to be county attorney? I'm not beaten yet." He stood up. "I hope you'll see it my way before the caucus."

"Don't count on it."

It was Van Alstine who first brought Sy word that Nels Cooper was trying to persuade other Democrats to back Ezra Black for county attorney. Black, an older man, had held the office years ago and had lost to a Republican after two terms. Within a week Susan heard the news, too.

"What's happened?" she asked. "I thought you were to be the candidate."

They were sharing a table that evening as they had been doing frequently since Susan's decision to remain in Hawthorne a while longer. Sy was encouraged by the resumption of their old relationship and was being careful not to jar it with reminders of the fact that he loved her. If he could maintain the status quo until after the murder trial, he believed he would be able to begin the courtship of a new Susan.

He hadn't told her about Nels Cooper's threat or about his shifting his support to Ezra Black, afraid she would sense defeat and decide after all to go back to Pennsylvania. Gazing at the beautifully structured face with its long line from high cheekbone to narrow chin, he sought a way to minimize the loss of Nels Cooper's support. "Somehow Nels found out about my plan to pursue the case against Ward's killers if I was elected county attorney. He knew I suspected Hap and that I had two other suspects as well. He asked me if they had families, and when I said yes, he argued that it would be better for them and the town if the case were forgotten. When I said I couldn't do that, he said I'd be hurting too many people and giving Liberty the ammunition it needed to try again to wrest the county seat from us, and, therefore, he couldn't support me."

Susan's eyes snapped. "I told you a year ago this town wanted to sweep Ward's murder under the rug."

"Nels isn't the whole town. I've sounded out men like Henry Sims who've been here a long time, and they told me Ezra Black wasn't very effective as county attorney when he held the job fifteen years ago. Most of them said they'd rather see me get it."

"That's what they say to your face." Susan had forgotten her food.

Sy added more catsup to his fried potatoes. "They can't all be lying. I'd stake my life on anything Henry Sims said." He cut off a bite of steak. "I told them why Nels had decided not to support me and explained that I thought this town would be in a lot more trouble if people in other parts of the county found out we were doing what you accused them just now of doing—sweeping a crime under the rug. I got a lot of agreement on that. That's the issue I'm going to campaign on."

Doubtfully, Susan asked, "Do you have any chance at

all without party support?"

"Townships will be holding caucuses in two weeks. I intend to call on leaders in every township and explain why Nels is trying to get me out of the race. It isn't a pretty story. I think it's going to make a lot of people mad."

"Including Nels Cooper."

"Yes, and I'm sorry. Nels and I have been friends. This will end that."

"Is there anything I can do to help you?"

"As long as you stay in Hawthorne you'll be a reminder to the whole county that this town still has an unsolved crime that I am promising to solve if I'm elected county attorney. That will be as effective as anything I can do." He grinned at her. "Cheer up. This is merely a setback, not a defeat."

"But you were so certain you would win. Now it's not certain at all."

"Still looking for guarantees," he teased. There was one he wished he dared give her: that he would love her forever.

Susan answered the knock at her door knowing who it was. Lettie had asked her at supper if she could come up and talk to Susan about something when she got off work. Then, as now, the small, fragile-looking body seemed aquiver with excitement. Lettie refused the chair she was offered, dropping to the edge of the bed, but only briefly, before springing up again and standing a few feet away from Susan and announcing, "I'm thinking about leaving Hap. Jerry Gibson wants me to run away with him."

It came as a real surprise. Cautiously, Susan asked, "Are you sure Jerry loves you?"

A dazzling light came into Lettie's pale face. "I'm sure.

Oh, Susan, nobody has ever treated me the way he does. I didn't know I could feel this—" She broke off, groping for words. "—this important. I don't mean the swelled head kind. I feel like I'm important to someone else. Jerry needs me. He wants me. He misses me when he's away, and he's happiest when he's with me." She had been flitting like a butterfly about the room as she spoke. Now she perched once more on the edge of the bed and added shyly, "And I feel the same way about him."

If Jerry is only half as much in love with her as she is with him, Susan thought, it will be all right. "Does Hap suspect anything?"

"He'd kill me if he did! I've got to keep it a secret until I'm gone. If I go," she added. "Do you think it would be terribly wicked if I did, Susan?"

"Wicked?" Susan thought about how Ward had died and about the men who had cold-bloodedly murdered him. Lettie was living with one of them. "I don't think it would be wicked at all, Lettie. In fact, if you have a chance to get away from Hap, go. Have you heard what Sy plans to do if he's elected county attorney?" Lettie obviously hadn't, so Susan told her. "Hap could end up in prison or worse. You'd be wise to divorce him as quickly as you can."

"You mean they might hang him?" Some of the light in Lettie went out.

Susan reminded her in quiet, even tones, "He helped kill Ward."

Lettie began to trace the pieces in the patchwork quilt with a small, work-roughened finger. "I've been his wife for three years. I even loved him once." She looked up. "Or could have if he had loved me." She was silent again for a while, then said, "I'll write to Jerry tonight after Hap is asleep and tell him he can send the money for my train ticket. He wanted to leave the money with me when he left last time, but I told him I needed more time to think."

"When will you leave?"

"Just as soon as I get the money. I'll need your help to get away."

"I'll do anything I can."

The blue and gold October afternoon had just enough of a bite in it to make Sy's wool suit feel good. Guiding the buggy back toward Hawthorne after meeting with some Democrats in the townships north of town, he asked, "How good do you think my chances are, Sal?"

Salvador Cross squinted as the breeze blew the smoke from his cigar back into his eyes. He had been accompanying Sy all over the county, lending his persuasion to Sy's in an attempt to win delegates to the county convention, which was now only two weeks away. "I think you'll get half of them in Ash Grove. You probably won't get any in Turkey Creek."

"That's the way I had it figured."

Sal had volunteered to help, and Sy was deeply grateful. Salvador Cross was known throughout the county, not only because of his big ads every week in the county paper, but as the man whose wife preferred living in the insane asylum to living a normal life at home. The tragedy had won him much sympathy. More important from Sy's standpoint was the fact that Sal's integrity was as well known as his personal problems. "It's going to be close. Damn Nels Cooper!"

Salvador Cross watched a jackrabbit spring up from the

dying prairie grass and go loping along the trail in front of them. "Nels thinks Hawthorne is his baby, and unfortunately for you, there are plenty of people who think Nels is a little wiser than most of us."

Sy glanced at the face with its deep lines of suffering. "I've got to win, Sal."

"I know." Salvador Cross's eyes followed the rabbit as it veered off the road and bounded across a plowed field. "The past can hang like a millstone around a person's neck. I hope for her sake as well as yours that you can cut it loose."

Susan stopped rocking abruptly; from the bed came Lettie's gasp. Their glances flew together. Hap's voice came loudly from downstairs. "Where's Lettie?"

They heard Rufus Lord reply without being able to make out his words.

"Well, she *ain't* at home," Hap said in a contradictory tone.

The murmur of Rufus's voice rose up the stairs once more, and then there was silence. Lettie slid over to the edge of the bed nearest Susan's rocker and whispered, "He's probably going to the kitchen to see if I'm still there."

Lettie had managed to sneak upstairs half an hour before, while Rufus, Sy, and two other men were deep in their card game. She was leaving on the eleven o'clock eastbound for Omaha, where Jerry Gibson would meet her. One by one she had secretly brought a few of her personal things to the hotel during the past week, packing them in a box that stood in Susan's room. Now the box was tied and ready to be carried to the train and Lettie was prettier than Susan had ever seen her, wearing a green dress with white ruching at the neck and cuffs. "It was my wedding dress," she explained when Susan told her how nice it looked. "I don't think I've worn it three times since Hap and I were married. I never seem to get out of calico."

The clock began to chime the hour, breaking the silence. Nine o'clock. Hap had been waiting for Lettie to get home and fix his supper. He'd be in a churlish mood; later his mood would worsen. Susan wished Lettie were already safely on the train and on her way to Omaha.

They heard him return from the kitchen and announce, "Ella said she let her go half an hour ago. Did you see her leave?"

After a reply that Susan and Lettie knew had to be a no, Hap said, "She must be upstairs visiting with that Maddox woman."

"Oh, my God!" Lettie breathed. There were steps on the stairs, heavy, angry ones.

"Stand in that corner," Susan said, indicating the one behind the door. "He won't be able to see you there." She picked up a book from the bureau and began rocking as noisily as possible. The rocker made a satisfactory and easily heard rhythm against the wooden floor.

With the book in her hand, she opened the door quickly to his peremptory knock, giving him no reason to suspect she was hiding anything.

"Is my wife here?" he demanded curtly.

The sight of that stumpy body and bearded face invariably sent fiery hatred flooding through her. Her hand tightened convulsively on the edge of the door, and she replied through tight lips, "No, she's not."

His narrow eyes glared at her suspiciously. "Do you have any idea where she is?"

"I haven't seen her since supper."

He was peering past her into the room. From his angle he could see the bed, the bureau, and enough of the rocker to see that it was empty. "Well, if you see her," he growled, "tell her I said to get on home."

Susan took her time closing the door, making sure he was on his way back down the stairs. She and Lettie stood where they were until they heard him speaking to Rufus, then they let out their breath simultaneously.

"Do you think he believed you?" Lettie asked, coming out of the corner on tiptoe.

"I think so."

"I wish it were eleven o'clock."

"So do I."

Lettie was too nervous now to sit still. She began pacing the small areas of space between the bed and bureau, between door and bed. As her fingers flew over her tatting, Susan felt the dread specter of loneliness, which she had come to know so well, confronting her with renewed oppressiveness. Lettie had become a dear friend; in fact, the first close woman friend she had ever had other than Coila. So long as she had been living at home, Susan hadn't felt the need for such a friend. She and Coila had shared everything; there was nothing they couldn't talk to one another about. Until Ward. Some things were too private to share even with one's best friend. Lettie's small, vivacious presence had helped fill the vast emptiness that Ward's death had left. Without her, the hotel was going to be a different sort of place. One fragment of the emotional life she had tried to piece together after her move into Hawthorne would be missing.

Looking up, she was struck again by how pretty Lettie looked tonight. Her red hair, darker in the lamplight, was neater than Susan had ever seen it. Excitement put color in her normally pale cheeks. In the stylish green dress, she was transformed from charwoman into a lovely lady. It was a side of Lettie she had never seen, and it brought a rush of new love for her. Overcome by sadness, Susan went to her and embraced her. "How I'm going to miss you!" she whispered past the ache in her throat.

Hugging her, Lettie urged, "Come and see me when I get settled. I won't know anyone except Jerry, and I'll be missing you something awful, too."

"If Sy loses the nomination, I'll be leaving Hawthorne, but I'll be going through Omaha on my way back to Pennsylvania. I'll stop a few days and visit with you."

"You'll know by tomorrow night whether you're going to leave or not, won't you?"

Susan's stomach curled with nervousness. The Democratic county convention was being held tomorrow in Hawthorne. "At least I'll know whether I'll be leaving right away or whether I'll be staying until the November election."

"I wish you were staying here for good. We could see each other once in a while. I'll be coming back now and then as long as Pa is alive. I went to see him today. I didn't tell him I was leaving, of course." Lettie spread her hands helplessly. "My emotions are all mixed up. I can't wait to be with Jerry, but I'm sad, too."

"I know."

They still had forty minutes to wait. Lettie alternated between pacing the floor and lying on the bed to rest as

Susan urged. Sleeping on the train would be difficult, and it would be midmorning of the next day before she arrived in Omaha.

"I'd better turn out the light," Susan said. "I'm usually in bed by this time."

So was almost everyone else in Hawthorne. The only place that remained open after ten o'clock was the saloon. The card game in the parlor had broken up fifteen minutes ago; Sy had come upstairs and gone to his room shortly thereafter.

Susan turned down the wick of the lamp on the bureau, casting the room into darkness. She waited until her eyes adjusted and went back to her chair. "Will you be working in Omaha?"

"I hope so. I want to help support myself until Jerry and I can be married. It will make living with him seem a little less sinful." Lettie fell silent, leaving echoes of her guilt floating in the dark room.

Susan said, "You're a fine, decent person, Lettie."

A whisper of thanks reached her from the bed, followed by a declaration in a firmer tone. "I mean to file for divorce the very first thing."

"Will that give your address to Hap?" There was no predicting what a man like Hap might do.

"I don't know."

"You must be very careful."

"I know."

Of course she did, Susan thought. Lettie had lived with him for three years. They were both victims of his brutality.

"Will Jerry quit his job? If I were him, I wouldn't want to come back to Hawthorne as long as Hap is here."

"I warned him about that, but he says he's not scared of Hap and he doesn't want to quit his job yet. He's making good money, and he's still a year or more away from having enough to start his own mercantile. I wish I could get a job that paid enough to help."

The clock struck the half hour. Ten-thirty. They had agreed to wait until ten forty-five before starting for the depot. They could walk it in ten minutes. Prudence dictated that they give as little notice as possible of Lettie's departure to the depot agent or anyone else who happened to be around when she left.

Suddenly someone began pounding on the front door downstairs. "Oh, no!" Lettie cried out. "He's come back."

Susan sat very still in her chair. Who else could it be? It wouldn't be anyone wanting a room; there hadn't been a train in since seven-thirty. In the moonlight she saw Lettie sitting up on the bed, a hand at her throat. "Don't worry," Susan told her. "If it is Hap, he won't find you. Not without breaking into my room, and Rufus won't let him do that."

A door closed, and a few minutes later they heard someone unlocking the front door. Hap's voice, raspy and angry, said loudly, "Lettie still hasn't come home. Are you sure she's not still here someplace?"

"He's drunk," Lettie whispered. "I can tell."

Rufus was saying, "What would she still be doing here? Everyone's gone to bed."

"I want to talk to that Maddox woman."

"You've already talked to her, Hap. Lettie wasn't with her, and she didn't come in after you left. Did you check with Frank?"

"He ain't seen her since this afternoon. I checked several

places. Nobody's seen her."

A note of worry crept into Rufus's voice. "That does seem mighty funny."

"She ain't never been this late before."

"Have you looked along the streets going to your house? She might have fallen and hurt herself."

"I've looked. I've been practically all over town. I want to see the Maddox woman. Them two are pretty thick. Maybe Lettie said something to her, or maybe she's up there."

"Why should she be up there? Unless you two had a fight. Did you?"

"She's got no call to be mad about anything. Let me go upstairs and see that Maddox woman."

Rufus's reply brought both Susan and Lettie to their feet. "Maybe it's best you talk to her. Sounds to me like something might have happened to Lettie."

"In the corner!" Susan whispered. "Quick." While Lettie sped silently to the same corner she had hidden in earlier, Susan opened the bed and mussed the covers. From a peg, she pulled her flannel wrapper and slipped into it, tying it tightly around her waist. Her shoes! The men were coming up the stairs. There was no time to get all those buttons unhooked. Hoping in the dark they wouldn't notice she was still wearing them, she sat down on the bed, knowing the springs would creak when she got up.

Rufus's knock was soft, tentative. "Susan, it's me."

Making her voice sound as sleepy as possible, she replied, "Rufus?"

"Sorry to bother you, Susan, but can I talk to you for a minute?"

"Is something wrong? Is Ella sick?" The bedsprings let

them know she was getting out of bed. She started for the door, trying to prevent her shoes from making any sound. All at once, she remembered her hair. Pausing, she jerked the combs out quickly, letting her braids fall down her back. When she reached the door, she opened it only a few inches, holding her wrapper closed at the neck. "Oh, it's you again," she said when she saw Hap standing in the small area of light cast by the kerosene lamp Rufus held.

"He can't find Lettie," Rufus said apologetically. His shirttail flapped over his trousers, and he was barefoot. "I wouldn't have brought him up, but I'm worried, too. She doesn't seem to be anywhere. We thought you might know where she might be."

"I haven't seen her since supper. She didn't mention that she'd be doing anything special tonight." Just that she'd be leaving town, Susan thought with unabashed glee as she glanced out of the corner of her eye at the disheveled, stumpy figure of the man who had helped murder Ward.

"Would you have any idea who she might have gone to visit?"

"She may have gone to see her father."

Hap declared tersely, "She ain't there."

"I'm afraid I wouldn't know, then."

"It's important, Susan." Rufus spoke placatingly, aware of the hostility between the other two. "Something might have happened to Lettie."

Pretending worry, she said, "Maybe she started home and fell or got sick or something."

"I looked," Hap said curtly.

Turning to him, Rufus said, "Maybe you should tell the sheriff."

Susan heard a small intake of breath over in the corner.

If Sheriff Van Alstine were told, he'd soon have the whole town alerted, including the depot agent. Running her hand up and down the edge of the door to disguise the sound Lettie made, she said, "I'm sure we're getting upset for no reason. Lettie has probably gone to visit someone and has simply forgotten the time."

"I hope so," Rufus said. "Come on, Hap. Good night, Susan."

The clock was striking ten forty-five as she closed the door. "I'm going to miss the train!" Lettie exclaimed in a loud whisper.

Throwing off her wrapper, Susan asked tensely, "Are you all ready to go?"

"Yes. Hap, for God's sake, leave!"

The two men's voices drifted up to them from the parlor. Susan retrieved her combs from the pocket of her wrapper and wound her braids back up on her head by feel. "There," she murmured and pinned on her hat, hoping it would hide her hasty job. Donning her coat she joined Lettie, who stood at the door listening, her box at her feet.

Hap was arguing with Rufus. "I ain't going to Van for help. I can find Lettie by myself, and when I do, I'll give her a talkin' to she'll never forget." There was a thud and a scraping along the floor as if Hap had stumbled into a chair. "I don't believe that Maddox woman. I think she knows where Lettie is."

"Why should she lie? Besides, she sounded worried, too. Wait here. I'll get dressed and do some looking myself."

Lettie let out a small cry between gritted teeth. "No, Rufus, no!"

Susan glanced automatically at the clock. It was too dark to see the hands, but its tick was loud in the silent room.

"I'm going over to the saloon," Hap said. "You can pick me up there."

Beside her, Susan felt Lettie wilting with relief. She remained taut with tension herself, realizing swiftly that in order to make the train on time they were going to have to squeeze their departure from the hotel between the time it took Rufus to put on his clothes and the moment when Hap was safely inside the saloon. She left the door and went to the window. The streets were dark except for the patches of dim light shining through the windows of the saloon. There was plenty of moonlight, however, more than she'd have ordered for this night. As she watched, Hap appeared in her line of vision, crossing diagonally from the hotel corner and heading for the saloon, which was located two doors up from Cross's Mercantile. "Hurry!" she breathed. Without taking her eyes from the blocky shadow that strolled toward the lighted windows, she said, "Go to the head of the stairs and be ready to run. But don't let Rufus hear you!"

"What if he comes out of his room? We've got to leave now or we'll never make it!"

"Maybe the train will be late." The words were scarcely out of her mouth when they heard its whistle, signaling its imminent arrival from the west. They couldn't wait any longer; they'd have to run all the way as it was. "Let's go! And pray that Hap doesn't look back this way when he goes into Mac's."

Moving as quietly as they could in their frantic haste, they ran down the dark stairway and out the door, taking time to close it noiselessly behind them. Moonlight fell full upon them. One glance told Susan that Hap had reached the saloon. Grabbing Lettie's arm, she pulled her tightly against the front of the hotel. "Don't move."

Hap stood silhouetted against the open door of the saloon for an instant and then went inside.

"Run!" Susan cried. Dashing around the corner, they made for the depot, a quarter of a mile away. Petticoats and skirts caught at their legs; hats threatened to bounce loose from pins. Lettie's box flew against her thighs and knees. Wordlessly, Susan took it from her on the run. Taller than her friend by several inches, she was able to manage it less awkwardly.

They passed the last of the houses. Only vacant lots lay between them and the depot. The train was pulling in. If there were no passengers to let off or waiting to board, it would halt just long enough to take aboard the mail pouch, then depart.

A quarter of a mile had never seemed so far before. Susan's lungs burned. They had left the sidewalks behind long ago and were running in the well-worn road that not only extended up from the depot, but carried traffic coming across the bridge from the far side of the river. At this late hour, however, it was deserted. With only moonlight to show them the way, they dodged ruts and peered ahead for low places that would break their stride.

While they were still a block away from the tracks, the train gave its warning whistle. With what seemed her last breath, Susan croaked, "Go on. Stop them."

Lettie flew off. Susan, unable to run another step, slowed to a walk. She saw Lettie burst into the light from the depot lamps and disappear around the corner of the building. A moment later she reappeared, waving Susan on. Having caught her breath, Susan ran the last half block to find Frank Cook and the train conductor waiting at the foot of the steps leading up to a car from whose darkened windows a few faces peered out. When Susan came into sight, the depot agent hurried forward to take the box from her hand, saying, "I hadn't heard you were leaving, Mrs. Maddox."

"I'm not," Susan gasped, trying to catch her breath. "Lettie is."

To forestall the question she saw rising to his lips, she turned to embrace Lettie. "Write me," she said breathlessly.

"I will. And thanks, Susan, for everything." With a brilliant smile, Lettie left her and climbed aboard. At the top of the steps, she waved, looking as joyous as a child on her way to a long-anticipated holiday.

The steps were taken up, a lantern waved, and with a puff of steam, the train began to move. Susan watched it for a moment, experiencing a mixture of triumph and sadness. When Frank Cook started in her direction, she pretended not to see and headed back up the dark road toward town.

{9}

THE NEXT MORNING Susan placed the letter to Hap that Lettie had left with her on Rufus's desk on her way in to breakfast. Rufus was waiting tables, delivering a stack of griddle cakes to a jewelry drummer who had arrived in town the previous afternoon and had joined last night's card game.

Going directly to the kitchen, she found Ella mixing up another batch of griddle-cake batter.

"Lettie still hasn't turned up," she said at once. Her moist, ruddy face was creased with worry.

"She's safe, Ella. She asked me to give you this." Susan handed her another letter Lettie had left with her.

Ella glanced at her sharply. "You say she's safe? Where is she?"

Susan told her the entire story while the older woman laid the letter aside and kept adding milk to the batter until it reached the consistency she wanted. Then she stopped, wiping up a spill on the tabletop with a corner of her apron. She seemed nearly speechless with surprise. "Well, I swan! I never knowed there was anything between them two. Rufus must not of, either. He sure never said anything." New moisture had popped out on her forehead. She bent and wiped it off with another corner of her apron. When she straightened, she shook her head wonderingly. "Isn't Hap going to have a fit when he finds out, though."

"She left a letter for him. I put it on Rufus's desk."

Putting one strong, reddened hand on her hip, Ella Lord asked, "Lettie's going to live with this Gibson while she gets her divorce?"

"Yes."

Ella absorbed this revelation thoughtfully for a few moments, then said, "I know Hap treated her bad, and I can understand her leavin' him, but livin' with a man she ain't married to ain't right."

Although she had never let on to Lettie, Susan didn't condone such an arrangement either, but what was the alternative? "She doesn't have any money and she doesn't have a job yet. She has to have a place to live. They'd get married today if they could."

"The sooner, the better." Ella picked up the batter bowl and returned to the stove. "Rufus will bring your cakes out to you in a few minutes. Help yourself to coffee."

Returning to the dining room with a cup of coffee, she saw that Sy had arrived for breakfast. Rufus was standing beside his table, and the two of them were engaged in an earnest discussion. Certain that she knew what it was, Susan joined them.

"Lettie is missing," Sy said at once, getting to his feet

and pulling out a chair for her.

"No, she isn't. She left last night on the eleven o'clock train. She's going to Omaha to Jerry Gibson."

Rufus stared at her dumbstruck. Recovering, he rumbled, "I knew that drummer was after Lettie! I never once thought she'd fall for his line, though. I thought she had more sense."

Said Susan, "Jerry really loves her. He'll make her happier than Hap ever tried to do. She left a letter for Hap. I put it on your desk, Rufus. She left one for you and Ella, too. It's in the kitchen."

The big wedge of Rufus Lord's Adam's apple bobbed. "So she was in your room."

"Yes, she was. I'm sorry I had to deceive you, but Hap would have dragged her back home if he had known."

"Lord a'mighty!" Rufus exclaimed and headed for the kitchen.

Sy said, "I knew there was something going on between Lettie and Jerry, but I didn't expect anything like this." His tone was faintly accusing. "You could have told me what she was planning. I wouldn't have told anyone."

"She and I thought it best if we kept it just between us. If Rufus had known it, he'd have given it away for sure last night when Hap kept coming here hunting for Lettie. Did you hear us?"

"No. What time was it?"

She told him about Hap's two visits to the hotel, ending each time with Hap coming to her room and questioning her, and about the excitement of Lettie's plan to run away.

Sy remarked, "I hope Hap never finds out that you helped her."

"He's sure to find out. Frank Cook saw me at the depot with Lettie."

Sy frowned. "Having the whole town know his wife left him for another man is going to be a terrible blow to his prickly pride. It's hard telling what he might do."

The possibility that Hap might retaliate against her had never occurred to her. "What could he do?" she wondered uneasily.

"I don't know," Sy replied, "but be careful."

"I will," she promised. Two men whom she recognized as candidates for county offices came into the dining room. "I almost forgot that the convention was being held today," she said. "I'm surprised you could sleep so well last night."

"I left the fingernail-biting for today."

"What time does the convention open?"

"Ten o'clock. By four this afternoon I should know whether I'm going to be my party's candidate for county attorney."

And I should know whether I'll be remaining here for another four or five months, Susan thought, or whether I'll be leaving Hawthorne in a week or two. Studying the handsome aristocratic face that had become so familiar to her, she realized how much she would miss Sy. She hadn't let herself think much about him since that evening down by the creek, maintaining a friendly but shallow relationship with him. For a moment, she permitted herself to acknowledge how fond of him she had grown. In many ways he had been able to fill one of the roles in her life that Ward had once filled—a strong, masculine presence to turn to for support and advice. She couldn't have managed without his assistance during those nightmarish months following Ward's death, and his warm friendship had been a desperately needed antidote to the feelings of self-doubt that had haunted her when she found herself so abruptly alone. It was good that she hadn't known at the time that he was in love with her. It would have put an intolerable strain on their relationship.

"You know I wish you luck," she told him.

"I know. If they nominate Ezra Black, we both lose."

Wincing with pain, Hap Turner raised his head from the kitchen table. The nearly empty whiskey bottle by his elbow reminded him why he was here and not in bed. Ignoring the misery of his hangover, he got up quickly and went to the bedroom. The bed hadn't been slept in. The fear he had drunk to deaden last night swept over him again. Where the hell was she?

When 1:00 A.M. came and went without her showing up, he was afraid something might have happened to her. Sitting alone in his house, he thought that if she'd walk through the door he'd be the happiest guy in the world. A few minutes later he'd be so mad, he would have hit her if she'd walked in.

This morning all that anger was gone. He took another swallow of whiskey and then headed for the hotel. There was a chance she had showed up there this morning.

The minute he walked into the hotel, he remembered what day it was. The parlor was full of men standing around, conversing intently, and the early morning smell of bay rum filled the room. Hap's heart gave a lurch. The Democratic convention was being held today. If Sy Harris was nominated he was going to be in big trouble. That drawling son of a bitch was out to get his hide. Fear joined hangover nausea in his stomach. Needing Lettie like he'd never needed her before, he started through the crowded dining room, praying she'd be in the kitchen.

Rufus glanced up from the table he was cleaning and called out, "There's a letter for you from Lettie on my desk."

"A letter. She isn't here?" Hap tried to fit this information into his splitting head. He watched the skinny hotelkeeper retreat to the kitchen before he could ask any more questions. Back in the parlor, he found Lettie's letter lying on the desk and ripped it open.

> Dear Hap,
> I'm leaving you. I'm going
> to Omaha. I'm going to get a
> divorce just as soon as I can.
> Lettie

Only on second reading did its meaning fully penetrate his throbbing skull. He thought he was going to be sick. Staggering blindly past a small knot of men to the door, he opened it and breathed deeply of the crisp fall air. She had left him. But why? They got along fine, better than some couples he could name. There wasn't another man in the picture, that was for sure. Jesus! He wouldn't have been able to hold up his head if she'd run off with some other guy. Damn her! Running away! People were going to think he wasn't man enough to hold on to her. He drew some more air into his lungs to cool the fury that was building inside him. By God, he wouldn't let her do it! He'd go after her and drag her back home. That would show everybody he knew how to handle a woman.

Whirling, he made for the kitchen. Ella was washing dishes; Rufus was filling plates.

"What do you know about this?" he demanded, holding out Lettie's letter and slapping it with the other hand.

"Nothing," Rufus answered swiftly. "We didn't know she was gone till this morning. I wouldn't have gone out to help hunt for her if I'd known, would I?"

"How'd you find out?"

"She left us a letter, too," Ella said without looking up.

"What did she say?" Hap asked suspiciously.

"She thanked us for all we'd done for her and said she was sorry to run away and not give us any warning..." Ella's voice trailed off.

"But what?" Hap demanded impatiently.

"She didn't want you to find out until after she left," Rufus finished.

"Did she tell you where she'd be?"

Rufus seemed surprised. "No, didn't she tell you?"

Hap didn't reply. "If she left here at the usual time last night, the only way she could have got to Omaha was on the eleven o'clock train. She must have been sitting down at the depot while I looked all over town for her." Why hadn't he looked down there? He'd have got her back again if he'd had to carry her every step of the way. "Are you sure she didn't say where she was going to be staying?"

"Not a word to us," Rufus replied firmly.

"I'll get her back. Wait and see if I don't. You got any coffee left?"

Susan held up one of the new winter hats she was unpacking so that Salvador Cross could see it. "Isn't this one pretty?"

Across the narrow store from her, her employer paused in his task of placing a new bunch of pocketknives in the glass display case. Susan thought she must have roused him from a reverie, and not a happy one. His sad eyes gazed at her blankly for an instant before lightening. "Yes, it is. From here the rosebuds look real."

"And look at this one! I believe these are prettier than the ones we had last year."

"I hope you'll be here to sell them."

"I hope so, too."

It was an hour before noon. The balloting at the convention was about to begin, if it hadn't already. Placing the hat with the pink rosebuds on its wooden display post, Susan experienced a keen pang of regret at the thought that she might soon by saying good-bye to Salvador Cross. He had been so kind. Business had returned to normal after the excellent crop year they had had, allowing her to see what a generous act it had been for him to hire her last year. Yes, leaving without knowing Ward's killers would pay for his murder would not be her sole regret.

After working silently for a few minutes, Salvador Cross exclaimed, "I can't get over Lettie running away like that. Was she afraid Hap might be sent to prison?"

Susan, who had told him immediately that morning about Lettie's flight from Hawthorne and her own part in it, explained, "She didn't know anything about Sy's determination to prosecute Hap until after she came to me and asked my advice about leaving him. Maybe afterward, when Sy began campaigning for the nomination and declared his intention of finding out who murdered Ward, she may have cast aside any doubts she had. I don't think it would have made any difference, though. She was really in love for the first time in her life. And loved in return."

Drawing another hat from the carton, she noticed that the blue velvet ribbon had come loose in one place, and she was about to get a needle and thread when the door of the store burst open and Hap Turner, his face tight and mean, came at her. If he saw Salvador Cross, he ignored him. Hands gripping the counter, he snarled at her, "You were hiding her all the time, weren't you? You helped her get away." The smell of whiskey was on him, both stale and recent; he was unshaven; his hair lay in its usual disorderly whorls.

"Yes, I helped her," she admitted coolly. Frank Cook's account of Lettie's departure must have finally reached Hap's ears.

"You bitch! You talked her into it, didn't you? She wouldn't have run away if you'd left her alone. Trying to get even with me, aren't you?"

Hap's epithet had brought a shocked remonstrance from Salvador Cross, who came swiftly across the room to catch Hap by the arm and command, "That will be enough of that! Get out of my store!"

Jerking his arm out of Cross's grip, Hap shouted, "Keep out of this, Sal. It's none of your business."

Susan didn't want her employer to throw Hap out yet. "What should I be getting even with you for?" she demanded.

Caught up by his own words, he retreated craftily. "You think I had a hand in killing your husband. Well, I didn't, and Sy Harris can talk as big as he wants to—he's not going to pin anything on me. You're the one he should go after, breaking up a man's home. I want to know where Lettie is."

Susan looked long and hard at his flushed, coarse-featured face. "Didn't she tell you where she was going?"

"To Omaha," he snapped. "That's all."

She had assumed Lettie had told him everything. I won't tell him where he can find her, Susan decided, but I am going to have the pleasure of telling him that she ran off to another man. "She left you for Jerry Gibson. He was meeting her train in Omaha."

All the color left Hap Turner's face; it was a moment before he could speak. Susan watched with bittersweet relish as he reeled against this blow to his ego. "I don't believe it!" he sputtered at last. "That's a lie!"

"It's true," Susan insisted calmly. "She's in love with Jerry, and he's asked her to marry him just as soon as she can get a divorce from you."

Ashen, the muscles of his face working, he leaned across the counter and demanded menacingly, "I want her address."

"Leave her alone."

He lunged across the counter. "God damn you, give it to me!"

She stepped to one side, but not swiftly enough. He caught her sleeve and yanked with such force that it ripped loose from its seam. In the next instant, Salvador Cross had an arm under Hap's chin, hauling him back, dragging him toward the door as he twisted and struggled. Susan wouldn't have believed Salvador Cross possessed that kind of strength. Apparently afraid that throwing Hap out of the store wouldn't end the matter, he drove Hap's head into the doorframe, knocking him unconscious. "Go get the sheriff," he said to Susan, his chest heaving from his exertions. "The only safe place for him is in jail until he cools off."

Avoiding the crumpled figure of Hap Turner, Susan ran

out of the store and across the street to the jail, holding her ripped sleeve together as best she could. "Where's the sheriff?" she asked at once of Deputy Crowder, who was sitting idly at the desk staring out the window.

"He's at the convention."

She had forgotten.

Catching sight of the torn sleeve, he showed instant concern. "Have you hurt yourself?"

"Hap Turner attacked me. He's over at the store. Mr. Cross knocked him out."

Kicking back his chair with one big foot and bringing his chunky body upright in one swift movement, he took her arm and led her back out the door without pausing for further explanations. Only when they were hurrying toward the store did he ask why Hap had assaulted her. When she told him, he said, "I heard about Lettie leaving him. I didn't know she'd left him for another man. No wonder he went crazy mad. He's been trying all his life to prove being short didn't make him less of a man than the rest of us."

Hap was coming to when they reached the store. He had turned over on his back and was blinking his eyes dazedly. A few feet away Salvador Cross stood, watching him warily. The deputy hauled Hap to his feet and, steadying him, sniffed and made a face. "Whew! I'll lock him up for being drunk and disorderly, ma'am, and if you want to charge him with assault, I'll add that, too."

"Just make sure you don't turn him loose until he's cooled off," Salvador Cross cautioned.

"I'll lock him up nice and tight. Come on, Hap. Can you walk or do I have to carry you?"

Fixing them all with a bleary, malevolent stare, Hap

Turner staggered out of the store without help.

"He may come after you again," Salvador Cross suggested uneasily.

Massaging her bruised shoulder, Susan said, "He wouldn't be that foolish, would he?"

"I wouldn't put anything past Hap."

When Sy learned of the incident that noon, his mouth drew to a thin line. "We'll charge him with assault, though I doubt that Judge Allen will give him a sentence long enough to keep him locked up until I can file murder charges against him."

"If you should lose today, it won't matter. I'll be leaving in a week or two."

He thrust his chin out combatively. "I'm not going to lose."

It began to look more and more as if he might. Expected to have ended by four o'clock, the convention was still in session at six-thirty. After finishing her supper, Susan brought her tatting down to the parlor to wait for Sy's return to the hotel. Shortly thereafter groups of men began coming in to take supper in the dining room. Sy, who was with one of the groups, broke away when he saw Susan and informed her that the convention was deadlocked on the vote for county attorney. He looked tired. She moved over to give him room to sit beside her on the sofa.

"This feels good," he said, sinking down. "How is your shoulder?"

A bruise had appeared where the seam of her sleeve had been ripped, and the abrasion burned, but it caused only slight discomfort, and she told him so.

"I'll file the assault charge against Hap tomorrow." His dark eyes were as angry as she'd ever seen them. "Van can hold him on the drunk charge until then."

"What about the convention? How much longer do you think it will take to break the deadlock?"

"I don't know. I've discovered that I'm not just running against Ezra Black. I'm fighting a county seat fight. The Liberty delegates are working against me because they don't want Ward's murder cleared up. They figure if Ezra wins the nomination they can hold that up to the whole county and say 'See, Hawthorne wants to bury the whole affair. She isn't fit to keep the county seat.'"

A note of discouragement had crept into his voice. It was the first time Susan had seen him betray even a hint that he might be defeated. Casting a sidelong glance at him and noting the fatigue lines around his mouth, she longed to reach up and smooth them away, but knew she dare not. He would read more into her sympathy than was there.

"And what the Liberty delegates are claiming is true, of course," she observed indignantly. "Nelson Cooper and a few others *are* trying to bury Ward's murder. It would have been an altogether different story if instead of Ward it had been a businessman or a longtime resident of Hawthorne." The old bitterness welled up in her again.

Sy stood up, and making an effort to sound cheerful, he said, "Well, we aren't beaten yet. I'd better go in and eat so I can get back to the fight."

"I'll wait down here until you come back tonight."

That promise seemed to genuinely cheer him. Giving her a smile, he went to the dining room.

Ella Lord yawned. She had been dozing on and off in her chair since she came out of the kitchen two hours earlier. The card game had broken up; the players had either given up and gone home or drifted over to the courthouse to await the outcome of the intramural fight among the Democrats. Rufus Lord remained at the table playing solitaire. Tired of tatting, Susan had taken a chair at the table to watch. She had left the door to her room open to let in some of the heat from the parlor stove. The hotel was so quiet they could hear her clock strike ten-fifteen.

Earlier in the day Rufus had hired a girl to replace Lettie, but she wouldn't be able to start working until the following Monday. That meant another big day for the Lords. They had served four times as many diners as usual that day, and with the convention running so late, most delegates would have to remain in Hawthorne overnight. Susan had helped Ella make up beds for the influx of men once the convention adjourned. They would all want breakfast before they started home, and their rooms would have to be cleaned after they left. Rufus was as overcome with fatigue as his wife. Susan frequently had to call his attention to a play he had overlooked.

"I've got to have some more coffee." Ella Lord was getting up from her chair when Sy came bursting in. He had been running. Beaming triumphantly, he declared, "I got it!"

"Oh, Sy, I'm so glad!" Susan rushed toward him instinctively in her happiness, then halted a step or two away. At one time she could have embraced him, but no longer. He noted her hesitation and made some movement that was never completed because by then Rufus had come forward to shake his hand and Ella Lord was congratulating him heartily. Almost at once men began coming in, seeking rooms for the night. The Lords moved off to take care of them, leaving Sy and Susan isolated from the noise and confusion in a corner of the parlor.

Grinning, Sy exclaimed, "I feel almost as if I won the election."

"It can't be any closer than this was, can it?"

"It won't be. There isn't much support for Jess. We were pretty confident that anyone we put up would beat him. So you can forget about going back to Pennsylvania for at least a month."

"I'm encouraged. I feel we're finally making some progress."

"You bet we are! I can name you three fellows who aren't going to be resting easy when they find out I'm the candidate. I'm going to file that assault charge against Hap tomorrow, and then I'm going to start campaigning immediately."

"I think you should rest for a day or two. You look awfully tired." Her concern earned her a glance so intimate she averted her eyes. "It's late, and it's been an eventful day. I think I'll say good night."

Sy stood up. "I'm ready to turn in, too. As you say, it's been quite a day."

They made their way through the crowd of men and went upstairs. At her door, Sy paused. "I can't remember a woman being concerned about my health since my grandmother died and Chloe left. Thank you. I appreciate it."

He had told her one evening at supper about his boyhood, how his grandparents had raised him and how their deaths had thrust him out into the world on his own when he was just a boy. Recalling now her mother's loving care and the affectionate humor of Ward's mother, she suddenly realized the poverty of Sy's emotional life. Smiling, she said, "If you won't take proper care of yourself, your friends must see that you do."

"I was hoping it was more than friendship," he said, pulling such a rueful face that she had to laugh.

"Good night," she said in a mildly reproachful tone, and went into her room.

{10}

As he delivered his campaign speech to the crowd that filled the opera house in Liberty, Sy knew something was wrong. Too many faces wore grins, too many heads turned to whisper. Moving his eyes over the crowd searching for someone who showed some interest in what he had to say, he found other faces that seemed to be frozen with some emotion far stronger than mere hostility to a political candidate. Only scattered applause greeted the end of his speech so it was easy to hear the man who jumped up to shout, "You ain't fit to hold office. Maybe you and that Maddox woman think you're gettin' away with somethin', but everybody knows what's goin' on between you and her."

Rude laughter broke out here and there in the opera house. Some of the women looked embarrassed.

Striving to regain his composure, Sy clenched his hands

behind his back and took a deep breath. "That is a dastardly accusation, sir, and an absolute falsehood. Mrs. Maddox's character is above reproach. I am her lawyer and also her friend. That is the extent of our relationship, and for proof I refer you to Rufus Lord and his wife, in whose hotel we live."

"They don't sit up nights to see whether you two stay in your own rooms, do they?" The heckler was clearly enjoying the sensation he was causing.

"What is your name, sir?" Sy demanded.

"Jimmy Evans."

"Mr. Evans, you are defaming the name of a good woman, and I intend to file charges of slander against you tomorrow morning." Sy turned and stalked off the stage. Every eye in the place followed him as he headed for the door, and another voice, undeterred by his threat, hurled one final insulting question at him.

"Why don't you make an honest woman of her and marry her?"

Shaking with rage, he descended the long flight of stairs that led up from the street. Once outside he made for his rented buggy, parked in the vacant lot next door. With several flicks of the whip, he put the mare into a fast trot and set her head toward Hawthorne, barely aware of the passing countryside.

He had made three campaign appearances last week and felt encouraged by his reception. He had known today that he was entering unfriendly territory when he went to Liberty, but he hadn't expected anything like this. Who had started that rumor? It was someone who wanted to see him defeated, of course. That could be a lot of people. But who would have the most to gain by his defeat? The answer was obvious. Hap Turner, Phil Osborne, Pat Seavey, and a fourth man still unknown. It was a matter of life or death to them. Hap was in jail serving a thirty-day sentence for assaulting Susan. He couldn't be spreading the rumor, but it could have been his idea. It would help serve the dual purpose of defeating him and getting even with Susan for helping Lettie get away. How widespread was the rumor? he wondered.

That question was answered soon after he returned the rig to the livery barn and went to his office. Van Alstine came to see him, a strange look on his face. "I just got home from Empire. I was asked some questions that knocked me back on my heels. It seems there's some gossip going around about you and Mrs. Maddox."

Sy sank back in his chair and swore. "I know. Some fellow in the Liberty Opera House stood up at the end of my speech today and said I was unfit to hold the office and told me why. From the expressions I saw on people's faces, and the laughter, it sounded as if everyone there had heard the rumor except me." He pinched the bridge of his nose and drew his brows together. His skull throbbed with pain. "The man's name is Jimmy Evans. I'm going to sue him for slander in Susan's name."

"That goes into district court, doesn't it? The next term isn't until January. That's too late to clear your name and Susan's before the election."

"I don't care. I'm going to teach that man and some others that they can't say things like that about people and get away with it." Meeting the sheriff's eyes squarely, he declared, "It isn't true, Van. I'd be the happiest man in the world if Susan would marry me, but she won't. That's all there is between us."

Van Alstine nodded soberly. "I believe you."

Sy gestured helplessly. "How am I going to clear her name?"

"You probably can't."

Sy had come to the same conclusion on the long ride back to Hawthorne. Denials were useless; they were the automatic response of the guilty. And there was no way to *prove* that one wasn't having an affair with a woman. "After all she's been through, and now to have to cope with this!" He glanced up to find Van Alstine regarding him with an expression he couldn't read. "Is there something else I should know?"

"Aren't you worried about what this is going to do to you?"

"How bad do you think this will hurt me?"

"A lot. You can be glad of one thing, though. Women can't vote. If they could, you could say good-bye to any chance of being elected. That don't mean they won't hurt you. Plenty of men are going to be swayed by the way their wives feel about this." He bounced the heel of his boot against the floor a couple of times. "Someone wants you beaten real bad."

"And we know who three of them are, don't we?"

"They feel you breathing down their necks."

"Whose idea do you suppose this was?"

Van Alstine gave a dismal shrug. "Pat Seavey has been in several times to see Hap. They may have cooked it up between them."

"It sounds like Hap. He could get even with Susan and maybe save his own skin at the same time. Who else has been in to see him?"

"Nobody. Whoever that fourth guy is, he's sure staying away from Hap while he's in jail."

A despairing sigh came whistling out from between Sy's teeth. "Do you suppose we'll ever get them into court?"

"Our chances look a lot worse as of today."

After Van Alstine had gone, Sy slid down in his chair and closed his eyes against the stabbing pains in his head. Should he tell Susan? Wouldn't she find out sooner or later? Later would be better. She would be so ashamed. For a while he had doubted they would ever resume their friendship after that night in July. It had been days before she could meet his eyes.

He massaged his temples. He couldn't bear to think of the snickers, the nudges, the foul words that her name was probably summoning up this minute. If they could but know her as he did, they'd realize there could be no truth to the rumor.

"Why don't you marry her and make an honest woman of her?"

The remembered gibe brought him slowly upright. Half an hour later he went to the hotel and knocked on Susan's door.

She had been washing up for supper. The sleeves of her dress were rolled up slightly, and she was drying her hands when she opened the door. Above her brow her golden hair was a bit damp and her clear skin shone from its recent scrubbing.

"Susan, I have to talk to you."

She hesitated, but the urgency in his voice conquered whatever reluctance she might have felt to invite him into her room. "Come in."

Her room was so different from his; it was as near to being a home as a hotel room could be. It might have been due in part to the two plants that sat on the small table in front of the window, and perhaps to the pieced comforter on the bed. His own bed was covered by a gray wool blanket. There was something more, though, something intangible, an essence of comfort and peace that only a woman's presence could give a dwelling. For a moment, an acute longing robbed him of words.

She finished drying her hands, waiting.

Trying to remain as unintrusive as possible, Sy stood beside the door. He chose carefully planned words to break the news to her. Nonetheless, she blanched, then went to the washstand and stood with her back to him. After months of being too thin, her body once more curved seductively within her blue wool dress. Signs of grief still lingered, however. There were shadows in the depths of her flecked gray eyes that Sy knew would never go away.

"Did someone make that up out of whole cloth?" she asked in husky tones, "or do you think—" She broke off.

"I'm sure this rumor was put together out of thin air," he assured her, "to keep me from being elected county attorney. The men who murdered Ward are growing desperate."

She turned, sudden understanding in her face. "Hap," she said.

"He and Seavey for certain. Probably the other man, too."

Abstractedly, she dropped the towel on the bureau, where, lying between the clock and the gold-rimmed shaving mug, it injected a note of disorder on the otherwise tidy surface. Sy stared at the mug; it must have been Ward's. "How many people do you think will believe it?" she asked.

"Too many," Sy replied. "People like juicy gossip. It adds some spice to their lives."

"It's so shameful!" She covered her face with her hands.

It cost him a great deal of effort to remain where he was and not rush to take her in his arms. "We can stop the rumors."

She looked up, her eyes brimming with tears. "How?"

He felt himself drowning in those tears, in those eyes that were fixed on his so hopefully. He would ask for nothing more if he could spend his life saving her from trials like this. "We can get married. That will stop the gossip."

She made no immediate response. She picked up the towel from the bureau and, as absentmindedly as she had dropped it, hung it up on its nail above the washstand. She walked slowly to the window, peering silently through it for what seemed to Sy an intolerably long time. "You know I love you," he reminded her when he could bear the silence no longer.

"I know," she said softly. Facing him at last, she said, "It wouldn't stop the gossip. If I married you, it would convince everyone that it was true, that there really had been something between us."

That had already occurred to him, and there really was no argument against her logic, but he tried nevertheless. "They might think that, but they couldn't continue to make up new gossip. And we'd be man and wife. Legitimized intimacy doesn't arouse prurient interest."

Turning back to the window, she stood in thoughtful silence again. This one didn't last as long. "I'll be leaving Hawthorne, if not in a few weeks then in a few months. I survived the murder of my husband. I can survive ugly gossip for as long as I'll be here." She came toward him, halting beyond the reach of his arms to smile faintly at him. "I'm sorry, Sy. I wish I could have given you the answer you wanted, but I still feel like Ward's wife, and as long as I feel like that I can't marry anyone."

Just for a moment he hated Ward Maddox for the hold he continued to have over Susan. Although he managed to shake it off, he could do no more than nod his understanding. "I'll see what I can do to stop the rumors," he promised, and left.

The hotel was wrapped in Sunday afternoon quiet as Salvador Cross climbed the stairs and knocked at Sy's door. There was a faint creak of bedsprings, then Sy opened the door. "Sal! Come in."

"I'm sorry if I woke you."

"I wasn't taking a nap. I was reading."

Salvador Cross stepped into the room; his eyes quickly took in the spare furnishings. There was little to distinguish this particular room from one that rented by the day. Clearly this was not Sy's home. He slept here, but he lived in his crowded office and the parlor downstairs. Cross accepted the only chair in the room, a castoff from someone's dining room. Throwing one leg over the other, he gripped his ankle and came right to the point. "Did you know there is a filthy story going around about you and Susan?"

From the edge of the bed where he was sitting, Sy said, "I heard it yesterday in Liberty. Van came home from campaigning in Empire and told me it was making the rounds there, too. Where did you hear it?"

"I visited for a few minutes after church with Con and Nels. Con heard it last night in the saloon." The outrage he had felt was still as keen now as it had been when Conrad Wirth had told it. "I want you to know I don't believe a word of it!"

"Do they?"

Cross shrugged and waggled his foot in distress. He wished Sy hadn't asked that question. "You know how people are. They get a kick out of hearing stuff like that."

Sy burst out with an expletive and bounded to his feet. "How can they believe anything like that about Susan? What can I do, Sal? As soon as I heard it, I asked her to marry me, but she won't. She said it would make it seem as if we really were guilty. I suppose she's right."

Salvador Cross had been watching for some indication that Susan was beginning to feel the same about Sy as he did about her, because, in his opinion, they belonged together. Once Susan's grief had faded, she was going to need another man to love her and one whom she could love. She'd find no finer man than Sy. Tragic as her husband's death had been, she was lucky; she was free to build another life. He thought of Maude, of her shining hair and delicate-featured face, of her soft body that had responded to him for a few years and then had grown cold as she withdrew into a world from which he was shut out, condemning them both to a half life, each as unnatural as the other's. Cruel as death could sometimes be, there were worse things.

"I know what I can do about it," he declared, answering Sy's question. "I'm going to start campaigning for you again. Susan can run the store like she did before. I'm going to every town in the county. I'm going to brand this rumor a lie, and I'm going to explain why it was started."

Sy, who had begun pacing the bare floor, paused to say gratefully, "I can't think of a better character witness for Susan and me. Thanks, Sal. If you can convince even a few people that there's no truth to the gossip, you'll be doing us a great service. I can't bear to have people thinking

Susan is that kind of a woman."

"How's she taking it?"

"She says she's weathered worse than this, and besides, she's only going to be here a few more weeks or months."

The only thing keeping her in Hawthorne was the desire to see retribution done. Salvador Cross wanted that, too, never more than now when those who killed Ward Maddox were causing Susan further pain with their vile stories. He hadn't the slightest doubt that they were responsible. "We want to keep her here as long as we can, don't we?"

Hands on hips, Sy asked soberly, "Is it that obvious?"

Salvador Cross replied, "It is to me. I don't know about other people."

"I'm not making much progress with her."

"We've got to get you elected. That will give you more time."

"I wonder if it will be enough."

Susan bore the speculative glances with a dignified demeanor that concealed the guilt that she had managed to shut off in a corner of her mind where it could be forgotten for long periods. If it had not been for a moment of weakness that hot July evening, she might have felt a fresh bitterness toward the people of Hawthorne, but the gossip came too close to the truth. She felt shamed by the loyalty of her friends who refused to believe her capable of such behavior.

It was impossible to determine how effective Salvador Cross's efforts to combat the rumor were. He campaigned alone, never missing a chance to show up at a rally or a meeting anywhere in the county to inform the audience that there were four men in Hawthorne who would stop at nothing to save their necks from the hangman's noose and that they were ruthlessly smearing a decent woman's name in order to defeat the man who had vowed to bring them to trial if he were elected.

It soon became apparent that his efforts were striking fear in the hearts of Sy's enemies. One evening as Susan was crossing the street from the store toward the hotel, she saw Sy standing on the sidewalk in front of his office talking to a man from Green Willow, the easternmost town in the county. She recognized him as Ervell Smith, one of Sy's strongest supporters. Sy saw her, parted swiftly from the man, and hurried to join her. "They're attacking Sal now," he announced bitterly. "They've started gossip about him and Laura. Ervell made a special trip over here to tell me. He heard it just this morning. It's all over Green Willow."

Susan experienced a far greater feeling of outrage upon learning of the vicious gossip linking Salvador Cross and his sister-in-law than she had when Sy had told her about the rumors concerning themselves. "Will they stop at nothing?" she cried helplessly.

"Apparently not." His mouth was hard, dangerous. "I'm going to fight them on this one. I don't know how yet, but I'm not going to stand by and let Sal and Laura be hurt. Two more decent people never lived."

"Do you suppose Sal has heard it? He was going to Liberty this afternoon."

"Whether he has or not, I think we should go there this evening and warn them."

Laura Knapp opened the door to them. The flesh on her face seemed to have shrunk, giving it a skull-like appearance. Susan embraced her silently before she led them into the living room. The house was, as usual, scrupulously clean, and the fragrance of the day's baking still lingered in the air. Through the doorway to the kitchen, Susan could see the remains of supper still on the table. Only a major catastrophe would have induced Laura to get up from a meal without at once cleaning the table and washing dishes.

Queena was sitting on the sofa. She had been crying; her eyes were reddened, and she avoided looking at them. When Salvador Cross rose from his chair, his movements were slow and heavy.

"You must have heard the things they are saying about you," Sy said as soon as they were all seated in the Cross living room.

Salvador Cross replied quietly, "Someone in Liberty was kind enough to tell me. Where did you hear it?"

"Ervell drove over from Green Willow. It's making the rounds there, too."

"I suppise it's all over Hawthorne, too," Cross suggested.

"If it is, I haven't heard it." Sy added, "I don't think it will find fertile ground here. Everyone knows you and Laura too well."

Queena, who had been sitting beside Laura on the sofa, cried, "If just one person believes it, I'll die!" She burst into tears, burying her face against Laura's shoulder.

Putting her arm around her niece, Laura glanced at the three of them, asking fiercely, "Isn't there some way we can stop this?"

Sy replied, "The first step is for Sal to quit campaigning for me."

"They aren't going to force me to do that," Salvador Cross declared firmly. "Getting you elected is becoming more important every day."

"Daddy! What about me?" came Queena's agonized cry.

Her look was accusing. "Don't you care how I feel?"

"There, you see," Sy said to the older man. "Forget about me and my election. You've got Queena and Laura to consider."

"The gossip isn't going to die if I stop campaigning for you." Salvador Cross's face contorted under the force of his distress.

"I think you're wrong. If you don't go around calling attention to yourself, it will fade and people will forget."

"Isn't there something more we can do?" Susan asked. "Sal has gone around explaining that the gossip about us is a lie. Can't we let people know that this latest story is a lie, too, and was started by the same people and for the same reason as the one about us?"

"Oh, yes, let's do that!" Queena exclaimed.

"Y'all got any ideas?" Sy asked. "I don't think sending someone out to defend Sal the way he's been defending me will work."

"Could we write a letter and get it printed in the paper?" Susan asked.

Laura Knapp took up the idea immediately. "We could ask our minister to sign it."

"I think all three ministers would sign it." Sy tapped a finger on the arm of his chair. "So would a lot of other people. I think some of them would be glad to donate a small amount to help pay for the ad, too."

"It should cover a whole page," Susan insisted. "We want to be sure that everyone who takes the county paper sees it."

"We'll run it in the other three papers, too," Sy declared.

"That's going to cost quite a bit of money," Salvador Cross warned.

"We'll manage," Sy promised. "I'll write the letter to-night. Who do you suggest we ask to circulate it for sig-natures?"

Salvador and Laura looked inquiringly at one another. "Our minister," he said, with Laura nodding in agreement.

"Queena, honey, if you'll bring me some paper and a pencil," Sy said, "I'll write that letter right now."

{11}

SHAVING FOR SY that morning was not the routine task it ordinarily was. Guiding the bone-handled razor around the contours of his face demanded almost more control than he was capable of. This was the most important day of his life, yet he was powerless to determine his fate. It lay in the hands of the voters. He had done all he could, and now there was nothing to do except await the outcome. So eager was he to get the day started that the painstaking task of shaving became a teeth-gritting exercise in self-control.

He was very much aware that two doors down and across the hall, Susan was dressing and preparing for a day whose only significance to her was that victory for him meant the chance to see Ward's killers brought to justice. And perhaps in the end that was all the day would result in for him. He might never see Susan as she was now, slipping out of her nightgown, her body warm from the bed, her hair flowing over her shoulders and down her back like honey; never watch her in the process of covering that body—of which he had such achingly intimate knowledge—against the world's eyes with garment after garment until she became the demure woman the public knew her as.

Sy's hand paused, shaving soap dripping from the bright steel blade of the razor. His eyes met the brown eyes gazing back at him from the mirror. With a sudden movement, he dropped the razor, wiped the remaining soap from his face with a towel, and went to Susan's door.

"Who is it?" she asked, without opening the door.

"It's Sy. May I come in for a minute?"

"I'm not dressed."

"Please. It's very important." What excuse would he give her if she let him in? He cast about for some reason vital enough to force his way into her room at this hour of the day.

"Just a minute."

What was she doing? He didn't want to see her dressed; he could see her like that any time he wished.

When she opened the door, he let his breath out in a long, silent sigh. She had pulled a rose wool flannel wrapper around her; the high lacy collar of her nightgown was visible. Her hair, as he had imagined it a few minutes ago, hung in long, rippling lengths that fell over her arms and breasts, as well as down her back. Her face glowed from its morning wash. Desire paralyzed his tongue, and he was unable to answer when she asked him with some alarm what was wrong.

"What is it?" she asked again.

He forced words out, not caring whether they made sense

or not. "It's silly . . . I mean, I'm a grown man . . . today is so important . . . I've never run for office before."

Her face softened in a way that set his heart thudding against his ribs.

"Of course you're nervous," she said, "and you're exhausted. You've been fighting ever since you began campaigning. But the world won't end if you lose today."

Yes, it will, he wanted to tell her. If I lose the election, I lose you.

"You'll still have your law practice," she was saying, "and you can run next time if you still want the job."

"I want it this year." He dropped his mask, letting her see his love for her. "I want it for your sake."

Her eyes darkened; whether from displeasure or because of an emotion he only dared hope for, he couldn't determine. Her tone was equally unfathomable when she murmured, "Oh, Sy!"

He waited, drinking in the sight of her. As if mesmerized, her hand rose slowly to the lace-trimmed collar of her nightgown.

Downstairs, Rufus called out something to his wife, breaking the spell.

"You'd better go," Susan urged quietly. "Someone might see you."

He gazed at her one moment longer, then went back to his room to finish shaving.

Having cast his ballot for Jess Frazier, Hap Turner left the courthouse, sending a sour glance at the saloon, closed because it was election day. The pint he had bought yesterday was more than half gone. It wouldn't last the day. He headed for the livery barn and the bottle he kept hidden in a stall. He was going to need some help getting through this day. Damn the drys! Next thing you knew, they'd get an ordinance passed to close the saloon for good. Maybe it wouldn't matter. If Sy Harris beat Jess today, he'd be clearing out of Hawthorne, leaving with a thousand dollars in his pocket, courtesy of three guys who were afraid if he was arrested again he'd talk to save his neck and collect the reward. They didn't fancy having their necks stretched the way they had stretched Ward Maddox's.

He entered the livery barn. From the horse stalls at the rear drifted Pat's voice, talking to a customer. Coming from the brightness of the morning into the barn, Hap couldn't make out the customer, who stood in the middle of the room waiting for the rig. He stopped in the first stall, which was left empty and used for storage, and brought out his bottle from behind a pile of old sacks. He took a deep pull, clearing his throat noisily as the whiskey burned its way down to his stomach. Then he sauntered back to where Pat was working. Recognition hit him when he made out the tan suit the customer was wearing. Blood rushed to his head, nearly blinding him. This was the bastard who stole Lettie and made him look like a fool. With a bellow, he threw himself on Gibson, whirling him around. Savage satisfaction spread through him as his fist met that soft, pale face. Gibson staggered back, and Hap swung again, but before he could connect, Gibson ducked and drove a blow into his belly that felt like it went clear through to his backbone. His breath coming in painful grunts, Hap circled his opponent, trying to decide if Gibson's blow had been a lucky one or whether he knew how to fight. Warily watching the shifting, slender body, the white, womanish hands, and the almost pretty features, Hap couldn't believe the man was a fighter. He moved in again, aiming at the face that brought bile up into his throat. Again he experienced a keen sense of pleasure as he felt the soft flesh mash under his knuckles. This time Gibson didn't stagger. He absorbed the blow and at almost the same instant connected with Hap's chin. Hap fell back against a post, ducking swiftly as Gibson rushed him, grabbing the taller man around the waist and burying his head against Gibson's chest. But there was no escape from the drummer's fists. Hap's head flew back against the post as Gibson's right hand came up under his chin. A left almost put him down. With arms that felt like rubber, he struck out at the pale blur of Gibson's face. A blow that felt like it separated his head from his neck was the last thing he remembered until a splash of cold water on his face brought him to.

Pat Seavey stood over him, a pail in his hand. Too dazed to move, Hap peered up at his employer, blinking away the water. There was the taste of blood in his mouth.

"Here, let me give you a hand up," Pat said.

"Leave me alone."

Pat shrugged and walked off.

Gathering all his strength, Hap pushed himself to a sitting position. His head felt like it had been kicked by one of the horses. He spit and cursed when he saw the blood. Groaning, he got himself up on his feet, clinging to a post until his brain stopped spinning. When his vision cleared, he spied an envelope at the base of the post. It was addressed to Susan Maddox in Lettie's handwriting. It must have fallen out of Gibson's pocket during the fight.

Bending to pick it up brought the pain in his head and face to an excruciating pitch. With the letter clutched in one hand, he leaned against the post, eyes closed, until the throbbing ebbed to a tolerable level.

He thrust his finger under the flap of the envelope and ripped it open. "Dear Susan," he read,

> I've changed jobs. I'm working in a lunchroom, cooking and baking pies. I don't wait tables. I quit the bakery because of the bad hours. Jerry didn't like me getting up so early in the morning when he was home.

Hap paused, unable to read further for the moment. The image called up by that last sentence hurt him as badly as his head did.

> I'm sorry you got into trouble for helping me. Hap's thirty days must be up by now. Be careful. I know how mean he can be. I don't see how I put up with it as long as I did. I didn't know it was possible to be so happy. Just three more months and then Jerry and I can be married. Everybody here thinks we already are.
>
> If you were here everything would be perfect. I miss you a lot. I don't expect to ever find a better friend. I could never have gotten away without your help. Write soon.
>
> Love,
> Lettie

Hap's hand closed convulsively on the letter. That bitch of a Maddox woman! If she hadn't hidden Lettie, he'd have found her before she left town. Mean, was he? Just because she hadn't been able to wind him around her finger like any woman would do if a man was a weakling. Gibson was probably eating out of her hand.

The throbbing in his jaw began a crescendo that had him gasping and clutching the post for support. He'd like to kill Gibson. When the pain eased a bit, he tore the envelope and letter to bits and threw it behind one of the horses before making his way back to the empty stall and his bottle.

The hotel parlor was uncommonly quiet that night without the usual card game filling the room with smoke and good-natured jibes. Sy, Rufus, and the regulars were over at the courthouse waiting for the vote count to begin. Susan glanced across at Jerry Gibson, who leaned back in one corner of the sofa, one eye blackened, a cut across his cheekbone over which a scab was forming. "Wouldn't you like to lie down? I could sit in one of the chairs."

"It hurts less if I sit up. The blood all seems to rush to my head if I lie down and throbs like the deuce."

He had told all of them—Sy, the Lords, herself—about his fight with Hap. Susan had listened with keen relish as he recounted how he had given Hap the worst of it and left him lying unconscious on the floor of the livery barn. It had surprised her that Jerry, slight and boyish, could more than defend himself against a bully like Hap. "Where did you learn to fight like that?" she asked him.

"I probably learned to fight about the same time I learned to walk. I had five brothers, three of them older than me." He laughed. "I had to learn to defend myself. It was a matter of life or death."

"Hap must have wondered what he got himself into."

"I think he realized right away he'd picked on the wrong guy. He'd been drinking, too, and that didn't help any."

He touched his cheek gingerly. "I'm sure he's hurting a lot worse than I am."

Dora Atherton, the girl Ella Lord had hired to take Lettie's place, entered the parlor. Smiling shyly and with downcast eyes, she headed for the door. She was almost a total contrast to Lettie: tall, large-bodied, scarcely able to meet anyone's eyes, speaking rarely and then so softly it was difficult to hear her. Only in energy and willingness to work long hours were she and Lettie alike.

"All through for the day, Dora?" Susan asked.

"Yes'm." The girl paused, her hands clasped in front of her, giving the two of them a fleeting glance that fluttered ultimately to an area of the floor halfway between them.

"And you're in a hurry now to go meet your beau," Jerry teased.

"No," she said, coloring.

"No beau or no, you aren't meeting him?"

"I only see him on Saturday nights."

"I knew a pretty girl like you would have one. He must be a farmer."

"Yes."

"I suppose you'll be getting married one of these days and Ella will have to hunt around for help again."

"Not for a year yet."

"He'll be a lucky man." Gibson's teasing tone was gone, and he spoke kindly. "Good night, Dora."

After she'd taken her leave, Jerry said, "I shouldn't tease her. Did you ever see anyone so bashful?"

"Quite a change from Lettie, isn't she?"

He chuckled. "Lettie doesn't know what bashful is. She took to city life like she'd been born to it. When she isn't working and on those days when I'm out of town, she rides the streetcars, and not just around South Omaha, either. She goes into Omaha and visits museums and places even I've never been."

"She sounds happy."

"If I hadn't lost her letter to you, you'd be able to read it in her own words. If Hap found it and read it, I'm sure he's feeling even worse than he would otherwise."

Ella Lord came in, without her ubiquitous apron, the sleeves of her dress still rolled above her elbows to reveal her thick, freckled arms. "Quiet in here tonight, ain't it?" she said, sitting down at one of the straight chairs at the table. Susan suspected that it was the only time she had been off her feet since five-thirty that morning, except for when she sat down to eat, if she even did that. "I don't suppose Rufus has been over to give you an idea of how things are going," she said.

"We haven't heard a word from anyone," Susan told her.

"Do you want some more cold packs for that eye?" Ella asked Jerry.

"Thanks, but I'm fine."

"Isn't Lettie going to have a spell when she finds out Hap took in after you?"

"She might have a spell, but she won't be surprised. We both suspected he might want to beat me up."

"Did she know you was this good with your fists?" There was surprised admiration in Ella Lord's expression.

"I tried to tell her so she wouldn't worry, but I don't think she believed me. She hasn't got to know me that well yet."

While the two of them talked about Lettie, Susan's mind drifted. Sending the needle in and out of the hem she was taking up in a new blouse that was too long for her, she contemplated with keen regret that this might be one of the last evenings she'd spend in that parlor. During the previous fifteen months it had provided her with comfort, the companionship to fill some unbearably lonely hours, and amusement as she listened to the exclamations of the cardplayers. She had become very fond of the Lords, who treated her less like a guest than one of the family. As they did Sy.

At the thought of Sy, she flinched inwardly. His appearance at her door this morning before breakfast had set off waves of memory. There had been something about the sight of him without his collar and with a dab of shaving soap under his ear that reminded her of how much she had once enjoyed living with a man. She loved the sight and smell of a man, the sound of a masculine voice. She liked the way their minds and hands put broken things aright. And seeing Sy outside her door that morning, not quite dressed and herself still in her nightgown, brought to life the need to feel the hard strength of a man's arms around her, an eager body seeking hers. Not just any man's arms, of course. She still wanted Ward, but he was beyond reach, sometimes even beyond clear memory. There were days when she could see his lean muscular body topped by the mat of blond wool that was his hair, yet she couldn't bring his features into focus. She remembered clearly the shape of his hands, but not the shape of his nose.

Too often now when she tried to recall his caresses, it was Sy's kiss, Sy's body that forced itself on her memory. It seemed traitorous because she didn't love Sy. Those forbidden emotions had surfaced this morning when he stood at her door and confessed his nervousness about the balloting that day. She had wanted to reach out and comfort him. When she saw the blazing desire in his face, it set her body on fire. She couldn't speak until some sound from downstairs broke the spell. It was dangerous for her to remain here, but as long as there was a chance that she could see Ward's murderers sent to prison, she would stay. Tonight's vote count would decide that.

At nine-thirty Rufus entered the hotel, beaming. "It's a landslide. Sy has it won!"

A ripple of excitement swept through Susan. "Thank God!" she breathed. Now Sy could proceed with the case against Hap and the others. Then the rest of Rufus's announcement sunk in. "A landslide? How can that be? Everything was against Sy."

"They're saying it was the dirt someone tried to smear on Sal and Laura that did it. Most people must have figured then that the rumor about you and Sy had to be a lie, too. It must have turned them against Jess and his backers."

"As it should have," Ella declared stoutly.

Jerry stretched and got to his feet. "So Sy is going to be the new county attorney."

"This town will see some fireworks once he takes office." There was satisfaction in Rufus's voice.

Touching the cut on his cheek tentatively, Jerry asked, "Are they through counting votes?"

"No, they've still got several hundred to count."

"But it's certain?" Susan wanted to know.

"As certain as the sun is coming up in the morning," Rufus declared.

Susan secured the needle and thread in her blouse, which she folded carefully and put on top of her sewing basket. "Would you tell Sy for me that I'm very happy for him?" she said to Rufus.

"I sure will."

Bidding them all good night, she went up to her room. Sy would take office the first week in January. She would be here at least two more months.

She was undressing slowly, enjoying the knowledge that people were no longer whispering about Sy and her. They never need know how close to the truth the gossip had been. Marrying him would have made this vindication impossible. Just as she had argued, it would have confirmed the gossip. Now they were cleared; no taint remained on their relationship. Except in her own heart.

She had been in bed only a few minutes when there was a knock at her door. She knew who it was without asking. Grabbing her wrapper, she padded barefoot across the chilly floor. Opening the door a mere crack, she saw Sy standing out in the hall, which was lit by only one wall lamp. His tie was askew and his dark, wavy hair mussed. At first glance she suspected he'd been drinking, but he smelled only of cigar smoke.

Drunk on the heady wine of triumph, he forgot the proprieties and burst into her room, exuberantly proclaiming, "We won!" He caught her around the waist and whirled her around, sending the skirts of her gown and wrapper billowing. Releasing her, he strode several steps farther into the room, then spun and cried, "Didn't we whip them though! Their dirty tactics backfired. You should see Sal; he's beaming. As soon as he saw it was a landslide, he went home to tell Laura and Queena, then he came back and cheered every time another precinct's vote was posted."

The knowledge that almost no one any longer believed the scandal about Salvador Cross and Laura gave Susan even more joy than the clearing of her own name. "I'm so happy for them!"

"Your reputation has been restored, too."

"I know, and I'm grateful, but I don't have to live here the rest of my life like they do."

Just for an instant his glow lost a bit of its wattage, then it resumed its full brilliance. Nothing, it seemed, could cast a shadow over today's victory. "I'll have a new county judge to work with, too. Taylor won."

Susan had forgotten that race in the excitement over the size of Sy's win. "You should have things pretty much your way once you take office."

He stuck his hands in his pockets, saying soberly, "Taylor won't let me tell him what to do the way Judge Allen lets Jess. He'll be an impartial judge, but I'm not afraid of that. The case I've prepared against Hap is so strong he can't rule any way other than to bind him over to district court for trial. And once we have Hap facing a charge of murder, Van and I can begin working on him. Speaking of Hap," he added, "someone told me he and Pat Seavey have been over at the livery barn drinking all evening. My win is bad news for them."

"I hope they're worried to death."

"I don't think there's any doubt about that." He pulled his hands from his pockets and flung them outward, exclaiming, "I feel like celebrating, but there's no place to go and nothing to do."

"I could go down to the kitchen and make coffee. Ella wouldn't mind. I realize that isn't the sort of celebration you have in mind, but I can see you're in no shape to go to your room and try to sleep."

"I think that would be a great way to celebrate."

"I'll get dressed."

"Why? You're decently clothed. Just put some shoes on. Besides, who's going to see us?"

No woman would be compromised in a kitchen, she decided. "I'll be down in a minute."

She eschewed her high-topped button shoes, opting for the blue felt slippers that sat beside her bed. She did take the time, however, to pin up her hair and secure it with the tortoiseshell combs. It made her look less like she'd come straight from bed.

A lamp sat on the large worktable, and when she reached the kitchen Sy was stoking up the fire in the big cookstove, making so much noise she was sure the Lords, whose room was behind the kitchen, would hear. In fact, in a few minutes Rufus appeared in bare feet, wearing only his trousers over his long underwear. When he found out what they were about, he sat them both down and took over. "There's some cake left, too," he said, indicating part of a yellow cake with white frosting that sat on top of the cupboard. "Divide it up, Susan."

While they sat drinking coffee and eating the cake, Sy's excitement spilled out in a steady flow of words as he told them in great detail about the vote in each precinct. His memory for the many totals was amazing. Recalling how skillful he had grown at campaigning, Susan wondered aloud if he shouldn't go farther in politics. "Why don't you run for the state legislature?"

Her suggestion pleased him. "Maybe I will. For the time being, though, I've got this murder case to prosecute. I'm not thinking beyond that."

"If you solve it and get convictions," Rufus remarked,

"you could get a lot of publicity. Herb will send the story to every other paper in the county. If he knew you wanted to run for the legislature, he'd send it to the Omaha and Lincoln papers, too. It would be a feather in Hawthorne's cap if you got to Lincoln."

Sy cut a bite of cake carefully with his fork, considering the possibility Susan and Rufus had introduced. "I hadn't given any thought to going into politics until the Democrats wanted to put me up for county attorney. I never had any ambition beyond being a lawyer." A zestful sparkle came into his eyes. "Now that I've had a taste of it, however, I might just try it again. The euphoria of winning is like nothing I've ever experienced."

"Defeat would have been bitter," Susan offered.

"Yes, things might have turned out very different tonight," he agreed.

"Right triumphed," Rufus declared, "but I don't suppose you can count on that happening every time."

"I'll bet I can count on one thing. No future campaign could be any dirtier than this one." As an afterthought Sy said, "That's what makes this victory so sweet. One of the things," he amended, sending Susan a meaningful glance.

His last remark slid innocuously past her. She was thinking that Sy was showing a side of himself that had not been visible before. Previously he had been gallant and affable, with the relaxed, almost lazy air of a gently bred Southerner. Tonight he sounded like a man who relished a fight and took great delight in defeating an opponent. How little she had known him.

"Well, I think I'll turn in again," Rufus said, getting up.

Susan gathered up the plates and cups from her place and Rufus's and took them to the sink. Bidding Rufus good-night, she lifted the teakettle from the stove and poured some hot water into the dishpan. She rubbed the dishrag briskly over the bar of soap until the water turned blue and sudsy. Sy appeared to be talked-out at last. He sat quietly, finishing his coffee while she washed the other dishes.

Tiredness had begun to creep over her. She was yawning when Sy brought his cup and slid it into the dishpan. Instead of moving away, he put his hands on her shoulders and pressed his cheek against her temple. His strong fingers pulled her back against him before his hands slid slowly down her arms, touching her breasts as if by accident on their way down to her waist. A melting weakness spread through her body. It would be lovely. She allowed herself to contemplate it for a moment; then she took his hands away from her waist and turned around. Love and desire blazed in his face.

"Good night, Sy," she said quietly.

He stood there so long that she began to think he wasn't going to leave. There wasn't a sound to break the silence. Finally, with a hoarse good night, he walked slowly out of the kitchen. Susan stared at his cup, lying on its side in the soapy water, then began slowly to wash it.

12

HAP SHIVERED AS he unlocked the livery barn and went inside; he was less cold, however, than scared. Only the necessity to save his neck was forcing him to leave Hawthorne and go to some strange place where he knew no one and didn't know his way around. A quick look at the square before he slipped inside told him that no one had seen him. The sky was dark; it had been overcast all day. It would be just his luck if it started to snow.

Having found the lantern that always hung beside the door, he lit it and went first to the office, where he took Pat's bottle from its drawer and helped himself to a stiff drink. He'd save his own whiskey for the drive to Empire. Packed in his valise were two more bottles. These wouldn't last until he got to California, but maybe there would be time at some of the train stops to get off and find a saloon.

Carrying the lantern he went to the rear of the barn and entered one of the stalls. He would take Chick. The black gelding was his favorite—submissive, easy to manage, and very strong. If he could have afforded a rig of his own, he'd have chosen a horse like Chick to pull it.

He led the gelding up front to the buggy Pat had bought only the month before. Pat's orders had been to take one of the older ones, but he wasn't taking orders from Pat any longer. He wasn't going to have to work for anybody for a long time, he thought, conscious of the one thousand dollars he had in his valise. Last week's election had made him a rich man, thanks to the guys who wanted him permanently out of the reach of Sy Harris and Van Alstine. All day, whenever he got that cold feeling in the pit of his stomach, he'd remember the money, and it made leaving seem a little less scary.

Chick stood patiently while Hap harnessed him to the one-seater. By the time it was done, his hands were trembling. It must be seven-thirty, he thought. Nearly time to go. He picked up the lantern and went across the dirt floor to the office for another drink. He was corking the bottle when he heard someone coming toward the barn. The footsteps thudded sharply on the frozen ground. Dousing the lantern swiftly, he peered out the window. It was the Maddox woman. He swore at her under his breath as she passed by. On her way to visit someone, he thought, probably Laura Knapp. Watching the slight figure wrapped in a heavy woolen coat, he felt his gorge rise. He'd bet his thousand dollars the bitch was responsible for more than hiding Lettie. She probably helped Gibson and Lettie meet in secret. Maybe she even loaned them her room. He knew she hated him. She had gotten even with him by making him a laughing-stock, making him look as if he had no more manhood than poor Chick here.

As she went by, he saw the white blur of her face so close he could almost have struck it. Damn it! If he didn't have to sneak out of town without attracting anyone's attention he'd show her that she hadn't evened things with him after all. The urge to run out and catch her was nearly overpowering.

Clenching his teeth, he spun away from the window and groped in the drawer for Pat's bottle again. The whiskey didn't cool his fury. Without another swallow, an idea came to him. He didn't have to catch the nine-thirty train from Empire; the eleven-thirty would do just as well. Hurrying outside, he saw her striding briskly a half block away. He watched, and when he saw her turn into the Cross yard, he returned to the office, sat down in Pat's swivel chair, and cradled the whiskey bottle against his stomach. Smiling grimly, he waited.

The first snow of the season had begun to fall by the time Susan left the Cross house and headed back to the hotel. There was no wind, unusual in this country where moisture was nearly always accompanied by winds. The snow had begun some time earlier; the ground was covered. The whiteness made the night less dark, and the large, thickly falling flakes muffled all sound, wrapping Susan in a soft silence.

She had never imagined, when she first made the decision to remain in Hawthorne, that she would be spending two winters here. Looking back, she recalled her militant determination to discover Ward's murderers and see them punished. Would she have stayed if she had known it would take this long to accomplish? Yes, there was little doubt of that. She had desperately needed some purpose in her life to fill the sudden and terrible emptiness left by Ward's death.

A fluffy snowflake landed on her cheek like a tear. It occurred to her that she hadn't cried for a long time. There were still times when she missed Ward dreadfully, but those times were rarer and the pain was not so keen. She couldn't envision the day when she would feel whole again, when Ward would be no more than a sweet memory. Yet she realized that that was where time was taking her.

The town square lay in silence as she approached it, glowing whitely in its coat of snow. The only lights visible were in the saloon and the hotel. It was nine-thirty, and as she watched, the saloon went dark.

Just as she started to cross the street between the livery barn and the lumberyard, she heard something behind her. Before she could turn to see what it was, an arm caught her around the waist and a hand clamped down on her mouth. She was pulled backward, throwing her off-balance so that for a few moments, while she fought instinctively to keep from falling, she was unable to make any attempt to escape the cruel hands that bit into her flesh. Her heel caught on the rough frozen ground just as she was pulled through the wide door of the livery barn. The struggle for balance was lost, and she sagged helplessly, her dead weight causing her attacker to stumble. The two of them fell. The imprisoning arms loosened, and her back struck a solid human body. In a flash, she rolled away and scrambled to her feet. She lunged for the door, falling again when a hand closed over her ankle and jerked her back.

Her scream was cut off abruptly by a fist smashing into her face. Pain exploded in her jaw. The little cry she was able to make was swallowed by the yawning space of the barn. Another blow struck her neck and another landed stingingly on her ear. Covering her head with her arms, she attempted to roll away from the rain of blows, only to find that her attacker was standing over her, one of his legs on each side of her body. Twice more his fists smashed into her head and face; then she felt rather than saw him run for the big door. Springing to her feet, she made for the wide opening. Hurling himself on her, he knocked her down; then the heavy door rumbled on its track as he shoved it closed, leaving them in pitch darkness.

She no longer needed light to identify her attacker. In the few moments he had been silhouetted in the doorway against the white world outside, she had recognized the squat, burly figure of Hap Turner. Did he mean to kill her? Gaining her feet in the pitch blackness, she sought some means of escape. She had never been inside the barn, but she had caught glimpses of the interior through the open door many times. She knew that the front part was used to store the rigs Pat Seavey had for hire. Behind that were the horse stalls, arranged on either side of a wide aisle. With her arms outstretched in front of her she walked to the left, where she had seen the larger rigs parked, hoping it would be possible to hide among them. Inching along, she wound her way past spoked wheels until she guessed she was close to the wall. Crouching down, she listened. He didn't seem to be coming after her. She heard a chair scrape as he bumped into it and knew he was in the office. The sound of another small scrape came to her, and the next moment, a lantern came to life and she saw him turn and come out into the main room, holding the lantern high and peering about in search of her.

Hardly breathing, she crouched behind the two-seater, following his progress through the spokes of a painted wheel. He was wearing a black suit and white shirt. She had never seen him in anything except work clothes, and even though the suit was smudged with dirt from their tussle on the floor, he presented so menacing an appearance in the stark black outfit that an icy tongue of terror licked through her. Why was he all dressed up? And then she saw it: the horse hitched to one of the buggies, a valise lying on the buggy seat. He was leaving town. He was fleeing to save his neck. And with him would go their only real chance of catching Ward's killers. Watching him work his way closer to where she was hidden she realized that before he left he meant to wreak vengeance on her for helping Lettie run away from him.

She prayed that someone had heard her scream, but held out little hope that anyone had. The snow was falling so thick and heavy that it muffled all sounds. The cold from the dirt floor began to penetrate her shoes, and her legs ached from maintaining her crouched position.

Holding the lantern above his head, Hap was searching among the various buggies and carriages, looking inside to see if she had concealed herself there. As he moved away from one, his roving eyes seemed to meet hers. Her breath stopped. Had he seen her? Setting the lantern on the floor at his feet, he took off his coat and threw it on a carriage seat. Then, with insultingly deliberate movements, he unbuttoned his fly.

Susan bit back a cry, but he had seen her. Leaving the lantern where it was, he started toward her. Knowing what he intended now and that he had discovered her hiding place, she screamed and kept on screaming even while she started up and made a try for the door, running around the buggy that had concealed her. Changing directions with a speed that doomed her, Hap made a grab and caught her. Although she was taller than he by several inches, her strength was no match for his. He wrestled her to the floor and began tearing at her clothes. Held to the floor by the weight of his body and unable to push him off, she used her hands to claw at him with such good effect that finally, with a curse, he struck her on the jaw, stunning her long enough that he managed to rip her underclothes and enter her. Pain shot through to her spine and all the way up to the back of her skull. Marshalling all her strength, she tried to roll her body and throw him off, but failed. His hands nailed her arms to the ground at either side of her head, leaving her helpless. She screamed. Halting his thrusting, he hit her again and then again.

When she regained consciousness, she was lying in total darkness. The only sounds she heard were those of horses breathing and the rustle of straw as one of them moved in its stall. Except for the fire between her legs, her body felt frozen. Pushing herself up to a sitting position awakened more pain; her face throbbed with it. Gingerly she examined it with her hand, finding dried blood beneath her nose.

Groaning and reaching out in the darkness for some support, she used the spokes of a wheel to pull herself upright, then stood for a few minutes, waiting for the waves of pain to recede, attempting to orient herself in the pitch blackness.

She followed the contours of the carriage with one hand, holding her other hand as a shield. She felt along the shafts to their end, certain then that she had found the aisle that separated the office from the line of vehicles. From there it was not far to the door. Whether from haste or indifference, Hap had not bothered to lock it when he left. She slid it open only far enough to let herself through, wincing as the strain pulled bruised muscles.

After the total darkness of the livery stable, the snow-filled world outside appeared as light as day. She made her way toward the now-sleeping hotel, aching in every muscle and sickened by the defilement of her body. She felt her way up the stairway, nearly collapsing before she reached Sy's door. With the last of her strength, she sagged against the door and turned the knob. When the door opened, she fell into the room.

She heard his startled exclamation and the rustle of his bedclothes. "Susan!" he cried when he reached her. He swept her up into his arms. His flannel nightshirt was soft and warm against her cheek as he laid her on his bed. When he had lighted his lamp and saw her face, she saw his body jerk from the shock. "My God, what happened?" he exclaimed and sat down beside her to brush the hair back from her battered face.

"Hap," she whispered. "He's skipped town."

Sy went still as death for a moment. The flesh of his face shrank against the bones. When he spoke his lips barely moved. "Hap did this to you?"

"And worse," she whispered. "I was coming back from a visit with Laura. He must have been waiting for me inside the livery stable. He dragged me in. Didn't you hear me screaming?" she demanded and began to sob.

Eyes dark with anguish, he said, "I didn't hear anything. Where did he go?"

"I don't know. He had hitched a horse to a buggy, and his valise was on the seat."

He stood up. "I'll go get Van. We'll find him." Slipping his arms under her again, he said, "I'm going to take you to your room and wake Ella. I'll stop by Doc Long's on my way and send him over."

Before leaving the room, he lit the lamp and sat down beside her again. Wordlessly he bent down to kiss her bruised face. "I'll find Hap, honey. He's going to pay for this, I promise you."

Susan clung to him, not wanting to let him go, knowing when he left it would come flooding back, the terror, the pain, the savage attack on her body. But she wanted Hap caught and he had a head start, how large a lead she didn't know. She wasn't sure how long she'd lain unconscious on the cold dirt of the barn floor. "Be careful," she murmured, and let her arms fall to her sides.

He kissed her once more and left.

The sheriff came to the door of his house in his long underwear and socks. It had taken repeated knocking and shouting to rouse him. "Sy?" he said uncertainly, peering out into the snow-filled night. "Come in," he exclaimed, coming awake all at once.

Sy stepped onto the linoleum floor of the Van Alstine front room, announcing as he did so, "Hap skipped town, and he raped Susan before he left."

A rumble started deep in the law officer's big chest and emerged as an outraged growl. "Where's the son of a bitch headed?"

"I don't know. Susan said he had a buggy ready to go and had a bag packed. I've got Doc Long and Ella looking after her. I figure he's headed someplace to catch a train. He knew we'd stop him if he tried to leave from here."

"What time is it?"

"Ten-thirty."

"He could be planning to take the eastbound from Green Willow. It gets in here about eleven-fifteen. That means it must leave there about midnight. The westbound leaves Empire a little after eleven."

Sy had already decided that Hap was heading west. That was the best place for a man to hide. And he wanted to intercept Hap. He had a score to settle with him before Van took him into custody. "I'll borrow Sal's buggy and start for Empire. You head for Green Willow."

There must have been something in his voice that worried Van. The big man cautioned him, "If you catch up with him, leave something for the law. If you wind up in jail you can't help Susan." Without bothering to reply, Sy opened the door and went back out into the thickly falling snow.

He took Sal's rig without waking him. He had less than an hour to catch Hap before the train left Empire. A quick search in Sal's barn turned up a lantern. Within minutes, he was driving out of the yard and heading out of town.

The road lay before him in pristine whiteness. Not so much as an animal track was to be seen. If Hap had taken this direction, the snow had hidden the evidence.

He flicked the horse's rump with the whip when it slowed, disoriented by the featureless white carpet under its feet and the smothering veil of snow that enfolded them. It required several licks with the whip to coax him back into a gallop. Heaven protect them from a frozen rut or a hole concealed by the growing blanket of snow.

He had gone half the five miles to Empire when he thought he could discern wheel tracks in the fluffy whiteness ahead. He reined in the horse and got out to investigate. There was no doubt about it; a buggy had been over this road a very short time earlier. If it was Hap, he had not been pushing his horse as fast as Sy was pushing his, believing apparently that even if Susan was able to go for help, pursuit could not be started until too late to intercept him.

Once again aboard the buggy, he set the horse at a gallop, leaning forward as they flew over the sugary ground, urging on the horse with voice and whip. He was almost upon the other buggy before he caught sight of it through the polka-dotted snow curtain that hung between them. Not until then had Hap been able to hear him. He laid on the whip, but too late. Sy's buggy drew up beside his. He saw Hap leaning forward, pressing his horse to go faster. Under another snap of the whip, Sy's horse sprang ahead, enabling Sy to grasp the lines of the other buggy. Yelling "Whoa!" he fought to bring both horses to a halt. Hap jumped out of his vehicle before the wheels stopped turning, and fled. Sy yanked on the reins, leaping out of the still-rocking buggy, and sped off after him.

Short, stumpy legs were no match for long, lean ones, and there was no place to hide. The woods that lined the river were at least half a mile away. Hap's futile dash for them ended when Sy hurled himself on the bulky body and brought it down into the featherlight snow. Hap fought desperately, but he was fighting with a savage. Something alien took possession of Sy when he finally got his hands on the man who had raped his beloved. If Hap landed any blows, Sy didn't feel them. Aware only of the yielding flesh beneath his fists, he pounded the face until he was forced to stop by arms that were too weak to obey his commands. Head hanging, gagging for breath, he sat astraddle of Hap's unconscious form until, finally able to rise, he lifted the dead weight and carried it to his buggy. Tying the second buggy behind his own, he started back toward Hawthorne.

The sight of Susan's battered face gazing up at him from her bed relit the fires of rage that he thought had died in the aftermath of the beating he had given Hap. Her body seemed to have shrunk; she was scarcely visible beneath the patchwork comforter. Ella sat in the rocker facing the bed. The dim light of the lamp etched lines of fatigue on her ruddy face.

"I caught him," Sy announced at once as he went to the bed and sat down beside Susan, taking her hand. "He was on his way to Empire to catch the train. We don't know where he was heading. He wasn't in any shape to talk when I got through with him." Recalling that fact for the moment afforded him a fleeting pleasure. "I rousted Earl out of bed, and we locked him up. Doc Long is taking a look at him. I've sent a wire to Green Willow so Van will know when he gets there that I caught Hap."

Not caring that Ella was watching, he raised Susan's hand to his lips and kissed it. "How do you feel?"

Beneath swollen lids, her eyes were dark as a winter night. "Like I'll never be clean again."

Ella asserted in troubled tones, "She's had a bath. Rufus and I brought the tub up here and filled it with nice hot water, but she keeps saying she still feels dirty."

Lifting a tendril of hair away from a bruised cheek, he asked, "Did Doc Long give you anything to make you sleep?"

"He gave me something for the pain," she murmured. "He said it would make me sleepy, and it has."

"Good. You'll feel better in the morning. And Hap won't

hurt you again. At the very least he's going to prison on this rape charge. We can hold him in jail until the next court term." Over in her chair, Ella was yawning hugely. Sy stood up. "Go on to bed, Ella. You've worked twice as hard as I have today. I'll sit with Susan the rest of the night." When the older woman started to take exception to the idea, he declared, "Go on, now, Ella. You know I'll take good care of her. If she needs a woman, I'll wake you."

Ella Lord sent a skeptical glance at Susan, who backed up Sy in a small voice. "Do as he says, Ella. You need your sleep. I wish I could say I didn't need anyone with me, but I don't think I could stand to be alone." Her voice broke.

Coming over to the bed, Ella patted Susan's shoulder with rough gentleness. "Put this out of your mind. When you wake up tomorrow morning, tell yourself it was a bad dream. That's the only way you ever have to think of it again."

Susan nodded like a dutiful child. When Ella had left, she asked, "How can I make believe it never happened? I couldn't feel more degraded if I had been taken by an animal."

Sy heard the self-hatred in her voice and was puzzled. "He forced you. You fought him as hard as you could. You're a virtuous woman. A man like Hap Turner can't destroy that."

"I'm not a virtuous woman." Her eyes fixed him with an uncompromising stare. "You know that better than anyone."

Deeply wounded, he protested, "You can't be comparing what Hap did to you to what happened between us!"

"Maybe I deserved this."

Exasperation over her need to accept punishment because of one moment of weakness brought sharp words to his lips. He bit them back and took her hand again. "Susan, what happened between us was the most beautiful thing I've ever experienced. When it was over, I loved you more. You had become more in my eyes, not less. You are everything a woman should be. That includes being able to love a man with your body as well as your soul."

"But I didn't love you."

The words cut like a knife. Not knowing what else to say, he laid his lips against her temple, urging, "Try to sleep now. Once you're rested, you'll be able to deal with this more rationally."

After putting some more coal in the small stove and turning the lamp as low as it would go, he settled himself in the rocking chair, easing off his boots and stretching out his legs. He leaned his head back and tried to find some measure of calm, without much success. A few minutes later Susan said quietly, "Take this pillow and put it behind your head."

He rose, and as he took the bed pillow she held out to him, she told him gratefully, "I'm glad you're here."

Touched deeply, he could only smile at her before returning to the chair. Placing the pillow behind his head, breathing in the scent of her that clung to it, he soon slept.

{13}

SHE WAS LATE for church and entered just as the congregation and choir began the first hymn. Tiptoeing down the aisle to an empty seat, she became aware that the voices were thinning. Heads turned her way; the church fell silent; faces registered shock and revulsion. It was then she realized she was naked. With a cry, she tried to cover herself with her hands and arms. Sobbing with shame, she turned to flee.

"Susan, wake up! It's only a bad dream!"

Opening her eyes, she saw Sy bending over her and shaking her shoulder gently. Relief washed over her, but the mortification would not be banished. Still sobbing, she clung to him. He sat on the edge of the bed and took her in his arms, murmuring soothingly to her until she quieted. Around the edges of the window shades she saw thin lines of light. "What time is it?"

"Seven-thirty. How did you sleep?"

"Heavily when I slept, but I kept waking up and remembering."

"How do you feel?"

"I ache all over."

Drawing back, he gazed into her face. The strained look that came to his mouth told her as much as a mirror would have. "Did you get any sleep?" she asked. Beneath a stubble of beard his face was haggard.

He smiled. "Thanks to the pillow you gave me, I slept quite well." Sometime during the night he had gone to his room for a blanket. It lay puddled on the floor where it had fallen when he rushed over to wake her. He had put his boots back on for warmth.

"Did you let the fire die out?" she asked, realizing that the room had grown very cold.

"I didn't want to wake you."

"But you must be half frozen!"

"I'll start one, and then I'll go shave and bring you some breakfast."

She lay there after he left, listening to the fire begin to draw. Sy had raised the shades, and although the sky was still gray, the room was bright with the white light of the snow. And empty. Loneliness seized her, rendering her vulnerable to the emotions that she had fought to keep at bay during the night. Self-disgust, rage, and a sense of powerlessness combined to leave her so enervated that even breathing required almost more strength than she could muster. Maybe she had been wrong to want revenge and to stay in Hawthorne. Maybe she had been vindictive and this was her punishment. If she had gone back with Coila she would have spared herself several memories that would haunt her until the day she died. She had been debased, in one instance by her own actions and now by rape. How would she ever cleanse herself?

"How's the fire going?" Sy asked, returning. A shave and a change of clothes had given him back his healthy glow. After making certain that the room would grow warm for her, he started to fetch her breakfast.

She stopped him with a halting request. "Would you ask Dora, or someone . . . would you ask them if they'd bring up the tub and some hot water again?"

He regarded her with troubled eyes before saying, "Yes, of course." He pulled the door shut behind him very quietly.

While she picked at her breakfast, he brought up the tub and two pails of water, which he set on her stove. "When I'm through eating, I'll bring up some cold water for you in case you need it. Can I get you anything else?"

She assured him she had everything she needed.

"Try to eat those eggs," he urged.

"I will," she promised.

Van Alstine set the basket containing the prisoner's breakfast on the desk and asked, "How is everything?"

Leaning forward from the desk chair to sniff the coffee aroma appreciatively, Earl Crowder replied, "He's been quiet as a mouse. I peeked in a couple of times to make sure he was still there. You here to stay?"

The sheriff nodded. "Go on home. If I need you later, I'll send someone over."

"No need to tell me twice. I'm hungry as a bear." He raised his solid, chunky body from the chair and pulled his coat off a hook beside the door. "Where do you suppose he was heading?"

"Maybe he'll be a little more talkative this morning." Van Alstine picked up the keys off the desk as his deputy left and carried the basket into the cell area. "Mornin', Hap."

There was no reply from the sullen-faced man lying on the bunk. Van Alstine unlocked the cell door and went inside. "You want some breakfast or aren't you eating either?"

"Set it on the floor. I'll eat. And put some more coal in the stove. It's freezing in here."

"I don't remember you ever caring much whether it was warm in here or not when you were on the outside and someone else was in here." Van Alstine studied his former deputy, who looked so unfamiliar in his black suit and white shirt. Hap hadn't moved. Why the hell was he lying there like that? The feather pillow, covered in blue ticking, was propped against Hap's scuffed valise. Or was the pillow hiding the valise? "What you got in there?" he demanded, pointing at the bag.

Hap stiffened. "Shaving stuff. Clean clothes."

The high windows didn't admit a lot of light to the room, but Van Alstine was able to see that Hap's face had gone very still. "Maybe I'd better have a look."

This brought Hap springing up to a sitting position, his hand going out protectively to the leather bag. "There's no gun in it if that's what you're worried about. Earl searched it when Sy brought it in."

The sheriff reached out and yanked it from beneath Hap's hand. Opening it revealed two work shirts and two pairs of work pants, the shaving things Hap had mentioned, and some underwear. Van Alstine shot a speculative glance at Hap and found his former deputy watching him with the unblinking tension of an animal that hopes to avoid discovery. Van Alstine began shaking out the clothes. A deep, narrow clasp purse fell out of one of the shirts. Retrieving it from the floor, he snapped it open and stared in surprise at the thick wad of bills that it contained. Earl's search hadn't been very thorough. "What did you do, rob the bank, too?" He counted and whistled. "A thousand dollars!" He threw the valise into Hap's stomach, keeping the purse and the money. "Where'd you get this?"

"I saved it."

"Like hell you did! Deputying and shoveling horse manure don't pay that well. Where'd you get it?"

"It's mine, I tell you!"

"Sure it is, but you didn't save it." Van Alstine pushed out his lower lip as he fingered the money. "They paid you to get out of town, didn't they? Seavey and the other one. I don't suppose Phil came up with any of this. He lives hand-to-mouth, same as you do."

Hap sat clutching the valise, a stubborn, closed expression on his face. Van Alstine peered at him, wondering how an ugly mess like this Maddox business could have happened in a nice quiet town like Hawthorne. When he'd been elected sheriff he hadn't expected to have to do much more than break up fights and run drunks into jail. The job hadn't amounted to much more than that until the Widow Brown's murder. That had put him in over his head. He felt the same way now, and he was just as mad as he had been then. "You're as good as in the penitentiary, Hap. We've got you cold on a rape charge. If I had my way, you'd be hung for that. And maybe you will be. Folks here in town have grown mighty fond of Mrs. Maddox. Some of them might take it into their minds to lynch you the way you did Ward Maddox. I'd guess that not a tear would be shed or that anyone would give a damn about catching those that did it."

Some of the color left Hap's face. He countered defiantly, "I didn't have nothin' to do with hanging Maddox. When you going to get that through your head? You want to send me to the pen for raping that Maddox bitch, go ahead. I ain't sorry, and I'm man enough to take what's coming to me, but you ain't going to get me on a murder charge."

"You ain't a man, Hap. You're a dumb little runt who thinks talking tough and bullying other people is going to convince people you are."

The valise went crashing to the floor as Hap lunged up off his bunk, fists clenched, his face working. "If you weren't sheriff, I'd show you how much a man I am!"

Van Alstine gazed down at him, letting contempt show in his face. "Ain't you glad I'm sheriff? Eat your breakfast, Hap. Maybe it will help you grow some." He picked up the valise and left the cell, making a show of locking it. Withdrawing the key, he gave Hap one last parting shot. "If you decide you want to tell me where you got this money, I'll stay here nights and hold off any lynching party that might come after you. Otherwise... well, I'll let you think on the otherwise."

He shut the door between the office and the cell area. Let the little bastard freeze in there. Tossing the money on his desk, he went to the window and stared across the street, not really seeing the different businesses that faced the courthouse and jail. He had never spoken to a prisoner the way he'd just talked to Hap. It wasn't right, he knew that, but they were going to have to scare the liver out of him if they were ever going to solve this Maddox case.

• • •

Two hours later, Pat Seavey came to the jail. "I hear Hap's in trouble again," he said, the color high in his fair Irish face. Cold as the morning was, he wore no hat, and his prematurely white hair had been tossed by the wind until it lay in disorderly waves upon his head. "Can I see him?"

Van Alstine regarded the Irishman coldly, willing to bet his life that part of the one thousand dollars Hap had been carrying had come from him. "What do you want to see him for?"

Seavey pretended surprise. "He works for me, and besides that, he's my friend. Who else has he got now that Lettie is gone?"

"You still call him a friend after what he did to Mrs. Maddox?"

"He must have been drunk. Besides, he blames her for Lettie running away."

"So it's all right if he evens the score by raping her?"

"I didn't mean that," Seavey amended hastily. "I just meant he was probably half out of his head."

"Did you know he was skipping town?" Van Alstine sent his glance boring into the livery man.

Seavey's glance wavered slightly. "I heard."

Van Alstine waited. He wasn't going to reveal that he had found the one thousand dollars Hap was carrying with him. The lengthening silence made Seavey shift his weight uneasily. "Where do you suppose he was going?"

"It doesn't matter now, does it? He ain't going to get there."

After another deliberate silence, Seavey flared, "Well, can I see him or not?"

"I ain't letting anyone in to see him yet except his lawyer, and he hasn't got himself one yet."

"You're acting mighty high-handed, aren't you, Van?" Seavey's temper was rising fast.

"I'm only going by the book."

Growling a curse, Pat Seavey stomped out.

Susan looked up dully from the bowl of chicken noodle soup that Dora had brought up to her just moments before Sy came in. "Hap was carrying a thousand dollars?"

Sy pulled up the rocker and sat down. "Van found it in Hap's valise. It isn't hard to figure out where he got it."

Susan regarded him blankly for a moment before her sluggish mind grasped the situation. "Of course. They wanted to get rid of him so he couldn't talk."

"Exactly. And guess who was the first one who came to the jail to see Hap this morning. Pat Seavey. Van wouldn't let him in. He told Pat he wouldn't let anyone in to see him except his lawyer and he hadn't hired one yet. Not more than an hour later, Ezra Black showed up saying he was Hap's lawyer. When Van asked Hap if he wanted to see Ezra, he said sure. So now he's represented by counsel."

"Is that going to make things harder?"

"A little, but we want to keep everything legal." His glance went from her to the nearly untouched bowl of soup. "Eat your soup," he coaxed.

"I'm not hungry," she responded wanly and settled more deeply into the pillows at her back.

"People are mad as hornets about what Hap did to you. You have the sympathy of the whole town."

Susan flinched. "I wish no one knew."

"There's no need to feel ashamed, Susan. You're the

victim of a crime, not the criminal."

"But it's such a shameful thing."

"You may feel that it is. Other people don't. They feel only pity for you. What if Hap had done this to Dora instead of you? How would you feel toward her?"

Susan tried to imagine it, but it was her back she felt pressed against the icy dirt floor, her thighs that were forced apart, her body that was brutally violated. She turned her cheek into the pillow. "I don't want to think about it!"

"No, of course you don't." Sy's voice was full of self-reproach. "I'm sorry." He rose and placed himself on the edge of the bed. Filling the spoon with broth, he held it out to her. "Eat a little of Ella's soup. Just for me."

If it hadn't been for his Southern drawl, it could have been her father wheedling her to eat and hastening her recovery from one of the many childhood illnesses from which she had periodically suffered. Obediently, she opened her mouth.

She had a visit that afternoon from Laura Knapp, who brought a note from Queena, decorated along its borders by watercolors and telling Susan she loved her and hoped she would soon be feeling well again.

"I discouraged her from coming with me," Laura said. Her thin, severe features, framed by her graying blond hair, were softened by the affection and the pity she felt for Susan. "It was frightening enough for her to know this had happened to you without seeing you like this. I'm afraid Hawthorne has treated you very cruelly since you moved here."

"Only a few of the people." Susan managed a faint smile. "I've found many good friends here."

More than she had believed. Gifts began arriving: handkerchiefs, a book, food. Mrs. Solomon, the sheriff's wife, and several other women called on her. The minister's wife came every day to see her.

Sy couldn't have been happier to see proven his assertion that she had the sympathy of the whole town. He had been worried by her refusal to leave her room even after the bruises began to fade from her face. She couldn't bring herself to go down to the dining room, however, or out on the street where she would be seen. Salvador Cross told her not to come back to work until she felt like it, but Sy kept urging her to break out of her isolation, as did Ella.

Her self-esteem repaired by the outpouring of sympathy and affection, she dressed one morning, and leaving the door of her room open, she waited until he came out of his room and joined him in the hall. The sight of her dressed and obviously ready to meet the world again brought a look of pleased surprise to his face. "I thought I'd go down to breakfast this morning," she murmured, feeling suddenly shy.

"In that case, madam," he said, making a courtly bow and offering his arm, "I beg the honor of escorting you."

She took it and clung to it, needing his presence and his support as she exposed herself for the first time to the curious glances she so dreaded. There was no one in the dining room that morning, however, except the two of them and Rufus. Ella and Dora came out of the kitchen and fussed over her until, laughing ruefully, she protested that she had played the invalid long enough and wanted nothing more than to have everyone forget anything had happened to her.

Upon arriving at work, she caught Salvador Cross by surprise. "Susan!" he exclaimed, hurrying toward her from the stove, where he'd been warming himself in the still chilly store. With eyes suspiciously shiny, he kissed her cheek. "Have you come to visit or have you come back to work?"

"I've come back to work," she responded, smiling.

Guiding her toward the stove, he declared, "I'm not the only one who will be happy about that. Your lady customers have been asking about you. We've all missed you."

"And I've missed all of you," she confessed. Letting her glance sweep the store where she had worked for more than a year, she experienced the warm feeling that the return to the familiar brings. "You've sold the pink lamp," she observed.

"Mrs. Vingers bought it. A group of friends are going to present it to Fred and Molly Gray for their twenty-fifth wedding anniversary."

"What's in those boxes back there?"

"Our Christmas things. Nuts, candies, and other things. They just came in yesterday."

"Is Christmas so near?" she exclaimed. "How time flies!" With amazement, she realized that once again it was true. Time was flying. For so long after Ward's death it had dragged with such slowness that she felt trapped forever in grief and pain. Someday the anguish would end altogether; it was already absent for long periods of time. What was still needed to restore serenity to her soul was to see the men who had killed Ward and shattered her life brought to justice. That task now lay in Sy's hands. All she could do was wait and pray.

Van Alstine awoke and sat up, yawning and rubbing his face, trying to clear away the heaviness in his eyes and head that an afternoon nap always left him with. He didn't like to sleep in the daytime, but invariably, if he was in the office after dinner, he grew irresistibly sleepy. It was those heavy meals his wife sent over. He had tried to tell her he was better off eating less at noon, but she kept packing the basket full. And as long as it was there, he ate it. He peeked into the cell area. Hap, too, had succumbed to sleep after the roast beef and chocolate cake.

Feeling bleary-eyed and headachey, Van Alstine went to the window and peered out at the town. Across the street a wagon stood in front of the flour and feed store. The breath of the two horses formed spurts of steam in the brittlely cold air. Van Alstine recognized the team and wagon as Phil Osborne's. He sucked air through his teeth disgustedly. Osborne would think nothing of loafing for a couple of hours after he'd bought what feed he needed, leaving his team uncovered in the extreme cold. After locking the door between the cell area and the office, he drew on his coat and went over to the lunchroom and bakery to visit with Oscar Nelson for a few minutes. By the time he had crossed the courthouse yard and the street, the biting cold had cleared his head.

Phil Osborne's wife came out of the feed store carrying her child, who was invisible beneath the blanket in which she had bundled him. Harley Bronson followed, carrying a sack of feed, which he threw into the wagon.

Van Alstine paused and greeted her, adding, "It's a mighty cold day for you and the youngster to be driving to town. Where's Phil?"

Small and thin as she was, she was not prevented by the child's weight from spinning around in alarm. "Oh, sheriff, I didn't see you! Phil hasn't felt good for a couple of days. We were out of feed, so I had to come in."

"It's awfully cold weather to take your boy out in. Couldn't Phil have looked after him while you drove to town?"

She fussed with the blanket, pulling it over the child's face. Van Alstine wondered how the boy would breathe. "I didn't think Phil was able to watch him so I brought him along."

Drunk most likely, Van Alstine thought. If Osborne wasn't scared with Hap in jail, he was an even bigger fool than he'd figured him to be. "Let me hold the boy while you climb up," he offered, taking the child from her.

Her first attempt to climb on the wagon was so hasty she missed her footing, barking her knee against the wheel so sharply she grimaced with pain. Harley came out with another sack of feed to throw in the wagon while she tried again, successfully this time. Settling herself quickly, she made room for her child on the seat. Without looking at the sheriff, she thanked him and started the horses moving.

Van Alstine headed once more for the lunchroom and bakery, gazing after the woman speculatively.

"What's Gracie Osborne doing in town on a day like this?" Oscar Nelson asked when the sheriff entered. The baker was a blond, pale-skinned man with a thin nose. His apron was as spotless as the cloths covering the six tables in his lunchroom. Smells of yeast and fruit from the bread and pies he baked filled the place.

Van Alstine went to stand beside the other man at the window. "She said Phil was sick, but you know, she was acting awfully funny."

"Phil was probably drunk."

"That's the first thing I thought, but why should she be so nervous about that? There's nothing unusual about him being drunk."

"Maybe it's just you that makes her nervous. She and Phil must know that you're just itching to arrest him."

"That could be it."

The more he thought about it, though, the more he felt that he should make a trip out to the Osborne farm to see if things were all right. Hitching up the buggy the next day, he drove through the bright, frigid morning to the river. There was no wind; nonetheless, before he'd covered the mile between town and the Republican, his face and hands and feet were stinging from the cold. The farm Osborne rented lay two miles east on the river road, and by the time Van Alstine arrived, he was more than ready to get next to a stove. When Gracie Osborne, who was clearly startled to see him, did not invite him in, he said, "I'm on the verge of being frostbitten, Mrs. Osborne. I've got to get inside."

Her young, already faded face came to life with an emotion Van Alstine couldn't quite define. "I . . . I can't let you come in, sheriff."

Trying hard to read her face, Van Alstine asked, "Why not?"

"Phil is . . . I mean he's awfully sick, and it might be catching." She refused to meet his eyes.

"Has Doc Long seen him?"

"Not yet."

She was obviously lying, and he recognized the turmoil in her face as fear. "I think I'd better have a look at him," he said firmly and placed himself in the doorway so that she had to retreat. He went past her into the kitchen and on into the dining room, where the Osborne child played in front of the base burner. Pulling off his gloves, Van Alstine went straight to the stove and stood there holding out his hands to the warmth. To his left was a small unused parlor, which held an ancient horsehair sofa and little else. All the bedrooms were upstairs. "Do you want to take me up or shall I go up alone?" he asked.

Gracie Osborne had followed him in, scooping up her child as if she needed something to hang on to. Her mouth twitching with nervousness, she said, "He isn't up there."

Convinced now that he'd stumbled onto something, but not yet sure what, Van Alstine asked, "Where is he?"

"He... he's gone for a few days."

"Where'd he go?"

"I don't know." It was the first unequivocal statement she had made since he arrived.

Some of his mother's fear had been sensed by the boy; his eyes were round and grave.

"Phil has skipped, hasn't he? Did you know he was going or did he leave you flat?"

Showing some spunk for the first time, she responded heatedly, "He wouldn't go away and leave us for good. He said he'd send for us as soon as he was settled and had a job."

Was he paid off like Hap, Van Alstine wondered, or did he just get scared and run? "How'd he get away without anyone knowing?"

Still defiant, Gracie Osborne replied, "He said he was going to ride a freight train."

It would have been possible for him to sneak aboard a freight car at night without Frank Cook or anyone else seeing him. It would have been mighty cold, but he'd seen bums keeping warm in closed freight cars by building tiny fires in buckets or big cans. If a man was desperate enough to get away, he could manage.

Realizing she had said too much, Gracie Osborne was

frightened again. Hugging her little boy convulsively, she blurted, "Phil hasn't done anything wrong. He was just scared, that's all. He knew you and that lawyer were out to get him, and he didn't know what else to do except leave."

Van Alstine let her remarks pass without responding to them. Drawing on his gloves, he asked, "Are you going to be all right out here alone? Is there anything I can do for you before I go back to town?"

Sullenly she said, "I can manage."

"I'll be on my way, then."

On the ride back, he went over in his mind the things he'd have to do the minute he got to town. He'd have to wire all the depot agents up and down the line asking them to notify him if Gracie Osborne tried to board a train. He'd send a description of her and the child. She was their best chance to find Phil. He wouldn't wait for Phil to contact her, though. He would start sending out descriptions of Phil and say he was wanted for questioning in a murder case. It would probably be wasted effort, though. The country was big enough to hide any man who didn't want to be found. And unlike Gracie Osborne, Van Alstine had no faith in Phil's sending for her. He was the kind who could walk away from responsibility without a qualm. Once he experienced bachelorlike freedom again, he would more than likely drop out of sight for good. He shook his head, dislodging the muffler he had wrapped around his face. It was always a mystery to him how women like Gracie Osborne could stick up for no-good husbands like Phil.

Hap Turner sat on his cot after his lawyer had left, holding the envelope Ezra had brought him. Because Van refused to let him have any visitors except his lawyer, Ezra had delivered what he thought was merely a friendly note from Pat. The note was far from innocent, however. He tapped the envelope several times against his knee, grinning now that he was alone. Of course he'd keep his mouth shut for five thousand dollars. He'd have kept it shut for nothing; why would he put his own neck in a noose? They must really be scared. Pat thought Van and Sy Harris would put the screws to him and make him talk. There was no doubt in Hap's mind that they would try, but they wouldn't get anything out of him. It was bad enough that he'd be going to prison for raping the Maddox woman. He sure wouldn't be admitting anything else.

It was just his luck that she had realized that he was leaving town that night. Otherwise, he'd be in California by now. He wondered if that was where Phil was heading. He must have panicked. Anger spurted through him. Those guys must think he didn't have any backbone. Hell, they ought to know he wouldn't break down. He became aware once again of the envelope he was holding. Let them think it. He was going to end up a rich man because of it. After a year or two in prison, he'd be free to do anything or go anywhere he wanted. He might buy himself a business somewhere. People looked up to businessmen. He might be a member of a town board someday, like Pat.

He stood in the narrow cell and stretched. It would give him something to think about during the next two months while he waited for his trial. And during those months in the pen. Despair momentarily conquered the pleasant expectations for the future. After being locked up in a cell for two weeks without a drink, without being able to move more than a few steps in any direction, the thought of spending a year or two in prison was intolerable. How did men stand it? Wadding up the envelope, he threw it at the cot as hard as he could. It bounced off the wool blanket and landed on the wood floor. Turning his back on it, he gripped the bars and pressed his forehead against his hands.

Susan had just reached the bottom of the stairs on her way into supper when Sy entered the hotel. A few grainy snowflakes dusted the shoulders of his black overcoat and the brim of his hat. On one of his eyelashes a melted flake glistened in the light of the already burning parlor lamps. "You worked late tonight," she remarked.

Wiping his boots on the rag rug in front of the door, he said, "Van stopped by my office on his way home. He got a wire a little while ago from the sheriff in Buffalo County, Nevada. A man they've identified as Phil Osborne fell from a freight car and was run over by a train."

The news of the sudden violent death of any person, even Phil Osborne, was lamentable. "Are they certain it was him?"

Sy straightened. "He was carrying a packet of pills with his name on it from Doc Long. The physical description matched, too. Van wired them to ship the body back here. He's gone out to tell Gracie."

Memories of that hot July morning a year and a half ago when the sheriff had brought similar word to her swept over Susan. It was the cruelest news a wife could hear; her heart ached for Gracie Osborne. "She'll need someone with her tonight."

"Van is taking her mother along."

Susan said, "It's a terrible way to die."

"So is hanging."

"Yes," she conceded, wondering if this way wasn't perhaps better after all. Better for Gracie Osborne, at least.

Her second Christmas in Hawthorne was spent at the Cross home. Sy and the Lords were also present. Invitations to Sy by the young ladies of the town and their mothers had gradually diminished when it became apparent that Sy's only interest was in Susan. She found it slightly embarrassing that people should think he was courting her. She still felt like a widow; in fact, still considered herself Ward's wife. How eager most people were to rush one through one's grief. There was evidence that she was recovering, however. Christmas this year did not bring with it the desolation she had had to struggle to overcome last year. Sadness, yes, but even at its worst, it was manageable. One reason for that, she believed, was that she was so near to seeing Ward's death avenged. She wondered if, once that was accomplished, she would be rid of the seething sense of outrage that she had carried inside herself these long months.

The day had been one of keen longing and frustration for Sy. He would have been miserable spending Christmas apart from Susan, yet sharing this most family-oriented of all holidays with her without possessing her robbed the day of some of its cheer. He had camouflaged his emotions successfully, he thought, and there was the moment to look forward to that night when he gave her the gift he had for her. There was a chance—there was always a chance—that she would discover that she felt more than just friendship for him.

They walked back to the hotel with the Lords. After bidding them good night, Sy followed Susan up the stairs, pausing at her door to ask, "May I come in for a minute? I have something for you."

"Sy, you didn't—"

Cutting her off, he said, grinning, "No protests now. After all, it's Christmas."

She left the door partway open, giving them some privacy without flouting propriety. While she lighted the lamp, he took from his pocket the tiny box he'd been fingering all day, its presence furnishing a tingle of anticipation. "I realize it's late in the day to be wishing you this, but Merry Christmas anyway," he said, offering her the gift.

Smiling, she took it and tore off the red tissue paper with which it was wrapped. Upon opening the box, her mouth formed a silent O. "It's beautiful," she said slowly, "the most beautiful brooch I've ever seen."

He had never seen one lovelier either. The many-faceted amethyst caught the lamplight and sparkled within its circlet of tiny pearls. "I special ordered it from the jewelry salesman who calls on Ed Padey."

Raising her eyes, she started to protest. "Sy, I can't—"

"Of course you can," he interrupted impatiently. "You don't have to tell anyone where you got it if that's going to cause a problem for you. Don't deny me the pleasure of giving it to you."

She hesitated only for an instant, then smiled. "Thank you, Sy. It's the prettiest, most extravagant present anyone ever gave me."

"Put it on," he urged.

She went to the mirror that hung above the bureau and pinned the brooch just below her chin where the two round wings of her white collar met. It showed up well against the dark wool of her dress. He stepped behind her and watched while she pinned it on. "There," she said, "I shall be the envy of every woman who sees it."

He turned her to face him. "Don't I get a thank-you kiss?"

A faint flush colored her skin. "Of course," she said and pressed her lips softly against his cheek. When she drew back, he caught her forearms, then bent his head slowly toward her mouth. Her eyes locked with his, she made no attempt to evade his kiss. Her lips, warm and soft, were still at first, but under the demanding pressure of his, they came to life. She turned her head, the better to meet his, and her breath quickened. Much too soon, she pulled away, turning her back to hide her expression from him, forgetting that the mirror would betray her. Suddenly her eyes found the gold-rimmed shaving mug; she stiffened, and he felt her recede from him. Damn the mug! he thought, wanting to sweep it off the bureau and send it crashing to the floor. When she turned to face him again, her eyes were remote even though her voice was warm as she said, "Thank you, Sy. Your gift has helped make this a wonderful Christmas. I'm very lucky to have friends like you and the Lords and the Crosses."

Accepting defeat, he said evenly, "I'm happy that it's been a good day for you." He went to the door. "Good night."

"Good night, Sy."

Walking to his room he tried to tell himself that all she needed was more time. But if she really wanted to adjust to life without Ward, wouldn't she get rid of that mug and the constant reminder it provided? The question wouldn't be put down. It followed him into his room and spent the night.

14

SY DIRECTED A level look at Ezra Black, who sat across the desk from him, and announced, "I'm prepared to file a first-degree murder charge against Hap."

The other lawyer's face was almost completely hidden behind a salt-and-pepper beard, but his dark, brilliant eyes didn't waver. "You were only sworn in yesterday."

"I've been preparing the case for months."

The man he had defeated for the nomination remarked, "You were awfully sure of yourself, weren't you?"

"Not that sure. It was just something I had to do, win or lose. I couldn't sit back and watch Hap and Osborne and Seavey going about their lives as if they hadn't murdered a man."

"What evidence do you have that they did it? You aren't basing your charge on Cal Rivers's statement, are you? No jury will convict my client on the word of a drunk."

"Are you prepared to risk Hap's life on that? You've dealt with juries for years. You know how unpredictable they are. Besides, Cal might be a drunk, but everyone knows he's not a liar. And don't forget, Van has those pieces of rope Hap was supposed to have been bound with. It's going to be obvious to any man on the jury that those ropes never had a knot tied in them." Sy watched the other lawyer take a cigar from his breast pocket and bite off the end. "I've got a good case against Hap, and you know it. I don't have to tell you, either, that this vigilante hanging has laid a stench over the entire county. I'm betting that a jury will be eager to punish anyone who looks even a little bit guilty." He paused and waited.

Ezra Black lit his cigar and asked through a cloud of blue smoke, "I take it you're about to make an offer."

"I'll reduce the charge to second-degree murder if Hap will name the other men who were in on it."

Ezra Black rolled the cigar around between his lips, wetting the end while he considered Sy's offer. Sy fixed an unwavering gaze on him. Getting Hap was important, but he wanted them all, and Hap was the only means he had of finding out who the fourth man was and of getting the evidence needed to convict him and Seavey. The other lawyer was silent so long that Sy couldn't hold his relaxed pose. He finally sat up straight in his chair and clasped his hands tensely across his stomach.

Blowing out a slow, thin stream of smoke, Black let his ashes fall in his lap. "There's no guarantee you'll get a conviction, and pleading guilty to second-degree murder will mean years in prison. I can't see that that's a very good bargain for my client. Now, if you'd drop the rape charge, that would sweeten it by several years."

Sy's gaze turned to an icy stare. "Not a chance. He's going to pay full price for that one. We've got him cold."

Black sat smoking for a few more minutes before he stood up. "All right. I'll go talk to Hap and pass along your offer. I'll let you know what he decides."

"District court meets in three weeks."

"I know when it meets."

"If Hap is going to accept my offer, I've got to know by the end of the week. I'll have to prepare the cases and have them ready when Judge Gaslin gets here."

"I'll tell him."

After Black had gone, Sy rubbed his face vigorously, trying to relax the muscles. Hap would be a fool to turn down the offer of a lesser charge. But Hap *was* a fool. Sy flung an oath across the empty office. Hap Turner would have been the last person in the world he would have chosen to let his personal happiness rest on.

"Hell no, I won't plead guilty!" Hap glared at his attorney who sat beside him on the jail cot. "I wasn't a party to no murder."

Ezra Black drew a freshly lit cigar from his mouth. "Sy has two good witnesses."

"I know what he's got and it's nothing. Who's going to believe Cal Rivers? And as for Van, his suspicions are flimsier than the pieces of rope he claims I was tied up with." With pleasure he regarded the cigar Ezra had given him. It was the first one he'd smoked in a long time.

"Sy thinks the jury isn't going to be too picky about the

evidence he presents against you. He says this vigilante hanging left a bad taste in everybody's mouth and the jury is going to want to make sure somebody pays for it. I think he's right. My advice would be to plead guilty to second degree."

"I don't want to spend years in the pen. These two months in here have nearly driven me crazy."

"A cell is better than a grave."

The word *grave* fell on Hap like a boulder. He couldn't speak for a few minutes.

Ezra Black said, "I tried to get Sy to agree to drop the rape charge if you would plead guilty to second degree, but he wouldn't even talk to me about that."

Because I got in where he hasn't been able to, Hap thought sourly. He had no regrets. That Maddox bitch had it coming to her.

"My advice is to accept the lesser charge and plead guilty. You risk your neck the other way. Sy is a damn good lawyer."

"How soon do I have to decide?"

"By the end of this week. District court meets in three weeks."

"I'll let you know."

"Well, it's done," Sy informed Susan that night as they sat alone in the parlor after supper. Rufus was still in the dining room visiting with a young man and his wife who had come to Hawthorne seeking land to buy. Susan had watched them surreptitiously during the meal. Had she and Ward looked that young when they arrived at the Lord's house for the same purpose?

"Ezra has explained to Hap that he can save his neck

from the noose if he'll testify against the other men. Apparently he's thinking it over."

"I wouldn't think he'd have to think that choice over for very long." Through the isinglass windows on the door of the base burner, Susan watched the orange flames.

"I wrote to Coila and Father today to expect me home before spring."

Sy, sitting with his feet stretched out toward the fire, was silent. She didn't have to look at him to know that her announcement would be a blow to him.

"I don't suppose there's anything I can do or say that will keep you here," he said at last.

"No, it's time for me to go home." She said it gently.

"I may not stay here either."

She glanced at him in surprise. "I thought you loved Hawthorne."

"I did." He recrossed his legs. "I've given some thought to going to Denver. It's bound to be quite a city some day. I could probably work up a practice there in time. Once your case is settled, there won't be much for me to do as county attorney. I might resign before my term is up."

"Hawthorne would be much poorer if you left."

"If Hap doesn't open up and if I lose the case against him, I'm going to leave for sure. I wouldn't want to go on living here."

Susan knew intuitively that unless Hap and the others were imprisoned or hanged, the burden of rage and bitterness she carried would take its toll of her like a chronic disease for the remainder of her life. "How long do you think it will take Hap to make up his mind?"

Sy stared at the glowing door of the stove and replied somberly, "Who can predict what a man like Hap will do?"

• • •

The end of the week came and went without any word from Hap or Ezra Black. On Monday morning Sy went to Black's office and was told by his colleague that Hap was still considering the offer Sy had made.

At the middle of the second week, Sy made another visit to Black's office. "What's Hap waiting for, a better offer? If he is, you'd better inform him that this is it. First or second degree—that's his choice."

"He's having trouble making up his mind. He doesn't like the idea of prison."

"Does he like the idea of hanging better?"

"There's a third possibility, you know. He might be found innocent."

Sy gave what he hoped was a convincing bark of laughter. "If you're giving him that advice, your client is being poorly served by his counsel." He didn't wait for Ezra Black's retort, leaving the overheated office to trudge back to his office through the snow.

Susan's anxiety was as great as his own. "He's not going to name those other men, is he?" she suggested that evening. "Do you suppose they've bought him off somehow?"

The same possibility had occurred to Sy. "I think it's very likely. They may have offered him so much money to keep quiet that he's willing to risk hanging for it."

"There wouldn't be that much money in the world to persuade me to risk my life for it."

"Me either, but Hap might not be able to resist the chance to end up a rich man instead of a dead one."

One week before district court was to convene, Sy got word to come to the jail. There he found Hap and Ezra Black sitting in the office with Van. Hap sat in the chair across the desk from the sheriff; Black was standing near the stove.

Speaking through the greetings, Van Alstine announced, "Hap has decided to talk."

Sy eyed the short, stumpy man coldly. "I was beginning to believe you were even dumber than I thought."

Hap Turner's bearded face reddened. He said something obscene, which Sy ignored. "Let's hear it. Who helped you hang Ward Maddox?"

"It wasn't my idea," Hap denied hotly. "It was theirs. I only helped."

"I'm waiting."

"Phil Osborne was one. Pat Seavey was another."

"And?"

"Nels Cooper." Hap's teeth flashed in a wolfish grin as his glance moved from one astounded face to another. "Never thought of him, did you? You don't expect higher-ups like him to go around breaking into jails and hanging people."

Van Alstine snapped, "You're lying. Nels Cooper not only wouldn't do a thing like that, he couldn't. He's too fat to wrestle a man into a noose."

"Why do you think he brought Pat and Phil along? It was as much Pat's idea as his, though. They had a town board meeting that night, and afterward, Nels and Pat stayed to talk. Nels was sure Maddox had killed the widow, and he was afraid Jess Frazier would mess up the case so bad that you would get him off," Hap said grudgingly to Sy. "Pat was just as mad. You know what a temper he has, and he never once doubted that Maddox was guilty. They decided to take care of Maddox themselves. Pat needed help, and he wasn't sure how I would feel about it, so he went over to the saloon and sounded Phil out. Phil was like the rest of us. He thought Maddox was the murderer."

Despite his loathing of Hap, and incredible as it seemed that Nels Cooper had been involved, Sy believed him. It explained why Nels had tried to persuade him to drop the case, why he had withdrawn his support and backed Ezra Black for county attorney. Nels might even have been behind the rumor that Sy and Susan were having an affair.

Van Alstine still had his doubts. He said, "If you're lying about Nels, this whole deal is off."

Glaring at him, Hap snarled, "I ain't lying. You just don't want to believe that the bigwigs in this town aren't any different from us little guys."

The sheriff glanced at Sy. "Have you got all you want?" When Sy nodded, he got up and jerked his head toward the cell area, saying, "Back you go, Hap."

As Van Alstine led him away, Ezra Black observed in a shaken voice, "No wonder Nels backed me against you. It was his own skin he was trying to protect, not the town."

"The damned fool," Sy said regretfully. "He let his desire to run things get out of control. He should have trusted the law to take care of Maddox."

Van Alstine came back, his face even more melancholy than it normally was. "How am I going to go to Nels Cooper and tell him he's under arrest for murder? He's been a leader in this town for almost twenty years. His wife is one of the finest women in the world, and his kids never got into a speck of trouble." He pushed some papers around on his desk. "I can't say the same for Pat Seavey's kids, but there are eight of them. How is his wife going to feed that family without Pat?"

If their actions hadn't put Susan through such hell, Sy could have felt more compassion for the men. "Don't forget for one second that they murdered an innocent man with a young wife and a dream. That will make your job a little easier."

Ezra Black was compulsively smoothing his salt-and-pepper beard. "It scares you, doesn't it, to think how much grief you can cause your family with one mistake."

They fell into a silence, each deep in his own thoughts.

"Will one of you go tell Earl I need him? I've got to get the warrants and then go serve them."

Sy hung back, letting Ezra offer. He wanted to go straight to the store and tell Susan. He left them immediately, using the excuse that he had the case against Nels to prepare and only a week in which to do it.

"Nels Cooper?" Susan repeated the name slowly. "He'd have been one of the last men in town I'd have suspected."

Sy had waited for an exclamation, a facial expression, something that would tell him that learning at last the identity of Ward's killers and knowing they were about to be arrested would crack the shell of outrage that had isolated her from her other emotional needs. She appeared to feel nothing except surprise.

Her surprise was nothing compared to that of Salvador Cross, who, upon hearing Sy's news, had come quickly to the millinery counter. "I remember that board meeting," he said in a stunned voice. "We couldn't keep our minds on the business at hand. All of us—Nels, Pat, Con, Henry, and I—were sickened by the thought of anyone killing and robbing Widow Brown. Pat was in a terrible temper, but he never once suggested a lynching. Maybe he was sounding us out and I didn't realize it. He'd been drinking pretty heavy, and he makes me nervous when he's like that so I wasn't paying much attention to him." He shook his head. "This is terrible! Nels Cooper sent to prison or worse! Belle has worried all these years about his diabetes and about him not following his diet. It would have been better if . . ." He let his voice trail off, refraining from finishing the thought aloud.

"It's over, then," Susan said. She spoke quietly, almost without expression.

Sy agreed. "Even if they refuse to plead guilty, Hap's testimony will convict them."

"Do I owe the reward to Hap?"

"Absolutely not! His reward for his information is his life. He's lucky to get that."

"It's over," Susan said again, as if she were having difficulty believing it. "I can go home."

Sy scarcely heard her thank him. He had expected her to feel the same exhilaration he felt. Certainly he hadn't expected this listless acceptance of the event she had lived for this past year and a half. Had he been wrong all this time in believing Ward's unsolved murder had shackled her to a former life, leaving her unable to contemplate a future? When he left a few minutes later, he felt the finality of Susan's remark that it was over.

Van Alstine kicked the snow off his boots with more force than the light coating of snow required before entering Nelson Cooper's hardware store. The store, one of the biggest in Hawthorne, was crammed with everything from nails to stoves. In the lot behind it were parked buggies and wagons and a few farm implements.

Bud Cooper, Nels's son, was in the process of removing everything from the window to the left of the door. "Going to change your display?" Van Alstine asked the dark-haired young man.

"No. No new stuff." Bud Cooper held up a pair of grimy hands and grinned. "Mother told us it was time to do some dusting, and it looks like she was right, doesn't it?"

"Sure does," Van agreed hoarsely. "Is your dad here?"

"Over there in his chair." The young man waved toward a rear corner of the store where Nels could usually be found ensconced in a big leather chair from which he seldom moved, unless there was more business than Bud could handle.

Van Alstine covered the distance as slowly as he could, his heavy steps loud on the wooden floor. When he was a few yards away, Nels Cooper hailed him. "Howdy, Van."

Van Alstine hadn't seen Cooper for a week or longer and was struck by the sickly appearance of the man. His multiple-chinned face was pasty; his dark eyes, usually bright as beads, were dull and lifeless. I don't think this is going to come as any surprise to him, Van Alstine thought. He brought the warrant out of his coat pocket and held it up. "I've got a feeling you know what this is."

"I think I could make a good guess."

"Hap talked this morning. He named you and Pat."

Cooper's eyes seemed to sink back into his head. He nodded and called to his son, "Come back here a minute. There's something I want you to hear."

Bud Cooper joined them, dusting his hands together. The dark eyes and nose were like his father's, but there was no other similarity between the lean young face and the other one. His inquiring glance moved between the two older men. Without explaining, Nels Cooper addressed Van Alstine.

"I thought Maddox killed the widow."

"I know you did," said Van, "but you should have let the law take care of him."

"I've been in politics for fifteen years. I've worked hard to get men like you elected so we can have good government in this county. I thought that the election of Jess as county attorney was a mistake, and when Widow Brown was murdered, I decided justice wouldn't be done if it were left to him."

Van Alstine listened patiently, knowing that Nels Cooper had to explain his action, that he was pleading for understanding, both from him and from his son.

"I didn't consider it murder. I looked on it as an execution. I never doubted for a single minute that he was the one who murdered the widow. Neither did Pat." Cooper, who had become increasingly short of breath, began to talk in short bursts, taking wheezing breaths in between. "I went to a board meeting that night... and when I saw... how riled up Pat was... I stayed behind with him... to talk about it.... When he said he'd like to... string Maddox up with his own hands... he was more or less... saying what I'd been thinking... all day. I put the idea up to him... and he was ready to go.... I had to calm him down.... make him wait till later. He said... he'd get somebody to help him... in case Hap wouldn't go along." Here Cooper paused, letting his head fall against the back of his chair. With his eyes closed, he said in a voice that had grown weaker, "I had never seen... a man die by hanging before. . . . I don't think there's been . . . a single night since . . . that I haven't had a nightmare . . . and seen him kicking and trying to breathe."

Van Alstine felt sorry for the boy. He had gone as pale as his father; even his lips had lost their color.

Nels said to him, "You'll have to tell this to your mother. I don't want her coming to the jail to see me." Unable to speak, the boy swallowed and nodded. "You can run the store by yourself. It will keep your mother as long as she lives, and you, too. Mary has a husband to take care of her. You'll all be all right. Now help me up."

Bud Cooper heaved and pulled the sick, corpulent man out of his chair, then embraced him, clinging to him until he could speak. "I'll get a lawyer from Lincoln, Dad. Maybe he can get you off."

"I don't need a Lincoln lawyer. I'm going to plead guilty."

Van Alstine had to look away from that young face so twisted with anguish.

"You'd better help Van get me over to the jail. I'm not sure I can make it."

With one of Nels Cooper's arms around the shoulders of each of them, they walked slowly across the street to the jail.

The sheriff found Pat Seavey in his office, far gone in drink. His eyes were bloodshot and unfocused, his speech slurred. "Howdy, Van. Need a rig today? Aldie's back there someplace. He can help you."

"I'm not going anywhere. It's you I want to see. I've got a warrant for your arrest."

"Now, Van, I'm not causing anyone any trouble. I've

had a little too much, but I'll go home and eat a good dinner and sleep it off."

"I'm not arresting you for drunkenness, Pat. Hap decided to talk. He told us all about what happened the night the four of you hung Ward Maddox."

The blue eyes came slowly but sharply into focus. "I didn't have anything to do with that. If he said I did, he's lying."

"That's for the jury to decide. My job is just to take you to jail."

"You're not taking me over there!"

Van Alstine took the document from his pocket. "I have a warrant that says I can."

"I didn't have anything to do with Ward Maddox's hanging! I'm not going to let you take me to jail on the say-so of a sawed-off little runt like Hap Turner who goes around raping women."

"You can tell your story in court. Meantime, I've got to lock you up until then. It's only a week away."

"You're not locking me up for something I didn't do!"

The sheriff's patience was running out. Not wanting to have to take Pat by force, he tried another tack. "I've already arrested Nels. He told me how you and him got together that night after the town board meeting and planned the hanging."

Fear and disbelief chased one another over Pat Seavey's fair-skinned face. "Nels couldn't have said anything like that!"

"He knew the minute I walked in his store what I was there for. He didn't fight it. He called Bud over and told us both the whole story."

Seavey's temper took off. "That fat son of a bitch! He's

just trying to take me to prison with him. But he won't get away with it. I told him that night I didn't want anything to do with hanging a man. He must have got someone else. I should have told you about him a long time ago, but I didn't want to get Nels in trouble."

"You're wasting your time telling me all this, Pat. My job is to take you to jail. The rest is up to the judge and the jury. Are you going to come along peaceable or are you going to make my job hard?"

"You aren't taking me to jail!"

Van Alstine gave a small, resigned sigh. "One way or another, you're going." With a swift movement he pulled Seavey out of his chair by one arm. Seavey came up swinging; the sheriff absorbed a blow at the same time his own fist was connecting with the livery man's chin. Pat Seavey crumpled like a bag full of rags. Hoisting him over his shoulder, Van Alstine left the barn and made for the jail.

Sy flexed his shoulders, trying to relieve the ache in his back. It seemed as if two days had passed since Van called him to the jail this morning to hear Hap's confession. Much of his enthusiasm for pursuing the case had waned after he observed Susan's apathetic response to his news that Hap had identified his cohorts, robbing the work that followed of the significance it would otherwise have had. While he was engaged in preparing the cases for court next week, Earl Crowder had come to his office to inform him that Nels Cooper had had a spell with his heart and that Doc Long was on his way to the jail. When Sy got there, Nels was still alive but in great pain. There was no possibility of getting a signed confession or a deposition to buttress the testimony against Pat Seavey that Hap would give.

Sy pulled out the heavy gold watch that had been his grandfather's. It was seven-thirty. He had skipped supper and still wasn't hungry. He was calling it quits for the day, however; his mind had rebelled. It would be useless to try to work any more tonight. At any rate, some of his incentive was gone.

He buttoned himself wearily into his coat and turned out the lamp, then headed for the jail to see how Nels was. Both Van and his deputy were there. They sat talking quietly in the office. "How is he?" Sy asked as he entered.

"About the same," replied Van Alstine. "Mrs. Cooper and the doc are with him. Bud was here until a little while ago. He went out to eat and get some food for his mother and Doc."

Doc Long heard his voice and came out. In answer to Sy's question about Nels's condition, the bald, portly man said in a voice that wouldn't carry to the cell area, "It's heart failure. He could go any time."

"Could he be moved back home?" The thought of Mrs. Cooper sitting in that cell sharing her husband's final hours with the two other prisoners seemed unnecessarily cruel to Sy.

Doc Long said, "If he were a smaller man I might try it, but I'm afraid the job of moving him would kill him."

"My wife brought some blankets," Van informed Sy. "We hung them around Nels's cell so they can have a little bit of privacy anyway. Bud brought a comfortable chair for his mother."

They fell into a silence, contemplating the vast proportions of this entire tragedy. Sy left a few minutes later.

• • •

Susan moved about her room restlessly. The small patches of bright wool in the pieced comforter glowed softly in the light of the kerosene lamp. On the bureau, the clock ticked quietly. It was nearly eight o'clock. Where was Sy? He hadn't shown up for supper. She hadn't seen him since he brought her the news at the store that Ward's killers were at last in jail.

The full impact of what had happened had gradually built an elation in her that she could scarcely contain. She needed to share it with Sy. To no one else could she express it so freely. The town was stunned by the revelation that two of its businessmen had been arrested for murder. Observing the sadness displayed by Salvador Cross and the Lords and their concern over the anguish this would mean for the Cooper and Seavey families, Susan realized that a full expression of her joy would be unseemly. Only Sy would understand. She had to share it with him or burst.

She went to the half open door and glanced out into the hall. Surely she hadn't missed him. Certain it was futile, she nevertheless went to his door and knocked on it. There was no answer. Going to the head of the stairs, she listened. From below came the voices of Rufus and the two drummers who had eaten supper in the dining room. They were playing a three-handed game of high five.

As she started slowly back toward her room, she realized that those companionable evenings she had spent in the parlor, listening to Rufus and Sy play cards with whomever else happened to drift in, were about to end. She had forgotten in her exultation that she was free now to go back to Pennsylvania. She yearned to see her father and Coila. Then why this feeling—it was regret, wasn't it?—when she thought about leaving here.

She left the door to her room half-open as before and went to her rocker, but she didn't sit down. Idly brushing her fingers across the polished cherry wood, she sought the reason for this regret.

I'm not the same woman I was two years ago when I left home, she decided. Looking back, she realized how immature, how untested she had been. I've known the bliss of being a wife, and I've experienced a widow's grief. It gave her no pleasure to contemplate sharing a house with Coila and her father. They expected her to be as they remembered her. They would be puzzled and hurt by the emotional distance from them that she had developed. And she would feel constricted living in a house that was not hers. Did she want to remain in Hawthorne? She considered the possibility for the first time. She had made some dear friends, and she had a job. She glanced around the room. If she stayed, she wouldn't want to continue living here. It was confining and lonely and had never provided anything more than a temporary living arrangement. She could afford a small house.

Aware that the room had grown chilly, she dropped a few pieces of coal in the stove. Any house she bought would be better than the one she and Ward had lived in. Where, then, was the sense of anticipation that she should be feeling at the prospect of fixing one up? She hadn't forgotten the fun and excitement of creating a home out of a sod house.

Wandering aimlessly around the room, she watered her plants from the pitcher and pulled the curtains aside from one of the windows to look out into the night. Clean snow and starlight faded the darkness. Lights shone from the saloon and the jail. At that moment, someone left the jail and headed across the wide courthouse yard toward the street. There was no mistaking the wide brimmed hat and the graceful stride of the man in the dark overcoat. Suddenly her elation returned. She watched him cross the street to the hotel, heard him come in, and waited impatiently for him to come upstairs. She went to the door. She heard the murmur of his voice and Rufus's. Was he going to join the game? she wondered in dismay.

A few minutes later she heard his step on the stairs. Opening the door fully, she saw that beneath his unbuttoned overcoat, his shoulders sagged with fatigue. His face failed to light up as it usually did when he saw her.

"I've been waiting for you. Come in. Have you had supper?"

He stepped inside her room, seeming to fill it. Removing his hat and gloves, he said, "No, I haven't had supper, but I'm not hungry."

By the light of her lamp, she saw how deeply weariness had carved lines around his mouth. "You worked very late. Sit down. You look as tired as I've ever seen you."

If he heard her invitation to sit down, he didn't accept it. "I've just come from the jail. Nels is sick. Doc Long says it's heart failure. He doesn't expect him to live. He and Mrs. Cooper are sitting with him."

"At the jail?" she asked. "That must be terrible for his wife. Couldn't they move him back home?"

"Doc doesn't think he would survive being moved."

So Nels Cooper wouldn't go to prison. His death would be a blessing, Susan thought, sparing him and his family the humiliation and perhaps the horror of execution.

"Pat's in jail, too. He was drunk when Van went to arrest him. Van had to hit him when Pat took a swing at him."

"Will he plead guilty?"

"I don't know. Maybe when he sobers up and has time to think it over he will. I hope so. I can put Bud Cooper and Van on the stand and let them repeat Nels's confession to the jury, but I hope I won't have to do that. The Coopers and Pat's family will be a lot better off if this whole mess doesn't have to be dragged through court."

"Won't Hap's testimony be enough?"

"Probably, but I wouldn't take any chances. I'd use all the evidence I have."

Susan made no further comment, allowing a brief silence to fall between them, which she broke in an apologetic tone. "I realize this is a great tragedy for many people, but"—here she threw back her head and stretched out her arms, crying—"I feel like I could fly. It doesn't seem as if there's anything holding me to the ground anymore. And it's all due to you. I can never thank you enough." She kissed him exuberantly.

When she tried to draw back, he held her and kissed her fiercely. She sensed his despair, his love, his need. All of it was there in his face when he pulled his mouth from hers. Her heart aching for him, she put a tenatative hand up to his cheek and whispered his name. His unhappiness touched her with an intensity that it could not have had twenty-four hours earlier. Then it would scarcely have penetrated the shell of fury and outrage around her heart. Now she wanted to comfort him, care for him, end his despair. Leaning back in his arms, she gazed with fresh sight at the aristocratic yet strong face, the dark eyes that at the moment held such pain. She loved him. Her hands moved with the thrill of discovery across his shoulders as this knowledge began to fill her. One hand went to his face, caressingly tracing his features, one by one. Without being aware of it, I've grown to love him, she thought with a sense of wonder. Would she have realized it had Ward's killers never been caught? Perhaps not. Recognizing that as a real possibility, she caught her breath, appalled to think what she might have missed.

That event had freed her emotions. She was whole once more. It was like recovering from a long illness. Acutely conscious of the hard pressure of Sy's arms around her, she knew for certain that this was where she belonged.

Catching sight of Ward's shaving mug on the bureau, she went over and picked it up, holding it in both hands. In the lamplight the gold trim and the wheat design glowed softly, striking a core of sadness deep inside her that she would carry for the rest of her life; but like a scar, it would fade with the years.

She felt Sy's eyes on her as he watched her silently. "I'm going to ask Rufus if he'd like to have this," she said. "It's of no use to me anymore."

She set it down and went back to his arms, smiling.